T0285445

"There are fast reads, and then there are reads that throw you right out of your chair. *Alias Emma* is in the latter category."   —LINWOOD BARCLAY

"Pure candy for those of us who love a good spy story— this is a novel you'll struggle to put down."
                                                —*Business Insider*

PRAISE FOR

THE TRAITOR

"*The Traitor* delivers everything fans of spy fiction could want: an absorbing plot, shadowy characters, page- gripping tension."   —*The Washington Post*

"A million-mile-an-hour thrill ride set in the glorious Mediterranean . . ."   —*The Big Thrill*

"Glass has delivered an un-put-downable winner. Here's hoping this series has a long life."
                                        —*Publishers Weekly* (starred review)

"I nominate Charlize Theron for the role of Emma Make- peace if there is ever a film adaptation of this series, which it richly deserves."   —*BookPage*

THE TRAP

THE
TRAP

A NOVEL

AVA GLASS

BANTAM
NEW YORK

A Bantam Books Trade Paperback Original

Copyright © 2024 by Moonflower Books Ltd.

Published in the United States by Bantam Books, an imprint of Random House, a division of Penguin Random House LLC, New York.

BANTAM & B colophon is a registered trademark of Penguin Random House LLC.

Originally published in the United Kingdom by Penguin, an imprint of Penguin Random House UK.

ISBN 978-0-593-97221-2
Library HC ISBN 978-0-593-97219-9
Ebook ISBN 978-0-593-97220-5

Printed in the United States of America on acid-free paper

randomhousebooks.com

2 4 6 8 9 7 5 3 1

Book design by Jo Anne Metsch

For Jack, forever

THE TRAP

MONDAY

7 October

SPECIAL TO THE PRIME MINISTER
INFORMATION: PUBLIC COMMUNICATIONS G7
SECURITY LEVEL: LOW
RISK LEVEL: LOW

*Below, please find the daily roundup of press in advance of G7
Summit in Edinburgh.*

BBC TODAY PROGRAM TRANSCRIPT,
7 OCTOBER, 07:10 HOURS

JULIAN CASEL: Now work is well under way in Edinburgh as
the city, police, and security forces prepare for the G7 summit.
Sarah Lams is our Scottish editor, and she's keeping an eye on it
for us up there. Sarah?

SARAH LAMS: You're right, Julian, things are really kicking off
now, as the clock is ticking down to the moment when those
planes touch down at Edinburgh Airport. In one week, the leaders
of the seven most powerful democracies will gather here in the
Scottish capital to discuss the most pressing issues facing the
world.

   This meeting of the Group of Seven, as it is officially known, is
particularly anticipated, as tensions have been rising between the
West and the twin titans of the East—Russia and China. Russia is

4 | AVA GLASS

known to be fuming about statements made by the British Prime Minister and the President of the United States criticizing the Russian conflict in Eastern Europe and its continual suppression of the production of oil that is sending prices soaring around the world. There's an expectation that the G7 leaders might decide to take a united front on sanctions. If they do, that could cripple the Russian economy, sending it into a downward spiral. Certainly the signals are there that strong action may be taken. This week both the British and the American governments issued statements, accusing the Russian government of, and I quote, "holding the world to blackmail."

Russia responded with a strongly worded statement, calling both the US President and the British Prime Minister "liars and cowards." The Chinese government issued a separate statement in more measured but still pointed terms, which said, "We support the Russian government's right to use any means to defend and support itself." That may not sound like much, but it sends a clear signal that the relationship between China and Russia is tightening.

It's in this febrile atmosphere that the gathering will begin next Monday, ostensibly to discuss ways to improve the global economy and stabilize democracy, but also surely to talk together about how they can rein in our neighbors to the east.

7 OCTOBER
THE SCOTSMAN

EVERYTHING YOU NEED TO KNOW ABOUT THE G7

As the world turns its eyes to Edinburgh next week, locals are preparing for traffic snarls, crowds, and press that history shows will make the city feel busier than the annual arts festival.

Here's what you should know as we brace ourselves for a very busy week.

WHAT IS THE G7?

The Group of Seven is an informal grouping of western democratic nations. Its members are the US, the UK, Canada, Australia, France, Germany, Italy, and Japan. Representatives of the EU also normally attend. Technically it has no leader, and no legal standing. But this alliance of nations is incredibly powerful.

WHERE WILL THEY MEET?

The main meetings for this year's gathering will take place Monday and Tuesday at Carlowrie Castle, a privately owned gothic manor house near Edinburgh Airport. These meetings will be closed to the media, and it's unlikely we'll get even a glimpse as the castle is tucked away amid dozens of acres of grounds, shielded from prying eyes by high walls. However, early meetings and bilaterals—meetings of just two or three nations–will take place at the Balmoral Hotel in town, and some leaders are arriving early for this reason. Carlowrie can't hold all the support staff, so some will be staying at the castle, others will have rooms elsewhere in town and will travel by convoy to the castle every morning. Along with the press and other staff, this means every hotel in the city is booked solid.

HOW WILL THIS AFFECT ME?

In short: traffic will be a nightmare. Starting tomorrow, road closures will be in place—some announced, some not announced, so prepare for the unexpected. When the US president arrives, stretches of the motorway into Edinburgh will shut down for hours for security reasons. The worst traffic will happen on Sunday, when the King and Queen are hosting a party for the leaders at Holyroodhouse. This will result in the closing of the Royal Mile and other major arteries within the city. Basically, if you can work from home, this is the week to do it. Expect chaos.

Just after midday on the second Monday in October, a long, black Mercedes made its way across London. It was one of those rare, crisp autumn afternoons when the blue of the sky was almost blinding, and the sun cast the city in melting golden light, but the man in the backseat barely glanced up from his phone.

The phone was Russian-made. Secure. Unhackable.

At the wheel of a nondescript Ford a short distance behind him, Emma Makepeace spoke into the microphone embedded in the lapel of her jacket.

"Unit Twelve. Target traveling east on Cromwell Road. I have eyes on."

"Copy that, Twelve." Adam's gravelly voice sounded clear through her earpiece.

Adam Park was Emma's colleague. Except his name wasn't really Adam, and hers wasn't Emma. Both of them were intelligence officers who worked for an agency so secret it had no name at all.

Emma watched the man's bowed head as the bulletproof sedan slid to a stop at a red light. She longed to know what he could be reading that was so fascinating. The Agency had spent all morning trying, unsuccessfully, to find out what he was doing in England.

Vladimir Balakin's private jet had landed two hours ago at an airport in Farnborough, 40 miles south of London. He'd been tailed ever since—first by Special Branch, and then a team from MI5. Ten minutes ago, Emma and Adam had picked up the chase. In all, twelve separate cars were pursuing him on parallel streets. This meant the cars directly behind the Mercedes kept changing, leaving nothing for its driver—a Russian intelligence officer with years of experience—to notice.

As the car idled at the light, Emma saw Balakin glance up at last and speak impatiently, gesturing at the cars around them.

"Don't like waiting, do you?" she whispered.

Back in Moscow he would have had a police escort rushing him through every red light because, while his true job title was a closely guarded secret, he was believed to be the second in command of the Russian military intelligence agency, the GRU. One of the most feared intelligence organizations in the world.

As far as the British government was concerned, he had no business being in the UK at all. It wasn't normal for someone that senior to travel to a country Russia counted as an enemy. It wasn't how things worked.

As soon as his plane had registered a flight path to England, a pursuit team had been assembled. There might have been no legal or diplomatic means of stopping him from entering the country but Balakin would not have a single unwatched moment on London's streets.

The light turned green, and the long Mercedes purred forward. Emma shifted into first gear and dropped back just far enough. Balakin turned his attention back to his phone.

Among the many things no one knew was precisely where he was headed. Russian officials usually preferred the Savoy and the Dorchester for their stays in town, but he hadn't chosen the obvious route to either of those hotels. Instead, he was driving down the Cromwell Road, which led, as far as Emma was concerned, nowhere interesting.

So when the Mercedes signaled and moved into the turning lane, she tightened her grip on the wheel.

"Target turning left on Gloucester Road."

"Copy that. Do not follow," Adam growled through her earpiece. She could hear the roar of his engine as he floored it.

"Copy." Emma bypassed the Mercedes without a sideways glance.

Adam had been traveling on adjacent streets, staying as close to parallel as he could with her. He would pick up the surveillance now.

At the next corner, Emma turned left and hit the accelerator, thumping hard over a speed bump. Somehow, she needed to get ahead of the Balakin's car on the narrow side streets.

It was a waltz of cars, each just out of sight of the other.

"I have eyes on," Adam announced a moment later. "Target heading north on Kensington High Street."

As she navigated London's twisting, narrow side streets, Emma was viewing a map of the neighborhood in her mind. Kensington High Street was a straight line to Hyde Park. And unless he was sightseeing, Hyde Park held nothing of interest except Kensington Gardens and the royal residence at Kensington Palace, and he certainly wasn't going there. The only place nearby was . . .

Her breath caught. She spoke quickly into her microphone. "The Russian embassy. That's where he's going."

There was a pause before Adam replied, "I think you're right."

"I'm heading to the Palace Green," Emma said. "Stay with him."

She hit the accelerator, racing down affluent streets of elegant townhouses, spinning the wheel as she navigated onto Notting Hill Gate, her tires squealing.

Just as she made the turn, a small woman in a pale blue uniform pushing a pram stepped out into the crossing ahead of her.

Emma slammed the brakes, bracing herself as her body was thrown forward. The car stopped with a shiver. The woman gave her an alarmed glance and hurried across the road.

Swearing softly, Emma accelerated more gently this time, fingers drumming the wheel when a slow-moving van pulled in front of her. Throughout it all, she could hear Adam's voice in her earpiece as Balakin's car made its way toward its destination.

Finally, she turned off onto a small side street, parking on a double yellow line before jumping out of the car and running down to a private lane, barricaded from traffic. She paused on the corner, pretending to look at her phone while in reality she was studying a sprawling Edwardian wedding cake of a building, half-hidden behind forbidding brick and metal walls topped with razor wire. The blue, red, and white Russian flag waved defiantly above the portico, the colors crisp against the backdrop of that peerless sky.

She didn't have to wait long. Two minutes after she arrived, the embassy's gates began to slide open. And a minute later, the black Mercedes rolled into view.

In the backseat, Vladimir Balakin stared straight ahead as the car turned slowly into the drive, its engine purring. Moments later, the gates shuddered and slid shut, hiding the car from view.

"Target inside the embassy," Emma said, softly.

For the first time that day, her boss's voice appeared in her earpiece.

"Abort this operation," Charles Ripley ordered. "All units, return to base."

But Emma didn't immediately do as she was told. Instead, she stared at those closed gates.

Something big was happening. She could sense it.

2

Twenty minutes later, Emma parked the Ford in an unmarked underground car park on a quiet Westminster street that curved like a scythe. The buildings here were classic Victorian red brick rowhouses, few were more than four stories tall. Beside each door a brass plate or tasteful wooden sign bore the names of the organizations inside. Most of them were true. The door she turned into had a sign reading "The Vernon Institute." That was a lie.

The plain, oak door opened into a small entrance hall that held nothing except a second set of doors. These were much more modern. And much more bulletproof.

Leaning forward, Emma stared into a small electronic device mounted on the wall. A red light blinked slowly. After a moment. the light turned green, and the doors unlocked with an audible *click*.

She walked through into a bustling office. Esther Fields waved from the comms desk, her blond hair a puff of vanilla tamed by the black straps of her headset.

"Ripley wants you to go straight up," she called.

Emma lifted a hand. "On my way."

She dropped the Ford's keys into the wooden box beside the

door with its perennial plea that the government's cars should be returned clean and with at least some fuel, before heading for the long oak staircase that dominated the room.

Everything about this building was a secret. Most people in the government had no idea it existed. Everyone who worked for the Agency was issued a fake name, fake identification, a fake background, fake lives.

There was a good reason for the secrecy, of course—the Agency hunted Russian spies.

Emma had barely put one foot on the steps when a voice called down from above.

"Stop." Charles Ripley emerged from his first-floor office with his coat over one arm and strode down to meet her. "Change of plans. We're going out."

Ripley was just over six feet tall, and narrowly built. Emma didn't know how old he was but he had to be at least sixty, although he looked younger. He'd cut his teeth with MI6 in the dying days of the Cold War, and there was nothing Russia had to offer that he didn't understand. The driving force behind the Agency's success, he was tireless, and when it came to his work, he was relentless.

He had a quick, athletic stride that belied the gray strands in his hair, and an authority that meant Emma turned around without question and headed back out the door.

As they walked down the curved road, he swept the black wool coat across his shoulders in one urgent movement and said, "There's a meeting. Secure location, high level. I want you there."

"About Balakin?" Emma asked.

"Yes." Ripley pulled a black cigarette case from his pocket. "It's the timing, you see. It's worrying people. It's worrying *me*." He lit a Dunhill with a worn gold lighter and took a long drag. "And then there was that knife attack last week."

Emma's eyebrows rose. The day before, a lone man with a

knife had attacked a group of tourists in front of Westminster Abbey. One person had died and three had been hospitalized. The attacker had been captured and arrested. Nothing further had occurred in the case, and to her, that had seemed to be the end of it. It was for the police to deal with.

"You don't think there's a connection, do you?" she asked. "That attack looked random."

"It *was* random, as far as MI5 can tell." Ripley glanced at her. "But the killer was Russian, you see. As were the victims. They haven't released that information yet."

Now Emma thought she understood.

"Was he FSB?" she asked, her tone doubtful. The brutal attack had held none of the Russian spy agency's usual . . . delicate touch.

"Not at all," Ripley said. "As far as we can tell, he was just what he seemed to be—a taxi driver who has lived in the UK for two years. We believe this was a mental health issue. All the same, the coincidence of timing . . ." He waved one hand expressively.

Coincidence didn't exist in their world. If something looked like a plot, it was a plot.

"Still," Emma said. "It can't be part of this. Vladimir Balakin wouldn't come over for a stabbing. He's too important."

"Agreed." Ripley waited for a jogger to run past them. Only when he was a block away did he continue. "You can have two terrible things happen at the same time, unfortunately. And this is our unlucky week. But everyone's nervous. There are a lot of itchy fingers on a lot of triggers this week, and Balakin will know that." He gave her a sideways glance. "His arrival means something."

They crossed a road, threading between the parked cars, before turning onto a leafy street.

When Emma spoke again, her voice was low. "Why do you think he's here? Is he just messing with us?"

It wasn't beyond the Russian government to send a senior official flying in, just to intimidate them. After all, they were preparing for a major gathering where Russia's own future was due to be discussed.

"I don't know." Ripley drew on his cigarette. "But I can't think of a single good reason for an FSB official at Balakin's level to fly to London to meet with the Russian ambassador a week before the G7 is scheduled to gather in this country." The words came out in a puff of smoke. "Unfortunately, I can think of quite a few bad reasons."

Emma thought of those black gates at the Russian embassy closing slowly behind the Mercedes. If Russia wanted to cause trouble for Britain, there would be no better time. Everyone was on edge. The whole world would be watching. For Russia every bad news story was a win. If it played its cards right, it could humiliate Britain and disrupt world markets all in one go.

She looked at Ripley. "You think he's brought something from Moscow. Something too secret to be transmitted in any other way."

"That is the concern," he conceded.

The more Emma thought about it, the more sense it made. Vladimir Balakin was ruthless. During his time with Russia's many spy agencies, he'd been personally responsible for massacres in Syria and Ukraine that had killed thousands of innocent people. He could be sitting inside that embassy now, plotting an attack on British soil, and there was nothing they could do to stop him. The embassy could not be touched—no embassy can, under international law. Their hands were tied.

No wonder there was an urgent meeting. No wonder people in very high places were panicking.

By then they'd reached Millbank and the Thames. Buses and taxis rattled by, and the cool autumn air smelled of diesel exhaust and river mud. Through the trees in Victoria Tower Gardens, Emma could see the water, deep blue in the late morning sun.

Ripley headed straight to an unmarked building with long marble steps and a grand portico. Emma followed, intrigued. She knew MI5 used many buildings under an assortment of identities and she'd been to a few, but she'd never been here before.

The atmosphere inside was cool and hushed. There was no biometric security, just a curved front desk where a small woman in a dark suit spoke quietly to Ripley, who nodded and handed over his phone. Emma followed suit without waiting to be asked. The woman put both devices inside a safe mounted in the wall behind her. And that was that.

"They're just about to start." Motioning for Emma to follow, Ripley bounded up a curved staircase with a marble balustrade, two steps at a time.

The building was almost surreally beautiful. Emma kept noticing things—the carved marble, an ethereal mural of a blue sky and white clouds on the soaring ceiling, the gilded plaster. It had the rarefied air of an art gallery.

As she climbed the stairs, Emma wondered if it had once been an oligarch's home. Not the current kind, but the nineteenth century variety—a shipping magnate perhaps. It was unfathomable how it had ended up in MI5's hands. But then, so many buildings did.

On the first floor, they walked down a long hallway to a door where a thin man with expensive shoes waited for them.

"Charles," he said, and his smile was as thin as his hair.

"Giles." Ripley stretched out his hand.

As the two men shook hands, Emma stood stiffly; her mouth had gone dry. The man talking to Ripley was the head of MI6, the most important person in British Intelligence. His real name was Giles Templeton-Ward but to everyone in the country he was known, as all heads of MI6 had always been known, simply as "C."

"Glad you could get here so quickly. The situation is developing," C said quietly. His accent was nearly identical to Ripley's, making him a product of Eton or Harrow and then Oxford, undoubtedly.

C glanced at Emma with inquiry, and Ripley said, "This is Emma Makepeace. The one I told you about."

"Ah, of course." In C's cold gaze Emma saw that he already knew everything about her. He knew about her Russian parents, the languages she spoke, her time in the army, and everything she'd done right and wrong in her three years at the Agency. He would have a list of all her weaknesses.

"Good to have you." Dismissing her with that short comment, he turned back to Ripley. "The prime minister is demanding answers about our plans for securing the G7. He would like those answers yesterday." Lowering his voice further, he added, "He's under pressure on this from the Cousins. They're threatening to withdraw if they don't have assurances our security is on track."

"The Cousins" was intelligence code for the Americans.

"Yes, I can't say I'm surprised," Ripley said, dryly.

"Indeed. Thinking hats will be needed." C glanced at his watch. "We better go in. They're waiting."

As she followed the two men through the door, Emma exhaled quietly.

Inside was a small antechamber that held another door, this one made of thick metal. It reminded her of a bank vault. Ripley and C walked through it without pausing.

On the other side of the door was a small, crowded space, more an oversized cupboard than a boardroom.

Although she'd never seen one before, Emma recognized it instantly. The Americans called them "Sensitive Compartmented Information Facilities," because of course they would. In Britain they were known simply as "Secure Chambers."

The steel-walled room would be bug-proof and safe from prying eyes, built in secret locations for situations like this one.

Three people already sat at the table. The first was Patricia Allan, the head of MI5, barely five feet tall and recognizable by her short, gray hair, which gave her a pleasingly androgynous look. Next to her was Dominic Larch, the Home Secretary. Not yet forty, he'd only been in the job three months. Everyone thought he was too much of lightweight to handle being in charge of police, security, and counterterrorism. Emma suspected they were right.

Beside him sat a confident, tall woman with shoulder-length blonde hair in a charcoal gray suit. Emma recognized her from news reports as Lauren Cavendish, the prime minister's special adviser.

She and Ripley took the two empty seats on the far side of the table, squeezing past in the confined space.

As she sat in a black leather chair, it struck Emma that there were no computers in the room. No phones. Not even a notebook. No records would be kept. When it was over, for all intents and purposes, this meeting would never have happened. But decisions would be made here.

The heavy metal door swung shut almost silently. She heard a faint, electronic buzz as it sealed that faded disconcertingly to silence.

Nobody spoke, but the tension was so palpable she could almost see it. Out of the corner of her eye she noticed that the Home Secretary's right foot had begun to jiggle unconsciously.

Sitting at the head of the table, C looked at them with weary solemnity.

"Let's begin."

There was no preamble. No one was introduced. Instead, he gave all the details of Vladimir Balakin's arrival. Occasionally he asked for additional information from one or another of the people present, gradually painting a complete picture none of them could deny.

His conclusion, when he reached it, seemed almost inevitable. "Our concern is that our Russian friends are planning to disrupt or attack the G7 next week, and that Vladimir Balakin has just arrived with the final instructions for how to carry out that attack."

It occurred to Emma that, outside of this small, airless space, an announcement like that might have resulted in panic. Here, though, the response was muted.

Patricia Allan, the head of MI5, spoke first. "What sort of attack are we looking at?"

"Our information is too poor at this stage to answer that. Listeners say chatter is increasing, but they have no specifics," C said.

"Listeners" were what intelligence officers called GCHQ—the government's vast monitoring and cyber agency.

"The obvious move would be targeted assassination but they know our security will be very high. That said, a drop of polonium . . ." C didn't finish the thought. He didn't have to. They all knew how easily polonium could be dripped into a teapot—it had happened before.

C glanced at Ripley. "What's your gut tell you, Charles?"

"Not polonium." Ripley's reply came without hesitation. "They can't afford to go to war with the world. Not now, anyway. They'll be looking at something else. A cyber-attack would embarrass us and leave the G7 looking vulnerable. Shut down the airports, perhaps. But I don't think that would bring Balakin here—it's not dramatic enough for him." He paused. "No. I think it will be bigger than that."

"What then?" It was Lauren Cavendish from Number 10. "We have to know what to expect. We have to prepare."

Her brown eyes were preternaturally alert, wary of anything that might damage her prime minister's chances for reelection.

Ripley spoke quietly. "Knowing Vladimir Balakin as I do, he'll be looking for the personal touch. A targeted assassination. That's his style."

The room had grown uncomfortably warm. A trickle of perspiration ran down Emma's spine.

"Even if that's the most likely, we have to prepare for any possibility," Patricia Allan pointed out. "But we're already stretched thin preparing for the G7. We're understaffed, and so are the police. In fact, because of cutbacks over the last few years, we're vulnerable on every front."

Cavendish waved a dismissive hand. "Leave the politics out of this. The prime minister doesn't want to hear complaints. He wants to hear *plans.*"

Allan fixed her with an icy stare.

The Home Secretary, who'd sat silently through all of this, spoke for the first time. His voice was surprisingly authoritative. "Cancel all leave. Call everyone back." He turned to Cavendish. "Will the PM authorize raising the threat level?"

She considered this. "Yes. We can arrange a meeting with the Cabinet Office today."

C held up one hand. "I'm afraid I don't recommend that."

Silently, Emma agreed, although, as the lowest-ranking person in this room, she didn't dare say a word.

"Raising the threat level is a public act. It would inform everyone, including our Russian friends, about what we know," C explained. "It could make an attack more likely."

Patricia Allan nodded. "Agreed. The fewer people who know about this the better."

"Then what the hell do we do?" Dominic Larch's face had gone red. "Wait to be attacked? That's simply not acceptable."

"I suggest we assemble a team." Ripley's commanding voice silenced the argument. "Small and agile, carefully targeted. We'll put our best people on it. Emma will lead it."

Emma drew in a sharp breath. So *that* was why she was here.

The others glanced at her curiously as Ripley kept talking to Allan. "It needn't interfere with the work your people are doing right now. And the same goes for the police. They can continue to prepare as normal. This unit will stay below the radar, focusing solely on identifying the plans for an attack and stopping it." He looked at C. "It's the best way to handle this."

C considered this. "It could work," he said, after a moment.

"We can spare a few people," Allan said. "How many do you need, Charles?"

"I'd want at least twelve on the ground." Ripley opened his cigarette case and closed it with a click. "I can provide six people from my team."

C nodded and the speculative look in those cold eyes told Emma he thought Ripley could have asked for much more.

"Six can give you three people for this. If Five offers as many?" C looked at Allan.

She nodded. The deal was done.

"Right. Then that's the plan. We'll have a team of ten, with Charles's team overseeing the operation wherever it takes us. Of course, we'll need someone from Six to coordinate our side." He glanced at Ripley. "Andrew Field would be my first suggestion."

"I have no problems with Andrew Field," Ripley agreed.

"Good," C said. "So we have a unit. But what we haven't got is time. Seven days from now the G7 meets in Scotland. We have seven days to find out what attack they're planning, and to stop it. The world's media is here already." He glanced at Larch and Cavendish from Number 10. "None of this can leak. We need to operate in absolute secrecy. Are we agreed?"

"Of course." Cavendish sounded offended. "We would never leak this."

Larch merely nodded, his foot hopping nervously.

Patricia Allan made a faint, amused sound.

"Well then," C said after an almost imperceptible pause, "Charles, we're counting on you. Whatever they're planning, find out. And stop them."

The meeting ended moments later. As she exited the room, Emma took a deep, relieved breath—the air outside the chamber felt clean and cool.

Dominic Larch and Lauren Cavendish headed straight for the stairs without looking back.

C, Ripley, and Allan were talking in low voices as they walked out into the hallway. An assistant approached and C stepped aside to speak to him. When the man walked away, C returned to Ripley and Allan, his expression a mask.

"Balakin's pilot just registered a new flight plan. He's flying to Edinburgh." He glanced at Emma and said simply, "Your operation is underway."

3

Five hours later, Emma stepped out of Edinburgh Airport into an icy wind that cut straight through her coat to the skin below. Overhead, clouds scuttled across the darkening sky. Raindrops scattered across the pavement like chips of ice.

It was still autumn in London, but in Scotland, winter had arrived.

Following directions she'd memorized before getting on the plane, she strode quickly across to the multilevel car park and took the stairs to the second floor, where she found a black BMW parked in the third space from the end of the second row, exactly where she'd been told to find it. Setting down her suitcase, Emma crouched beside the front driver's-side wheel and retrieved the keys from the top of the tire.

She placed her small suitcase inside the trunk and got in behind the wheel. Inside, the car was spotless, the gas gauge showed a full tank.

"Nice," Emma murmured, appreciatively.

Clearly MI5 took better care of their cars than the Agency.

The BMW started with a powerful growl. Emma reached behind the visor to retrieve the car park ticket, which showed the car had entered the garage four hours ago. Just as she was about to shift into gear, her phone vibrated.

"Makepeace," Emma said.

"Message from Ripley." It was Esther's voice, from headquarters. "Balakin's plane is due to land in ten minutes. He wants you to be there."

"Copy that," Emma said, and shifted into gear.

"I'll message the details now. Good luck," Esther said, and the phone went dead.

Emma had been working since six o'clock that morning and yet she felt wide awake. Her body thrummed with energy. It was always like this at the start of an operation. There was so much to think about, so much information pouring in, so much to do, sleep became superfluous. Adrenaline became her rest, her food, her drink.

Right now, she knew the others were on their way, each traveling separately to avoid attention. Ripley was traveling by military jet—it was the only way to be sure nobody could track his movements.

They needed to be certain Balakin remained unaware his plans had been noticed. For as long as possible, the Agency wanted the plotters to feel safe. It's when you feel safest that you make mistakes.

Balakin's jet was due to arrive at the same airport, but at a VIP section used for private jets. Esther sent Emma GPS coordinates by secure message and a note about where she should park.

Emma hated using GPS—you might as well glue a target to the top of your car—but she had no choice. Normally, she'd memorize the route but there wasn't time. Everything was moving too quickly now.

With a squeal of tires she pulled out of the car park on to the confusion of roads and roundabouts. Dark rain tapped the windows and the windshield wipers thumped rhythmically as the phone's flat, automated voice directed her around the side of the long, low terminal building until she could see the runway stretching ahead of her.

The location Esther had sent her to was a shadowed spot at the edge of a sprawling staff car park with a perfect view of the section of the terminal where private jets unloaded.

She had just parked when a one-word message flashed on her phone from the Agency.

Landing.

Grabbing a pair of field glasses from her bag, Emma climbed out to get a better view. The wind snatched the door from her hand and flung it wide open, and sent her coat billowing like a parachute when she stood up.

When it came to weather, Scotland wasn't messing around.

Emma could hear the roar of a plane coming in to land, and pressed her back against the door to shut it, keeping her focus on the air strip.

The bright airport lights illuminated the scene on the tarmac like a film set. It wasn't difficult to find the plane she sought— Balakin's Dassault Falcon 900 was much bigger than the other private jets at the airport, with distinctive cream and red livery. She spotted it almost immediately, wings twitching in that gusting wind, the tail number V2691 clearly visible as the pilot brought the plane down, wheels skipping off the tarmac once before holding steady.

Camouflaged by darkness, she watched as it rolled to a stop at the end of the terminal closest to her. A nearby gate opened and a dark Range Rover drove through. Emma followed its progress around the terminal, where it drove straight to the Falcon. As soon as it stopped, two men emerged from the car and stood waiting near the plane.

Pushing a button on the modified binoculars, Emma began photographing the scene as the plane's door lifted and a flight attendant in a crisp beige uniform dropped the stairs into place before moving aside to allow a lone man to descend.

Tall and thin, with a tonsure-like bald spot, Vladimir Balakin was instantly recognizable, even when his face was turned away. When he glanced up, she caught a glimpse of his narrow eyes and sharp cheekbones. He looked cadaverous. It was rumored that he was terrified of poisonings so he ate almost nothing. There was no way to know if this was true but, looking at him, she believed it.

The two men who had waited for him were not so easily recognizable. One seemed to know him well, but the other—a dark-haired, stocky man in his forties in a well-cut suit—was visibly uncomfortable, his shoulders hunched around his ears. He stayed further back, while the smaller man leaned eagerly toward Balakin, talking rapidly.

After a moment, the smaller man returned to the Range Rover and backed it toward the plane. The nervous man and Balakin followed on foot.

Emma raised her eyes from the binoculars, frowning as the SUV stopped just near the plane's steps. The smaller man got out and raised the trunk, blocking her view of what happened behind it.

"Damn," Emma whispered, as all three men crowded behind the large vehicle. They seemed to be loading bags—presumably Balakin's luggage—but she couldn't see any of it.

Either way, the work took only a minute, and then the nervous man closed the boot and got behind the wheel. The smaller man held the door for Balakin, as he climbed into the back and then took the passenger seat. After a moment, the Range Rover was making its way around the long, low terminal building toward the gate.

Emma jumped back into the car, dropping the binoculars on the passenger seat. She turned the heater on with some relief, rubbing the blood back into her numb fingers as she waited.

She'd have given anything to see what they'd loaded into that car. It could easily have just been a few suitcases. Or it could have been a crate of explosives. Maybe the airport's security cameras could show them more, but somehow she doubted it. Balakin was too smart. She'd seen the way he looked around, checking the area. It had probably been his idea to back the car up. But at least she could discover Balakin's destination. There was only one way out for the rare VIP travelers wealthy enough to pay the thousands it cost to get authorization to have cars meet their planes. And that road was the one she was sitting next to right now.

Four minutes later, the Range Rover rolled past her. For the second time that day, and three hundred miles north of where she'd started, Emma pulled into the street behind Vladimir Balakin.

On this journey, there would be no dance of pursuing vehicles. It was just her—no cover, no backup.

She kept well behind the SUV, letting cars filter in between them, keeping her focus always on the Range Rover.

Once again, she had no idea where he was going. Edinburgh was not a favorite spot for Russians in the UK so there was little to go on in terms of where he might be heading when he filtered into the dregs of rush hour traffic on the motorway.

Emma hated not knowing things.

Still, it was easy to stay out of sight, shifting lanes long enough to be forgotten, and then swinging back again behind Balakin, just another pair of headlights.

After fifteen minutes, the Range Rover signaled and exited onto a quieter side road. Here, Emma had no choice but to drop much further back. Still, at least she had a clear view as the SUV turned left, then right, winding to the edge of the city center. Within minutes, the houses around her changed from modern subdivisions to Victorian stone buildings, their coal-blacked edifices jutting out ominously against the night sky.

Emma was completely lost by this point; she didn't know this city at all. It was unnerving to have no idea where she was when following someone as dangerous as Vladimir Balakin.

The closer she got to the city center, the narrower the ancient lanes became, making it harder to go unnoticed. A thick fog had begun to roll in off the River Lieth, and visibility was poor. Once or twice, she pulled over and switched off the car's headlights, waiting until Balakin turned the corner before starting up again and hurrying to catch up, hoping that in the dark she could be mistaken for a different vehicle in the rearview mirror.

During one of these maneuvers, she rounded a bend and found the Range Rover stopped in front of a tall black gate. Emma drove past the house without slowing and turned off at the first corner. The instant she was out of sight of the other car, she cut her headlights and pulled into a parking place in the darkness.

Snatching her phone from the dashboard holder, she jumped out and ran to the corner just in time to take a picture of the SUV as it pulled through the gates. Fog hung in the air like a milky veil but she caught a glimpse of a gabled manor house built of stone just before the heavy gates closed again and the view disappeared.

In the shadow of a tree, sheltered from the winds that had buffeted her at the airport, she studied the high garden wall. The house was completely hidden from the street but the house number was carved on a slate plaque, tastefully lit, beside a very modern electronic keypad.

Nothing told her what this place was. All she knew was what it wasn't. This wasn't the home of the Russian consulate general in Scotland. It wasn't the home of the ambassador's mistress, nor of any senior staff. She'd studied those buildings in the plane on the way here. This was an expensive house, and it was not on MI5's list.

There was no point in lingering where she might be seen by hidden CCTV cameras or guards and she returned to the car and sent the address to Esther with the message: **"Our friend has arrived."**

The reply came quickly.

"Good work."

For the next hour she sat in the dark, hoping for more information, or at least to see some action, but the gate stayed solidly shut. The winds had stopped as quickly as they'd risen, and the street had grown eerily quiet, the frigid air sheathed in slow-moving clouds of white. In fact, no one passed at all, except a man walking by with a briefcase, clearly on his way home from work.

A few minutes after the man passed through, a secure coded message told her an MI5 agent was nearby, and that she could go to her hotel and check in.

Emma was impressed. It had to be briefcase man. She hadn't clocked him as one of theirs. But then, she was used to working with ghosts. She'd done it many times. The fewer people you knew on an operation, the safer everyone was.

Suddenly, freed from the obligation to keep watch, she felt very tired, and she yawned widely as she started the car. She was more than willing to let the unknown man from MI5 take over while she got some sleep.

She shifted into gear and pulled out of the parking place, driving with no headlights for the first few seconds, just in case. Only when she was a safe distance from the house did she flick the lights on.

Again, she was forced to use GPS to find her way. As she drove across the dark city, with its gloomy buildings of coal-stained stone and the jagged outline of Edinburgh Castle standing watch from the promontory overlooking it all, worry nagged at her. She didn't know enough. She didn't know this city. She didn't know Balakin enough to know what to make of him. There'd been something in his confident swagger as he left the plane that bothered her. It was almost as if he knew she was there. As if he wanted to be seen. But that didn't make sense. Everything told them he was an incredibly secretive man.

Still, something didn't feel right. It felt as if the Russians were far ahead of them. There was a cockiness to their actions that showed they believed their plan, whatever it was, would work.

And if that was the case, Emma and the Agency were in deep trouble.

TUESDAY

8 October

SPECIAL TO THE PRIME MINISTER
INFORMATION: PUBLIC COMMUNICATIONS G7
SECURITY LEVEL: LOW
RISK LEVEL: LOW

Below, please find the daily roundup of press in advance of G7 Summit in Edinburgh:

BBC TODAY PROGRAM TRANSCRIPT, 8 OCTOBER, 08:23 HOURS

SARAH LAMS: I'm standing on the Royal Mile, at the heart of the action as the city of Edinburgh prepares for the first world leaders to arrive. It's a chilly morning, but work is already well underway, as you can probably hear in the background. Some workers have been out since before dawn, putting in place barricades along these narrow historic streets, creating the infrastructure that will be used to redirect traffic during the three days of the G7.

Early next week the convoys of international officials will travel down this very street to Holyroodhouse for a meeting with the

King and Queen at the royal residence. By then though, there will already have been multiple meetings here in the Scottish capital, and each journey—every single trip—must be choreographed down to the finest detail. Security is already intense, and it is going to be ratcheted up every day.

Roads are being closed, diversions are causing traffic snarls, and the locals are having to find a new way to navigate even on foot, as Edinburgh gets ready to take center stage.

But it's not just the traffic the government's worried about. Police continue to investigate the attack in London from earlier this week, and you can feel the tension in the air. Security forces are taking no chances. Every detail is being analyzed as they look for any weaknesses in their plans.

But there isn't much time. The media has begun to gather; the hotels are filling with advance teams from the various nations. And there is a sense right now that, if this goes wrong, Britain has a lot to lose.

4

Early the next morning, Emma walked through the Intercontinental Hotel's glass doors and out into Edinburgh at rush hour. The foggy weather of the night before was long gone, and the city's blackened jagged stone spires jutted up into a pale blue sky. The air was damp and cold, with a faint smell of diesel.

Emma had already mapped out her route and was moving quickly when she reached the corner and turned onto the busy main road, nearly bumping into a pair of police officers in full Kevlar, both carrying snub-nosed military rifles. Emma recognized the guns as the SIG 516, the weapon preferred by the Scottish armed response units.

"Sorry," she said, stepping hurriedly out of their way.

Both of them swept her with a swift, flat-eyed glance that rejected her as a threat in an instant. It was a look of absolute intensity that Emma recognized from her own time in the army.

The female officer, her fair hair pulled back tightly beneath a small cap, nodded with unsmiling politeness as they moved on, their attention already shifting to the next person.

Armed police are extremely unusual on the streets of Edinburgh normally, but there was nothing normal about this week.

Armed security would be dotted throughout the town center, on constant patrol until the G7 was over.

The sharp sound of clanging metal split the air, and Emma turned to watch as temporary barricades were unloaded from a flatbed truck, and dropped onto the side of the street. Those would be used to block traffic and close lanes whenever the motorcades were on the move. Edinburgh was getting ready.

The crowds of commuters on their way to work eyed the stacks of metal warily. It was only Tuesday, but getting around the city was already growing more complicated. In a day or two, simply walking from one street to another might be impossible.

Emma had made sure she looked like every other worker heading to the office, her jacket buttoned up, light brown hair pulled back into a ponytail. Like the street behind her, she appeared normal, unthreatening. But the bag over her shoulder was virtually empty, a prop to help her blend in. Everything she needed was in her pockets. Except the knife. That was tucked into her right boot.

Nothing about her was what it seemed.

She'd checked into the hotel last night under the name Anna Case, using a credit card provided by MI6.

In response to cheerful questions from the hotel receptionist, she'd explained that she was in town on business. Usually that was the end of it, but Liz, as her name tag identified her, had been chatty.

"There are so many reporters in town right now for the G7," Liz had remarked, her Scottish accent giving her words a musical note as she leaned forward hopefully. "Are you a journalist?"

"No," Emma had replied with a chuckle. "Nothing like that."

Liz had blinked at her. "Oh really? What business are you in, if you don't mind me asking?"

Emma hadn't missed a beat. "International distribution. Mostly oil industry equipment."

"How *interesting*," Liz said, her smile never fading. She handed Emma a room key. "Enjoy your stay!"

Emma had slept impatiently and minimally, rising before dawn, eager to get started. It bothered her that sleep was necessary; it was such a waste of time.

It had always been like that. When she was eight years old, she used to wake her mother up with a cup of tea minutes before her alarm clock went off almost every day. Her mother had told her that her father had been the same.

"He could not sleep," she'd said, in that velvety Russian accent she'd never lost, even after decades spent living in England. "'So much to be done,' he would say, when I fussed. 'No time for rest.'" Then she'd paused before adding, "He was right, of course."

Emma could never ask her father about his insomnia because weeks before she'd been born, he'd been executed by a Russian firing squad.

It was a brutal end. He had been guilty of everything they'd accused him of—he had spied against his native Russia, sending secret documents to Britain. But his motives had been good; he'd been trying to avert nuclear war, and the Russians knew that. They knew exactly how dangerous things had become in Moscow in those chaotic days after the Cold War ended. They simply didn't care.

They'd made an example of him and in the process, they'd made an enemy of his daughter.

That had been a mistake.

The unexpected memories reminded Emma that she hadn't told her mother she was leaving London. She pulled out her phone without breaking stride and dialed.

"Alexandra! Is everything fine?" The concern in her mother's voice sent a razor slice of guilt through Emma's heart. Guilt made her snippy.

"Of course everything's fine," she said. "Why do you always think something is wrong?"

"You never phone this early, so I thought something is not right."

It always amazed Emma how astute her mother was. She didn't know the truth about what her daughter did for a living, and yet whenever Emma was on an operation, she somehow sensed danger, like a bird senses a cat hiding in long grass.

"I'm only calling early because I wanted to let you know I'm going out of town," Emma said. "I'll be in Scotland for a few days."

"Scotland!" Her mother repeated the word with a kind of wonder, as if Emma had announced she was headed to Antarctica. "I have never been to Scotland. It is very beautiful, I believe."

Again, that unwelcome stab of guilt. This time, Emma controlled the urge to argue.

"You should go," she said. "It's only five hours on the train."

"Maybe," her mother replied, in a tone that meant the opposite.

Emma knew it wouldn't happen. Her mother had settled well in her new land but she had never fully recovered from the trauma of fleeing Russia while heavily pregnant, leaving her husband behind to die. Twenty-eight years after she'd made that journey, she was still shy and cautious, and she rarely traveled far from her home in the leafy, anonymous Surrey town of Guildford.

Everything worried her, but most of all she was terrified of spies. She blamed them for what had happened to her husband. The grudge she bore was unceasing, which was why Emma would never tell her the truth about what she did for a living. For all the time she'd been at the Agency, her mother believed her daughter was a low-level civil servant, working for the Foreign Office.

"But you are in Scotland for work. Not joy." Her mother's tone was disapproving.

"Yes, only a few days. But I don't want you to worry if you can't reach me. I'll be in meetings all day and I'll have to switch my phone off."

"Well, I hope you have a lovely time, even if you work too much," her mother said. "You are very busy always with your diplomats."

"They keep me on my toes," Emma agreed. "Listen, I have to go. I'll be home in a week. I love you."

Moments after she'd hung up, she turned a corner onto a quiet side street. The building she sought was right ahead of her. The crenelated nineteenth-century structure was hard to miss, built of dust-colored stone with a sign outside that read OFFICES FOR LEASE.

Slipping her phone into her pocket, Emma walked to the front door and typed a six-digit code into the keypad. The lock released with an audible click.

Inside, the lobby was small and quiet, and the air smelled not unpleasantly of fresh paint and plaster dust.

The building was still being renovated, and in the way of many buildings these days, the front desk was unmanned, which meant there was nobody to ask any questions. The new trend for empty front desks and automated entry systems was incredibly useful to spies. So little oversight. So few layers of protection.

Inside the lift, a Perspex plaque had been mounted to list the names of the companies in the building. All but one of the spaces were blank, as none of the offices were yet considered ready for occupation. The space for the fifth floor, though, had been freshly filled in with the words "Distinctive Exports Ltd."

This was the button Emma pressed.

When the elevator reached the fifth floor, she stepped out into an open-plan space that stretched the length of the old stone building. Martial rows of arched windows let in pale morning light, which flowed across bare plywood floors into a tangle of power cables.

Nothing was finished here. The Agency had paid to ensure the work would stop for a week.

The walls were cinder block, with wires stretching along the edge of the ceiling and dangling in corners. The huge space was as cold and damp as the street outside, and empty, aside from a single long table set up at the far end of the room, surrounded by a few plastic chairs and topped with multiple computers. Several screens had been mounted on the wall, while others leaned nearby waiting to be put up. All were blank except one, which held a steady shot of the gate that Balakin had driven through last night.

Ripley sat in front of it, a cigarette smoldering in one hand, contemplating the high gate like a cipher.

"You're early." He spoke without looking at her, and his voice echoed hollowly off the empty walls.

"So are you," she pointed out.

Glancing at the closed gate on the screen, she said, "Any action?"

"Nobody has come in or out since Balakin arrived." Ripley exhaled a stream of smoke just as a door at the end of the room opened and a tall, lanky man in his twenties emerged, carrying what looked like a heavy gray bag over one shoulder. His dark hair was a mass of curls, and he wore a Ramones T-shirt under a jet-black blazer. When he spotted Emma, a smile brightened his face.

"Hey, Emma. Welcome to our Scottish HQ," he said.

Zach Mason was the youngest person at the Agency, and a technical genius. Emma didn't know how Ripley had found him, but he'd been spotted while he was still a student at Cambridge University, coding computer games in his spare time. These days he was the Agency's technical wunderkind, maker of useful gadgets, and occasional hacker.

"I've got something for you," she said, handing him the SD card from the binoculars. "Pictures from last night." She turned to Ripley. "Two people came to meet Balakin's plane. I didn't recognize them."

"Cool. Let's have a look." Zach slid the card into a reader connected to one of the computers littering the table.

As he worked, Emma spotted a pod coffee machine propped on a chair in one corner.

"I see you brought the coffee with you."

"I go nowhere without it," Zach said, typing. "Help yourself."

Emma chose a blue pod at random and glanced at Ripley. "Two men picked Balakin up at the airport. I didn't recognize either of them. I think I've got good pictures, though."

"Good." Her boss pointed his cigarette at the screen. "We set up a camera across the street from the house but the fence is a problem."

"Can we get someone inside?" Emma asked.

"Maybe. But it would take time."

Ripley started to say more, but then stopped as images began to open on the second screen mounted on the wall. The shots Emma had taken of Balakin's plane and the group of men standing next to it were surprisingly clear. She could see all the features of the smaller man, looking eagerly at Balakin. And the thin Russian spymaster, his head tilted toward the other two.

"Zach." Ripley's voice was quiet, but the younger man looked up at him instantly. "Run a face match."

Zach typed a machine-gun volley of information.

Emma pressed the start button on the machine and the spicy-sweet scent of coffee joined the smoke of Dunhill Blues in the air. At the far end of the room, the elevator doors opened and three people walked into the cold, cavernous space.

"Are we late?" asked a stocky man with a subdued but intense demeanor.

Andrew Field was an ordinary looking man in his fifties, with thinning hair and a perpetually worried expression. If you passed him on the street, you'd never look at him twice, which would be a mistake. He was one of the highest-ranking officers at MI6, and an incredibly skilled spy.

He walked to Ripley first and shook his hand, a wide smile creasing his round face. "Good to see you, Charles."

"And you," Ripley said.

Andrew turned to her. "Emma." His tone was affable but a flicker in his small blue eyes betrayed a hint of hesitancy. Emma knew why.

They'd last seen each other only a few weeks ago, on the night the traitor Jon Frazer had been taken from prison and driven to Brize Norton Air Field in Oxfordshire. From there, he was to be flown to Vienna, where he would be exchanged in absolute secrecy for two British operatives who'd been arrested in Russia. It was a ritual as old as spying itself, but one witnessed by very few people. And one the government would never admit existed.

To avoid any risk of attention, the move had happened at midnight. Emma had stood on the tarmac in the vicious glow of the airfield lights, watching in silence as her former colleague and lover stumbled out of a windowless vehicle, his hands manacled, escorted by a phalanx of grim-faced military police.

He'd worn a sports jacket and trousers that must have once fit him but which were now loose and baggy. His wavy auburn hair had been cropped short. He looked pale and thin, as though he'd been in prison two years, instead of two months.

As he'd been hurried toward the waiting jet, he'd wrenched his head around, his eyes sweeping the darkened Oxfordshire landscape almost hungrily, taking one last glance at his homeland. He would never be allowed on British soil again.

In that moment, his eyes found Emma. And, even though her stomach had turned, she had stood still, barely breathing, unable to wrench her gaze away.

At first, Jon's expression didn't change. Then his lips formed a ghost of a smile. He raised his hand as much as the shackles allowed.

Emma made a soft, unconscious sound, as if he'd struck her, and recoiled.

Jon was a double agent. At MI6, he'd taken money from two Russian arms dealers in exchange for information that helped them avoid capture. In return for his help, he'd received more than five million pounds. But his actions had resulted in the deaths of two people, and Emma had barely escaped with her life.

She'd never seen it coming. She'd liked Jon. More than liked him. She'd let him into her life and into her bed, and the whole time he'd been selling her out for Russian cash. She blamed herself for not seeing the signs. She wouldn't make that mistake again.

Trust was an indulgence she could no longer afford.

When the plane at last took off, its lights climbing steadily into the sky, Emma had felt some of the weight of guilt and pain leave her shoulders. At least he was gone. At least she'd never see him again.

She'd almost forgotten Andrew Field and Ripley were standing next to her until Field spoke. "A crying shame," he'd said, unwisely. "A good man ruined by greed."

Emma had rounded on him. "There's *nothing* good about Jon Frazer," she'd snapped, her voice thick with pain. "There never was anything good in him. You made a mistake, Andrew. You took a viper into the nest, and you put it next to *me*."

Her voice had broken on the last word, and she'd strode away, fighting her fury and pain. In that moment, she'd been too angry and hurt to care about the fact that Field far outranked her.

Since then, she'd avoided him, mostly out of shame. And he'd had to deal with the fact that his own career had faltered.

But she liked Andrew Field. He was an incredibly skilled spy. And she owed him an apology. What had happened with Jon was no more his fault than her own.

"Hi, Andrew," she said, holding out her hand.

He took it in a firm grip, and the smile that crossed his face was fleeting but warm.

"Nice to see you again," she said, with meaning.

Beside him, the tall woman with hair cut in a sharp black bob introduced herself to Emma as Hayley Mir, a section head from MI5.

"And you're Emma Makepeace. I know all about you." Hayley eyed her with interest. "I'd poach you for my own team if I thought for one minute Charles would let me get away with it."

"I won't let you get away with it," Ripley warned, snuffing out his cigarette.

The man next to Mir was a few inches shorter than her, with graying hair and intelligent eyes.

"Graham Brodie." He spoke in a heavy Glaswegian accent as he shook Emma's hand with a firm grip. "I haven't heard of you, but if you're as good as she says I'd like to offer you a job with Police Scotland."

"If everyone's finished trying to hire my operative," Ripley interjected, "we should get to work." But he patted Brodie on the shoulder affectionately and glanced at Emma. "Graham's one of the best coppers I know."

"It's all lies," Brodie assured her, with a grin. "I'm actually terrible."

Everyone took a seat at the long table facing the screens. Ripley alone remained standing.

"My colleague Adam Park should be here, but he shared the night shift on surveillance so I've sent him to bed," he said. "But I'll fill him in on everything we discuss. We've got an ID on the house where Balakin's staying."

He nodded at Zach, and a new image opened on a large screen on the wall behind him.

"The house belongs to this man, Nikolai Orlov," Ripley said. "Born in Kazakhstan, he emigrated to Britain fifteen years ago on a high-income visa. Forty-seven years old. Received British citizenship three years ago. These days he calls himself Nick Orlov, apparently."

"He was at the airport last night, wasn't he?" Emma asked.

"Exactly."

Zach typed something and the image on-screen changed to the one Emma had taken the night before of Balakin and the smaller man speaking, their backs to the camera. The man next to them was clearly Orlov. He was staring away from the other two, his lips tight.

Graham Brodie leaned forward, studying the image intently. "Interesting. I've seen happier millionaires. Who's the other bloke?"

"We're still working on that," Ripley said.

"Get me a copy of that image. If he's local, I'll see if any of my officers can do better than your computer," Brodie said.

"Consider it done," Ripley said.

Hayley Mir typed into her tablet, a slight frown creasing her forehead.

"What do we know about Orlov?" she asked. "His name isn't giving me much on our system. Is he FSB?"

"Not as far as we can tell, and that's the problem. Nick Orlov isn't your usual Kremlin puppet." Ripley picked up his cigarette case. "He's self-made. He started an oil company when he was twenty-six years old, in Russia. His specialty was buying waste from the petrochemical industry and processing to extract usable oil. As oil fields became less productive, his business grew exponentially. Fifteen years ago, he moved the company to the UK and renamed it North Seven. North Seven is now one of the largest British petrochemical companies." He glanced at Field, who'd been typing into his laptop. "Has MI6 got anything on him?"

Field glanced up. "There's nothing in his file to indicate he's ever met any Russian government officials or their agents before now. He's so far off our radar, his file's almost empty."

"Aye, so what's changed, then?" asked Brodie. "Why's he carousing with a snake like Vladimir Balakin?"

"That's a good question," Ripley said.

"I've got my team looking into it now," Field said. "We'll trace

Orlov's travel. See if he's been to Russia recently. Perhaps he's fallen in with a bad crowd."

"My side is on this, too," Hayley Mir chimed in. "We'll look into North Seven, see if we can figure out if it's in any financial difficulties that might have led him to make poor decisions."

"Look at his family as well," Ripley said. "He's divorced; I believe his ex-wife lives in Russia. Find out if his parents are still alive and if they're connected to the Russian government. Balakin must have chosen him for a reason."

Field glanced at Ripley. "How can we organize this to avoid stepping on each other's toes?"

"I suggest we set up two units," Ripley said. "One to continue surveillance on Balakin. Another to investigate Nick Orlov." He pointed at Field. "Andrew, get your team working on Balakin. Try to figure out what he's doing here. That's the key issue, or we think it is. He'll need to be followed at all times." Turning to Hayley Mir, he continued, "Your side should focus on Orlov's company–who's he doing business with? Is he in some sort of trouble?" And, to Brodie, he said, "Let Police Scotland know we're doing advance security work throughout the area. We may need to call on them for help. If we do, we'll go through you."

"You've got it," Brodie said.

"Emma." Ripley turned to her. "I want you to head up the surveillance on Nick Orlov. Find out who he is, and what makes him tick. We don't have much time, so keep eyes on him."

Before Emma could respond, Ripley turned to Brodie and said, "Emma's going to need a guide for this—she's not familiar with Edinburgh. Do you have someone who can partner with her?"

Emma was horrified. A *partner*? She couldn't work with a stranger. They'd slow her down and she wouldn't trust them. She shot Ripley a fierce look, but he kept his attention fixed on the Scottish officer.

"Sure, we'll need someone smart for this," he said, thoughtfully. "Someone not easily intimidated."

Emma's brow furrowed. "I'm fine to work on my own."

But Ripley held up a hand to stop her. "A guide will help you work faster. We have very little time."

"I think I know the person," Brodie announced. "A good copper. Clever."

"Someone you trust?" Ripley pressed.

Brodie nodded. "Aye."

"Excellent. Then we have a plan." Ripley looked at the faces around him. "I want to say right now, I can't remember a more serious situation in the last few years. We need to move fast to stop any attack before it begins. Does everyone understand what they need to do? Any questions?"

No one spoke. The mood in the room had darkened, and a fine tension seemed to hum in the air.

"As you all are aware," Ripley continued, "this operation must be invisible. The prime minister has asked us to keep it under wraps. Use alternative comms channels as much as possible. If you have vital information for me, bring it in person. This room will be swept for listening devices every day." He took a breath, his expression deadly serious. "We have less than a week until the G7 meets. We need answers before then, or this could all get very ugly. I'm counting on you."

5

The minute the meeting ended, Graham Brodie broke off and strode toward the elevators, talking into his phone. Emma lingered at the table, reading through the intelligence files on Nick Orlov.

It was very odd that they could find no connection between him and Russian intelligence. Vladimir Balakin didn't mess around with amateurs.

The Russian organization *Federalnaya Sluzhba Bezopasnosti* was better known by a three-letter acronym: FSB. But it was the name it had before the Berlin Wall fell that everyone remembered. The KGB had been one of the most feared and respected intelligence organizations in the world. Its methods and ruthlessness were legendary. It had changed its name, but the malign tools of its trade remained the same. It had an ironclad system for choosing operatives around the globe.

And Nick Orlov didn't fit that mold.

According to his files, he hadn't stolen his money from the Russian people in the time-honored tradition—he'd earned his wealth slowly and steadily. He'd worked hard for everything he had, and as far as anyone could tell, he'd played by the rules.

Why would he risk everything by tangling himself up in Russia's network of spies now? It didn't make sense.

She pulled out the page about his family background. He'd married while still in Russia, his wife had moved to Scotland with him but then, after they'd divorced ten years ago, she'd moved back. There were no children, no further ties to Russia.

Both his parents were dead, and he himself rarely traveled back to his home country.

In short, there was nothing suspicious about him. He simply didn't act like a spy.

She looked up to where the picture she'd taken the night before was still displayed on one of the wall-mounted screens. His polished features and full mouth warned of self-indulgence and vanity, but Emma thought she saw desperation in his eyes.

"Emma," Ripley called, and motioned her over to where he stood with Brodie. "Graham's arranged a local partner for you."

"Oh good." Her tone was assiduously neutral, but the sharpness in Ripley's glance told her he knew exactly what she was thinking.

"Mackenzie's good at her job," Brodie assured her. "Very smart. Absolutely trustworthy. Perfect for this project."

Emma gave a silent inward sigh. There was no getting out of this. She was going to spend the entire operation dealing with a cop with no intelligence experience, who would probably feel threatened by her and want to prove himself.

"Well, fantastic," she said. "Where do I find this Mackenzie?"

"Downstairs and ready to go whenever you need," Brodie said. "Have you got a car? If not, you can use one of ours."

Imagining a battered police-issued Skoda, Emma replied quickly, "I have a car, thanks."

"Ah, grand. That's fine, then," Brodie said. "Mack'll meet you out front."

"Perfect." Ripley turned to Emma. "Keep your focus on Nick Orlov today. He's got to come out of that house sometime and we need to follow him wherever he goes. Don't lose him, no matter what happens." Ripley glanced at his watch. "You better get going. I'll walk you to the lift."

Taking the hint, Brodie stayed where he was as Emma and Ripley crossed the long, empty room. Once they were out of earshot, Ripley spoke quickly and quietly.

"I know you don't like this, but no one knows this city as well as a local. I can't have you getting lost. There's no time."

Remembering her journeys the day before on Edinburgh's tangle of streets, Emma abandoned her resistance.

"I know. It's fine."

"Listen, Emma," Ripley said. "Whatever the Russians are planning, I believe Nick Orlov is at the center of it. I can feel it. He's the link we can break. Stop him, and you'll stop it all."

"You're sure it's Orlov we should pursue?" Emma asked. "Balakin's the one with a direct line to the Russian government."

"That's why we'll never get anything out of him," Ripley said. "He's too good. Too savvy. If we're right, Orlov's got no business in this fight. Somehow we need to get to him and find out what he knows, and we have to do it quickly." He paused, a new tension in his face. "Something tells me you're going to need to go deep for this one, Emma. Be ready."

"You know you can count on me," she promised.

But as the elevator doors closed and she found herself alone, the first seeds of doubt planted themselves in her heart. Something in Ripley's voice had sent a chill through her. He was warning her, but she couldn't understand why.

There was no time to try and unpick it now, though. When she walked out the front door, a tall woman in a blazer a little too small for her long frame was waiting outside. As Emma approached, she watched with a wary mixture of resignation and caution, like a dog that had been kicked once and never forgot it.

"You're Mackenzie?" Emma looked at her doubtfully.

The woman gave a knowing smile. "You expected a bloke, right? I'm Kate Mackenzie. But everyone calls me Mackenzie if they don't call me Mack. I guess you're Makepeace?"

"Emma. Let's walk and talk." Emma gestured for her to follow and strode off.

Mackenzie hurried after her. "Hey, maybe you can tell me what the hell is going on? Why am I here, exactly?"

Her wavy brown hair was pulled back, and a scattering of freckles dusted her heart-shaped face. She wore no makeup. She looked cold, and Emma wondered why she wasn't wearing a coat.

"Nobody briefed you?" Emma asked.

"No briefing," Mackenzie said. "No information at all. Just an order to drop everything and come here straightaway. What is so important that I've had to drop multiple investigations? It's not like we're overflowing with manpower right now."

Emma didn't miss the bitter edge to her tone. But in her experience, cops were always angry about something.

"Well," she said, "I can tell you we're part of a much larger team looking into a suspected threat related to the G7. You and I will be conducting surveillance on one man in particular. It should be straightforward, and it won't take more than a few days. I don't know the area, so my boss thought I needed a local to help. I don't agree with him, but here we both are."

"So you're telling me I'm your guide to Edinburgh?" Mackenzie sounded incredulous.

"That's the idea."

"Astonishing." Mackenzie shook her head, her lips tight.

By the time either of them spoke again, they were nearly to the car park where Emma had left the BMW.

"So, I guess you're a spook," Mackenzie said, as they threaded through the rows of parked cars.

"I prefer 'intelligence officer,'" Emma told her coolly. "And you should know that you are covered by the Official Secrets Act.

If you ever tell anyone anything about what happens over the next few days, you could be prosecuted for treason." She pulled the keys from her pocket and unlocked the black car. "This is us."

If Mackenzie was cowed by her tone, there was no sign of it as she studied the sports car with disbelief.

"Spies get BMWs and we barely get bicycles. What a country." She opened the passenger door and climbed in without waiting to be invited.

Emma stood for a second looking at her through the window before getting into the driver's seat. She'd never forgive Ripley for this.

It was only when she backed out of the parking spot that she realized, humiliatingly, she'd need directions to get back to Nick Orlov's mansion.

"What's the fastest way to get to Wesley Coates Gardens?" she asked, brusquely.

"Well, as a homicide detective, I haven't had a lot of cause to spend time on such a posh street," Mackenzie drawled, donning a pair of sunglasses. "But I think I can find it. Turn left out of here, then take the second right and you'll be going in the right direction."

Emma gunned the engine, pulling away with a screech of tires.

It was nearly nine o'clock and morning rush hour was well underway. As they joined the flow of traffic, Emma decided she had no choice but to make the best of this situation. Clearly neither of them wanted to be here, but they had a job to do.

Talking as she drove, she explained the basics of who Nick Orlov was, and about Balakin, and their concerns about what all this might mean for the G7. When she'd finished, she said, "Any questions?"

Mackenzie thought for a long moment. Finally, she said, "It's Wesley Coates Gardens, right?"

Emma nodded.

The Scottish police officer pointed ahead. "Take the next left."

Emma didn't know what to make of Kate Mackenzie. Most police officers would at least be a little impressed by working with intelligence this closely. But she seemed utterly disinterested. Like the world had somehow let her down, and this assignment was just further evidence of that disappointment.

She had only a slight Scottish accent, which probably meant she hadn't spent all her life here. Her skin was largely unlined, and Emma didn't think she was yet forty. Her features were too strong for her to be truly attractive, but she had good bone structure, and her eyes were a striking shade of blue. The too-small jacket seemed to indicate she'd recently put on weight and hadn't yet adjusted to the change, or perhaps she'd borrowed it from someone smaller. Occasionally she tugged at the sleeves, as if this could make them stretch. That was the only indication Emma saw of nervousness.

When the forbidding gates of Orlov's mansion appeared in front of them, Emma slowed and found a parking spot a short distance away with a partial view of the entrance. When the engine was off, she sent a secure message to Zach. Just two letters.

"OS."

On site.

A few seconds later, she heard a car start on a nearby street. The last of the night team would be leaving now.

She pointed the house out to Mackenzie, and explained what they were looking for. After that, the two of them sat staring at the expensive gate in silence.

After several long minutes, Mackenzie asked, "Is this really all we do?"

"This is it."

"Hardly James Bond, is it?"

Emma shook her head. "Nope."

Another silence fell.

"If the guys in that house want to blow up the G7, or something like that, why don't they just cancel it?" Mackenzie asked.

"They can't," Emma told her. "We can't give in to every threat. Governments can't be manipulated by a handful of angry people or nothing would ever get done. The issues they're here to discuss are too important to be pushed aside because of fear."

"I guess you're right." Mackenzie turned to look at the stone houses around them with their neat window boxes filled with fading summer flowers. "Won't someone notice two women sitting in a car all day in front of their living room window?"

"You'd be surprised how little people notice." Emma shot Mackenzie an interested look. "So . . . you're a homicide detective?"

"I was. Until recently." Mackenzie kept her eyes on the gate. "Lately I've been on the drugs squad."

She tugged at her sleeves again, harder this time, as if she'd like to rip them off and throw them out the window.

"What happened recently?" Emma asked. "People don't leave homicide until they retire."

"Don't they?" Mackenzie's tone was sardonic. But when she saw that Emma was going to wait patiently until she gave a real answer, she sighed. "My boss and I had a disagreement. I lost. End of story. End of my career."

Emma studied her with new interest. "Did you disagree about a case?"

"You could say that." At last, Mackenzie released her tortured sleeves and turned to face her. "Eight months ago, a young woman walking across St. Mark's Park after a night out was attacked. She was raped, and her throat was slit. Her body was found the next day by a jogger." She recited the details without emotion. "She was a prostitute and drug addict, well known to the police." She met Emma's gaze, her eyes fierce. "She was *nineteen* years old."

She paused, letting the words hang there, before turning her gaze back to the gate.

"There was no DNA on the body. No fingerprints. Nothing to go by. Boss wanted to drop it after a week. But it looked to me very much like a case we'd had a few months earlier. Similar methods. Similar victim. I believed we were dealing with the same killer, and I found two more cases that might have been done by the same person. I thought I had a good idea who our guy was on this, but I couldn't pin it on him. There wasn't enough evidence. All I needed was a bit of time and I'd have had him, but my boss pulled us all off it, to put us on more 'high profile' cases." She made air quotes around the words. "I objected. My chief disagreed with me. I objected again in stronger terms." She slouched back in her seat, her face dark. "I was moved to the drugs team."

"This was punishment?" Emma guessed.

Mackenzie's only reply was an eloquent shrug.

"What happened with the case?" Emma asked. "The young girl?"

"Sod all." Mackenzie's voice was bitter.

Emma leaned back in her seat, happy, not for the first time in her life, not to be a police officer. It was a thankless job.

"If it's any comfort," she said, "Graham Brodie sang your praises. He clearly thinks you're a great cop."

Mackenzie's jaw tightened. "Well, that's unusual. Normally, he's too busy building his own reputation to worry whether any of us is any good." She gave Emma a defiant look. "I am a great cop. Show me a corpse and I'll find you a killer. But what do I know about all of this?" She gestured at the upscale houses around them. "Surely I'd be better used solving murders than guiding a Londoner around Edinburgh. There are bus tours, you know."

Despite herself, Emma laughed. She was starting to like this angry, complicated detective.

"Look, I'm sorry they've made you my babysitter, but I really need you. And you may actually help prevent multiple murders, if my people are right about what's going on in that house."

Mackenzie considered this, her skeptical blue eyes holding Emma's for so long it became uncomfortable. It was almost a relief when she turned back to look at the high gate ahead of them.

"What exactly do you think they're planning in there?"

"Not sure yet. A bombing, perhaps. But an assassination would be more likely. Both could be in the cards." Emma thought of the undercurrent of warning she'd detected from Ripley. "Whatever it is, it's big. We have to stop it."

"Right, then." Mackenzie slid her sunglasses on. "I'm in. Let's get the bastards."

6

The gates of Nick Orlov's house stayed stubbornly closed throughout the rest of the morning. After that early conversation, Emma and Mackenzie fell into a patient silence. They were both very practiced at waiting.

The sun that had brightened the early hours gradually disappeared behind a wall of gray clouds, and the icy wind blowing in off the North Sea had begun to take on a deeper chill by the time the gates at last shivered and, with a clang of metal, began to slide open. Emma picked up her phone.

As the tall gates parted, a sports car painted the bright crimson of fresh blood appeared on the other side, a winged "B" on the hood.

Quickly, Emma typed a three-letter code to Ripley and Zach ("OTM"), then started the engine.

She recognized the dark-haired man at the wheel from the picture of Nick Orlov she'd studied that morning.

"It's our guy," she said.

"He looks the type." Mackenzie clipped her seatbelt into place.

As the red car pulled out, it revealed a second vehicle waiting behind it. It was the black Range Rover from the night before.

"Who's that?" Mackenzie asked.

Emma hesitated as the Range Rover pulled into clearer view.

It held two men. One had a thin frame and dark hair, with a tonsure-like bald patch.

"It's Balakin," Emma said.

The Russian was in the backseat, his sharp eyes looking straight ahead. The driver was the smaller man from the airport. His wiry build and thick brown hair were unmistakable.

As Emma and Mackenzie watched, the Range Rover turned out of the drive in the opposite direction from Orlov.

Mackenzie turned to look at her. "Who do we follow?"

Emma hesitated. All her instincts told her to follow the Russian spymaster, but Orlov was her target. And his car was disappearing from view.

Muttering an oath, she slammed the gearshift into first, and sped after him.

MI6 better be on their toes, she thought, *or they'll lose Balakin.*

In seconds they again had a clear view of Orlov's red car far ahead.

"He's got good taste at least," Mackenzie observed, as they followed him through the quiet neighborhood. "That's a Bentley Flying Spur. It's pure class. Costs more than my flat."

"Cars are a good way to launder money," Emma told her. "Billionaires trade them like stocks and bonds."

Even as she said it, she knew this wasn't true of Nick Orlov. He owned three cars, according to the files she'd read this morning. A five-year-old Range Rover, an Audi, and the Bentley. Enough to show he had plenty of cash, but not enough to indicate laundering.

When they turned onto the main road, she dropped further back, giving Orlov more space.

Mackenzie observed this with a slight frown, but said nothing.

Emma allowed two cars to get between them but always she could see that vivid red car powering ahead. The scarlet was easy to track, glowing like a beacon.

Orlov stayed within the speed limit as they pursued him down narrow streets, passing rows of stone buildings blackened with ancient smoke, until the jagged outline of Edinburgh Castle appeared in the distance.

Finally, the Bentley slowed and turned into the curved entrance to a four-story glass office building. Emma slowed as she passed the structure. A sign in front held an artfully designed logo with an N and a 7 intertwined.

North Seven.

"This is Orlov's office." Emma was genuinely surprised. "I think he's . . . going to work."

It seemed ridiculous that he would spend all night with one of the most powerful men in Russian intelligence and then just get on with his life. But that appeared to be precisely what was happening.

Without being asked, Mackenzie raised her phone and took a quick series of shots as Orlov parked in front of the building and climbed out of the car.

And then they turned a corner and he was out of sight.

"Now what?" Mackenzie glanced at her. "We can't go in that building."

"We wait and we watch." Emma began to make her way around the block, looking for a place to park. Her voice was calm but her doubts were growing. Mackenzie was right—they couldn't go inside. They couldn't get close enough to get what they needed. There were too many locked doors between her and her target. But how could she open them?

Leaving the car parked on the street, she and Mackenzie staked out a spot at a coffee shop with a good view of the entrance to the glass building. It wasn't ideal, but Emma felt she had few choices. With so many police patrolling in the city center right now, lingering on the pavement would attract attention.

If she'd noticed Emma's frustration, Mackenzie had the good

sense not to ask any questions. She kept her focus on the red car, which remained parked in the driveway.

While they waited, Emma got her to send the photos she'd taken to an internet dropbox used by Zach.

Using her own phone, she sent a secure message to headquarters.

"O at the office. Where's B?"

A minute later, Ripley replied.

"MI6 is with B. Stay with O."

So MI6 hadn't lost Balakin. Everything was under control.

With no other choice, she and Mackenzie watched the glass offices, as the clouds gathered overhead and the day grew darker. Nick Orlov didn't reappear. The red car didn't move.

With every passing hour, Emma grew more certain that they were doing this all wrong. She'd spent all morning staring at a gate, and the rest of today staring at an office building. She'd wasted nearly a full day.

Maybe Orlov was at the center of everything as Ripley suspected, but watching his office door wasn't going to give them any information at all. They needed to try something else.

Emma stood up.

"Keep watch," she told Mackenzie abruptly, and walked across to the not-terribly-clean toilets and locked the door.

She splashed water on her face, drying it with the hem of her jumper. In the hazy mirror, her skin was smooth, her eyes untroubled. She gave nothing away, even to herself. But her concerns were growing.

The thing they needed most was time. The time to unravel whatever tangled plan the Russians had cooked up—a plan they'd undoubtedly been working on for months. But in a few days Air Force One would land at Edinburgh Airport.

Somehow, they had to figure this out before then. And right now, they had nothing at all.

. . .

It was eight o'clock when the night shift took over the evening surveillance on Nick Orlov and Emma returned to the offices of Distinctive Exports. The building was freezing. Through the windows she could see the dark sky; the only light came from the office buildings around them and the street lights below.

Zach, who wore a black down jacket and fingerless gloves, was at the far end of the long table typing furiously. He glanced up as she crossed the long room.

"How's Orlov?"

"Busy at work, apparently," Emma said.

"Well, things got a bit wild here today."

Emma looked at the wall-mounted screens. There were more of them now—five in total. Each held a separate image: the gate at Orlov's house, the gates of the Russian embassy in London, the black Range Rover, Vladimir Balakin's plane, and the fanciful gothic turrets of Carlowrie Castle.

"What happened?" she asked. "Where's Balakin?"

"In the restaurant at the Balmoral Hotel having a six-course dinner with a £300 bottle of wine," Zach gave her a look. "He's taken a suite there. But it's not where he's sleeping tonight that matters. It's where he was this afternoon." He gestured at the last image on the wall. "He spent an hour taking pictures of Carlowrie Castle."

Emma stared. "You're joking."

Carlowrie Castle was the planned meeting location for the G7. Over the last few weeks and months, the privately owned gothic manor house outside of Edinburgh had been bomb-swept, security cleared, analyzed by MI5, and thoroughly secured. Police were permanently positioned on the castle grounds for the next two weeks. It was an insane place for a Russian spy chief to visit.

"I wish I was." Zach tilted his head at the door behind him. "Ripley's in the back, talking to Six about it. Everyone's losing their minds."

Emma was stunned. "What about security? How did he get that close?"

"Look at this." Zach typed something and a series of pictures appeared on the screen. Emma saw the increasingly familiar black Range Rover, the sinewy driver with the angular face watching as Vladimir Balakin, pale and ascetic, held his phone up to take pictures, for all the world like a tourist. "He stayed off the property and took pictures from public roads, and then circled the castle, taking shots from other directions. He can't have got much because the house is set so far back from every road, but it was the most obvious reconnoiter we've ever seen." Zach held up his hands. "It was as if he was taunting us."

The door at the end of the room opened and Ripley stormed in, a cigarette smoldering in one hand. Andrew Field emerged seconds later, his phone against his ear, and walked toward the lifts.

"Emma." Ripley motioned her over. "Where's Orlov?"

"At home. Adam's taken over surveillance." She gestured at the image of Balakin. "Rip, what the hell is happening? What is Russia up to?"

"I have no idea what Russia is doing." Ripley stubbed his cigarette out viciously. "Balakin was all but measuring the G7 meeting rooms for new carpets. This is disastrous. The whole operation is in danger now. *Andrew.*"

He barked the name forcefully. Field lowered his phone and walked over to join them.

"It's all a bit of a tangle at MI6 now, I'm afraid," he said, glancing at Emma. "The foreign secretary's insisting on taking steps, but it's unclear what can be done. If they call in the Russian ambassador, it alerts everyone to the situation, including all the G7 leaders. If Russia isn't planning an attack, we risk looking like fools. If they *are* planning an attack, they're certainly not going to tell the foreign secretary." He ran a hand across his thinning hair. "Frankly, I've never seen anything like this."

"If the foreign secretary calls in the Russian ambassador, it's over. There will be no G7 meeting in Scotland. We are so far behind on this we might as well not be here at all. The Russian government is *laughing* at us." Ripley spoke with simmering fury. "Bloody hell. I will not be outsmarted by Vladimir sodding Balakin."

Field turned to look at the screens, his round face creased. "It's so odd. This was done for show. But why did they want us to see this? What are they showing us?"

Emma looked at him. "What if it's some sort of trap? Do they want us to cancel the G7? Is that the plan? After all, if the G7 doesn't meet they can't sanction Russia, and we'll take the blame for that."

Field turned his cool blue eyes to her. "It's possible. But it doesn't seem likely to me. It's not how Balakin works. We need more information, but with half the government now sticking its oar in, things are about to get much trickier." He glanced at Ripley. "The foreign secretary is very unhappy, and that will make the prime minister nervous. So much is on the line, you see."

Ripley gave a tight nod.

Emma looked from Field to Ripley. "We're not being pulled out, are we?"

"Not yet," Ripley said. "But I don't think I'll be running this operation by midnight. Do you?" He directed the question to Field.

Field met his gaze. The two men had known each other for decades. They'd worked together in Russia when both were with MI6 just after the end of the Cold War. Their friendship had somehow survived in the faithless world of espionage.

Field shook his head. "The foreign office will insist on taking over running things. They might let me lead on the ground, but I'll be taking instructions from headquarters."

Emma looked from one of them to the other. "What happens then?"

A faint smile crossed Field's face. "I suppose that's up to the prime minister."

In the silence that followed, Emma could hear the *tick tick* of raindrops tapping against the windows. It sounded so hollow. As if the building were empty. As if they were already gone.

"If the politicians start telling us what to do, it's over," Ripley said, with finality. "The Russians will win everything. We might as well pack and go home."

WEDNESDAY

9 October

SPECIAL TO THE PRIME MINISTER
INFORMATION: PUBLIC COMMUNICATIONS G7
SECURITY LEVEL: MODERATE
RISK LEVEL: MODERATE

THE TIMES
Page One

EVERYTHING IS ON THE LINE FOR
THE PRIME MINISTER

BY LAWRENCE CROWLEY

As preparations get into full swing for the G7 in Edinburgh, the prime minister remains in London, brooding over the details for the most important week of his career as chaos brews around him.

The venue is ready, security is in overdrive, the champagne (from Sussex vineyards) is ordered. The leaders of the free world will be served Scottish lamb with organic Highland potatoes and wild-caught salmon with samphire collected on the Scottish coast. There will be British cheeses and apple chutney. But it must go smoothly, or trouble will follow.

The prime minister's position has been in doubt since he barely survived a vote of no confidence in early September. His own ministers have been quietly telling journalists for weeks that he's "got to go." He's perceived as weak and ineffectual after losing several votes on immigration bills his party considered crucial. Now many of his own back benchers want to see him gone.

The G7 is his last hope to redeem himself and prove that he can pull off a major deal, uniting Britain's allies, and standing up to the Russian Kremlin over the illegal wars in eastern Europe.

For this to work though, he needs perfection. The Gathering of Seven must run like clockwork. If anything goes wrong, the prime minister knows it will be used by his enemies in his own party to hold him to ridicule or worse—contempt. And that would bring him down.

Knives are out in Westminster. And the nights are growing longer . . .

7

Emma was still in the office at one in the morning when Field received the call saying the decision had been made—MI6 and the Foreign Office were taking control of the entire G7 operation away from the Agency, with the prime minister and foreign secretary having direct say over major security decisions. Ripley was now a minor player in this game.

It was everything they'd feared.

"The government is making diplomatic enquiries behind the scenes," Field announced apologetically, as they sat in the cold office, clutching cups of Zach's super-strong coffee. "We're to back off all work for now. They are reconsidering our approach."

The mood in the office was funereal.

"They're idiots," Adam said, his wide brow lowering. "They'll get people killed."

"It's disastrous," said Ripley. "We don't have time to stop. By the time they realize they need us to start up again, it will be too late."

"I agree." Field pulled a cigar from his pocket and a lighter appeared in his left hand. "So, don't stop."

There'd been a pause before Ripley repeated those words as a question. "Don't stop?"

Field lit the cigar. When he spoke, his words came out in clouds of bittersweet smoke.

"Headquarters for the operation are relocating to Westminster. My team is stopping work, as instructed. If the Agency continues work without informing me, there's no way I could possibly know."

The look the two men exchanged contained volumes.

"You're not coming back to this office?" Ripley watched his old friend closely.

"This office is being disbanded, as far as I'm aware." Field took another contemplative draw on the cigar. "My people will be fully focused on Vladimir Balakin, whom we shall watch at a great distance. The Foreign Office would like a small group from the Agency to stay in Edinburgh and continue some surveillance on Nick Orlov. Those are the only orders I have for you, at this time. Everything else is to cease."

Ripley was still watching him. "And if we go beyond surveillance . . . ?"

"I would know nothing about that," Field said. "You will be solely responsible for your activity on this operation. You can approach it how you see fit as head of the Agency. The foreign secretary did not give specific details about how surveillance on Orlov should be conducted. That is at your discretion."

Emma had held her breath as she watched the two men. Nobody knew more about intelligence than they did. Field was fully aware that Ripley could lose everything if he disobeyed orders from Whitehall. And yet, both men knew terrible things happened when politics got in the way of intelligence. Each believed in breaking the rules when the cause was good.

Ripley sat for a moment, his head bowed, then abruptly straightened.

"Thank you for letting me know about all of this," he said, formally. "We're going to follow orders as given. If the prime minister needs anything from us other than surveillance, we'll be ready. I'll keep this office open just in case. But of course . . ." he said, gesturing at the wall of screens behind them showing Orlov's gates and the North Seven offices, ". . . we will focus exclusively on this."

Field studied his old friend with shrewd blue eyes, but all he said was, "Good." Still holding the cigar between two fingers, he stood. "I'm heading back to London at six hundred hours. I'll be in touch if anything changes. Good luck."

He walked to the elevators without looking back. When the doors closed behind him, Emma and Adam both looked at their boss questioningly, but he said nothing. Instead, he picked up his black cigarette case and pulled out a cigarette, tamping it on the lid before lighting it with the battered brass lighter. Curling strands of cigarette smoke soon overrode the cloying scent of cigars that Field had left behind, but still Ripley did not speak.

Emma couldn't bear the silence. "Are we really shutting down?" she asked.

"Of course not," Adam said, before Ripley could speak. But almost immediately a shadow of doubt crossed his face. "Are we?"

"We are not shutting down," Ripley revealed, definitively.

A thrill of excitement ran through Emma.

"I knew it," Adam said. "I knew you wouldn't walk away."

But Ripley, unsmiling, turned his focus to the screens on the wall. "We're continuing the operation but we need a new approach. We don't have backup anymore; we're on our own." He pointed his cigarette at the screen showing the forbidding gates of Nick Orlov's house. "First, we need to get inside that house. It's the only way to find out what the hell is really going on. Then—he pointed at the image of the North Seven glass door—"we have to get inside that office." He turned to them. "That's the job. Find a way. Do it fast."

The three of them had talked into the night, working out ways they might get closer to Nick Orlov. By the time they'd left, just after three in the morning, they still didn't have a plan. Everything they'd thought of would take too long.

Emma walked through the cold night back to her hotel. Her

head felt heavy with exhaustion and her eyes burned, but she hadn't gone to bed. Instead, she took a shower, changed clothes, and walked out to the car.

A mist fell as she drove across the dark town on quiet streets, windshield wipers thumping a steady heartbeat. This time she didn't need GPS or guidance; the landmarks along the way had become familiar—the gas station on the main road with only three pumps, the Victorian school with a distinctive wrought-iron fence, and then the long rows of three-story stone houses with pristine front gardens.

By the time she'd parked and shut off the car's engine, she was already deep in thought. If she was going to get close to Nick Orlov, first she needed to understand him.

She'd read his intelligence files so many times she'd committed them to memory. She knew about his background—a childhood of poverty out of which he had dug himself, the entrepreneurial streak that led him to start his own business and grow it with almost feverish intensity.

And then his curious decision to move it all to Scotland, a decision that had to have been personal, as he could easily have stayed in Russia where his wealth had grown. That indicated an emotional connection to this land.

She could use that. But she needed more.

Emma studied the peak of the roof she could see behind the tall fence. On this leafy upscale street, Orlov's fortress-like compound was an outlier. It was set further back than the other houses, and Emma wondered if that had been the attraction when he'd bought it ten years ago.

Taking out her phone, she connected to the internet and plugged Orlov's address into a property website. Outside, the sky was dark as pitch, and rain trickled down the windows of the BMW. With the engine off, it was beginning to get cold inside the car but Emma barely noticed as the photos opened. The shots were dated from the time of sale of the last sale of the house, and they showed an old stone-built manor in ragged condition, a square, sturdy nineteenth-century building with symmetrical front windows and two tall chimneys. It had been unloved for a long time, its windows had begun to sag, and the grounds were overgrown. It had no tall fence back then, no heavy metal gates. It faced the streets a little sadly, a scruffy neighbor to the prim houses around it.

So, Nick Orlov was responsible for the stone walls that encircled the property now, as well as the modern gates and CCTV cameras. It had been his intention to have a safe, hidden home. But safe from whom? Vladimir Balakin?

If so, that plan had failed. Because for some reason, Orlov had welcomed Balakin into his home. Why would he do that?

She was so intent on her research it was nearly nine when she suddenly remembered Kate Mackenzie. She'd been scheduled to pick her up on a street near the hotel an hour ago. Hastily she grabbed her phone.

It barely rang once before Mackenzie's voice, low and simmering, spoke. "Where are you?"

"I'm at the same place as yesterday," Emma said. "Can you meet me here?"

The phone went dead.

Emma winced.

That had been an error. And she got the feeling Kate Mackenzie wasn't the forgiving kind.

When she arrived thirty minutes later, Mackenzie's expression was thunderous. Her coat was soaked with rain, and her fair hair clung to her red cheeks. She shut the door carefully before exploding.

"What the hell, Makepeace. I waited in the rain for *an hour.*" Without giving Emma time to respond, she held up her hands, sending raindrops showering across the dashboard. "Do you know what? I'd be very happy not to do this. I was quite content in my warm, safe office, drinking terrible coffee and investigating drug dealers, all of whom will eventually get arrested, go to jail for a year, and then come out and sell more meth and coke than they did before. It was a joyous and rewarding life experience. So if you don't want me, please tell me."

The words poured out in a rush, as if she'd been bottling them up the entire time she stood on that corner, gradually getting soaked to the skin.

"I'm sorry I didn't come get you." Emma kept her voice even. "I lost track of time."

"*You* lost track of time." Mackenzie's tone was skeptical. "Come on. I've only worked with you one day and I already know you forget nothing. You're a machine." She paused. "Look, you don't want me here, you've made that obvious. And I'm not wild about this either. But I don't deserve to be just . . . just . . . abandoned."

Something in her tone had changed. In that instant she didn't sound angry. She sounded hurt.

An unfamiliar emotion wrapped itself around Emma's heart. It took her a second to recognize it as remorse. She liked Kate Mackenzie. She liked how straightforward she was, and that rare honesty she sensed in her. She liked her and yet she'd forgotten her.

"I'm sorry," she said again, with more feeling this time. "I really did forget." Seeing Mackenzie's unbelieving look, she reached out a hand and touched the cold fabric of her damp coat sleeve. "It really was a mistake. I didn't get any sleep. I've been out here five hours."

"Five hours?" Mackenzie's brow creased. "You got here at four in the morning? What's going on?"

As rain thumped against the roof of the car, Emma gave Mackenzie a brief version of the truth. What she didn't tell her was that operating off the books like this was incredibly dangerous. Technically, none of them should be doing anything other than sitting in this car watching those gates for the rest of the day. But they were about to go much further than that.

As she spoke, Mackenzie watched her closely, as if looking for something to distrust. When Emma finished, she looked out the window clouded with steam from their breath, strands of wavy hair clinging to her cheeks.

"You still think Orlov's at the middle of this?"

"I don't know," Emma said. "But there's only one way to find out. We have to get inside that house."

"How do we do that?"

"Well, there are two traditional routes," Emma said. "Either we break in, or he lets us in."

Mackenzie gave her a puzzled look. "Why would he let us in?"

Emma thought of the pictures she'd seen of Orlov—his carefully groomed hair, the polished appearance, the expensively whitened teeth.

"He's forty-seven, divorced, and vain," she said. "If we play our cards right, he'll open that door wide."

8

That morning, they followed Nick Orlov's red sports car straight to the North Seven offices, where Emma and Mackenzie watched their target walk inside and disappear from view. Two minutes later, Emma received a secure message from Zach.

"Come back to the office. Both of you."

When they stepped out of the elevators, Mackenzie paused to take in the unplastered walls and exposed wires.

"OK . . ." she said, quietly.

"What it lacks in décor it makes up for in dampness," Emma assured her.

As she spoke, a striking woman with dark hair curled in a nineteen-forties style hurried toward them. Wearing a red tartan jumper and matching lipstick, she seemed to glow in the drab surroundings—a bright star in a dark sky.

"Emma Makepeace, at last," she said, beaming.

"Martha!" Emma exclaimed. "When did you get here?"

"Early this morning. And so far, I've got to say the weather in Scotland is reminding me horribly of where I grew up," Martha said, in her thick Manchester accent.

Emma knew her presence was no accident. If the Agency's disguise specialist had arrived, then she was finally going undercover.

As if she knew what she was thinking, Martha gave her a significant look. "Ripley's waiting for you."

Turning to Mackenzie, she held out her hand. "I'm Martha. If you don't mind, I need to ask you a few questions."

As Martha chatted with Mackenzie, Emma headed across to where Ripley, Adam, and Zach were talking.

It was immediately apparent that nobody had slept. Adam's wiry hair was tangled and shadows underscored his dark eyes. Ripley didn't look much better: his long, craggy face was unshaven and pale. Only Zach seemed impervious to the need for rest, and appeared his normal self.

"What's going on?" Emma asked. "Why'd you pull me in? Who's watching Orlov?"

"Hannah came up from London this morning," Ripley informed her. "She's taking over daytime surveillance effective immediately." He turned to Adam. "Patrick is taking over the night shift from you. I need you both elsewhere."

Hannah and Patrick normally worked as a team on specific projects for the Agency. If they were here as well as Martha, then Ripley was going at this operation with everything he had.

"What's happening?" Adam's voice was low and serious. "Are we going in now?"

Ripley motioned to Zach and said, "Bring them up to speed."

The tech specialist picked up his mug of coffee and turned to face them. Emma could see the letters PEACE tattooed on the backs of his fingers.

"Overnight, I hacked Orlov's email," Zach revealed, his voice buzzing with energy. "It was surprisingly easy—my baby sister has a better password. From what I can see in there, Orlov seems to be a normal bloke. Hard worker, likes the ladies, fan of Scottish independence and making lots and lots of money. Nothing obviously scary in there."

"Did you find anything about Balakin?" Adam interrupted. "Something that explains what their plan is?"

"Not one thing," Zach told him. "They must be communicating another way. To be fair, the FSB prefers Whatsapp for that kind of conversation, and I can't access that unless we get our hands on Orlov's mobile phone. But, here's what I did get."

He set down his coffee and swung back to his keyboard and typed something. A calendar appeared on the wall screen.

Emma stepped closer. "This is Orlov's?"

Zach nodded. "He uses a standard internet calendar connected to his email. Honestly, if he's a Russian spy, he's a particularly crap one."

Ripley motioned to him. "Show them today."

Zach clicked on that day's date.

Orlov had meetings scheduled at the office at ten, eleven, and two. That evening at seven, he had noted "Dinner with V at the Balmoral."

"V?" Emma glanced at Adam and Ripley. "Any ideas?"

"That, among other things, is what I want you to find out," Ripley told her. "First Balakin relocates to the Balmoral, and now Orlov is meeting someone there. V could be Vladimir. They could be having dinner together tonight."

"Or it could all be misdirection." Adam's deep growl interrupted him. "Come on Ripley, why would they be this obvious? First Balakin's photographing the G7 site, and now Orlov's going to meet a Russian spy at a major hotel? They're messing with us."

Ripley's gray eyes considered him, his fingers drumming lightly on the table. "You may well be right," he conceded. "But the only way to find out what they're really up to is to get close."

"Maybe." Adam still looked dubious. "It just feels like we're being played. Why seek our attention like this?"

"I don't know. But there's not enough time to try anything complicated." Ripley turned back to Emma. "I want you to be at the Balmoral tonight. I've got you a booking in the restaurant at the same time. Meet Nick Orlov. Get close to him. Find out all you can."

Emma held his gaze. "How close?"

"As close as you can." Ripley's eyes didn't waver.

Emma's heart stuttered. They both knew everything left unspoken. He was asking her to be a honeytrap.

Adam watched the two of them, his brow creasing. Zach was typing again, but she knew he was listening.

"Are you ready for this?" Ripley pressed.

"Of course," Emma said, although her mouth felt suddenly dry. "Whatever you need."

So this was what Ripley had decided in the long hours when none of them had slept. She was going to seduce him to find out what the Russians were planning.

None of the spy agencies will admit to using honeytraps in modern intelligence, but it happens. When everything else goes wrong, sex is sometimes the only way.

"Good." Ripley turned to Adam. "I want you there too, keeping an eye on Balakin. Stay with him, but don't let his MI6 shadow see you. Both of you remember, *we are not here.*"

Ripley glanced over to where Mackenzie stood waiting uncomfortably near the elevator. Martha must have told her not to move.

"What do you think of her, Emma? Could she go with you? It would look more natural if you weren't alone, and I need Adam to focus on Balakin."

Emma followed his gaze. Mackenzie's hair was still lank from the rain, her raincoat rumpled and stained. She seemed to sense their gaze and glanced up, but she was too far away to hear what they said.

"She can handle it," Emma said. "She's a good cop, I think. Good instincts, anyway."

"Graham Brodie told me she's a bit of a rebel. Tends to speak her mind," Ripley said.

Emma gave a brief laugh. "Yeah, but that's not always a bad thing."

She thought about how upset Mackenzie had been this morning. She wanted to do this job; Emma could sense that. She wanted to be taken seriously.

"She can do it," she said, definitively.

"Good. Give her the brief. Let Martha fix you both up. You've got plenty of time to prepare. Your table is booked for seven. Get there earlier in case he shows up in the bar." He drew her closer, lowering his voice. "Get yourself into Orlov's life. Come up with a reason for him to know you, and want to see you again. We don't have much time for finesse but I know you can do this."

Emma hoped he was right. The idea of seducing Orlov sent a kind of sickening dread into her veins. Maybe she could do this without going that far. Maybe there was a way.

But she had very little time to find it.

When Emma joined Mackenzie a few minutes later, the Scottish detective seemed subdued.

"What's going on?" she asked, tugging unconsciously at the sleeves of her jacket. "Why are we here?"

The light from the bare bulbs didn't quite reach this part of the room, and the two of them stood in shadow as Emma said, "Listen, I'm going undercover to get closer to Orlov, and we'd like your help."

"Right . . ." Mackenzie sounded cautious.

"I'm going to be honest, it might be dangerous," Emma told her. "The people Orlov is working with are very bad indeed. If this is too much for you, I'd understand. I know you're only expecting to help me find my way around Edinburgh and now I'm asking you to take risks . . ."

"I'll do it," Mackenzie said cutting her off, mid-sentence.

Emma searched the outlines of her face. "You're sure?"

"Whatever you need." Mackenzie's voice didn't waver.

To her surprise, Emma found she was relieved. If she was doing this, she didn't want to do it alone.

"Good. Well, we start tonight," she said. "We're going for dinner at the Balmoral Hotel. Nick Orlov will be there. I have to try and get close to him. Did Martha tell you she specializes in disguise?"

Mackenzie nodded.

"Well, she's the best there is. You won't recognize yourself when she's done with you. Come with me."

If Mackenzie found any of this overwhelming, it didn't show on her face as they crossed the office to where Martha had set up a new table in a corner with a freestanding rack of clothes, and suitcases piled around her.

As they approached, she studied Mackenzie with the appraising eye of a car dealer approaching a ten-year-old Fiat.

"Size fourteen? Size seven shoes?" she guessed.

Mackenzie gaped. "Yes? But how . . . ?"

"Martha's the Einstein of clothes," Emma said.

"Flattery will get you everywhere." Martha tilted her head to one side. "Let's start with your hair, Kate. Do you mind if I color it just a little?" Before Mackenzie could argue, she turned to Emma and gestured at the rack of clothes. "Try some of those on. See what fits."

"It'll all fit," Emma said, pulling out a creamy Sézane dress and holding it up. "It always does."

Martha led a reluctant Mackenzie to a chair she'd arranged under a standing lamp that she seemed to have magicked from nowhere.

"Don't worry, you won't feel a thing," she said soothingly. "I've never lost a patient yet."

•   •   •

Five hours later, Emma and Mackenzie were in the back of a taxi driving through rain-slick Edinburgh streets. In the distance, the castle was a constant landmark, its uneven walls lit up like something from a dark fairy tale.

"I feel ridiculous." Mackenzie touched a strand of her hair, highlighted to golden blonde. She'd resisted the dresses Martha suggested, so they'd settled on a loose silk blazer worn with black pleated trousers. Over it all she wore a convincing fake Burberry raincoat.

The outfit really suited her. She looked sophisticated. Like she belonged in those clothes. But, her nerves were obvious. She kept touching her hair and fussing with the edges of her jacket.

"That." Emma touched the hand plucking at the silk sleeves. "That tells me you're nervous."

Mackenzie curled her hand into a fist. "Shit. I didn't know I was doing it again."

"You overcome a tell by paying attention to it," Emma told her. "Now you know this is your tic, when your hand reaches for your sleeve, you'll notice. Just straighten your fingers and take a breath. The more times you do that, the more aware you'll be." She shifted back to face the front. "You look great. Nobody's going to see anything when you walk in that door except a confident, powerful woman."

Mackenzie rested her hands flat on her knees, stretching her fingers out. "I hope you're right. I've never done undercover work. I was a street cop, then I was a detective. I solve crimes the old-fashioned way, you know? Asking questions, getting answers."

"In a way I do the same thing," Emma told her. "I just do it wearing someone else's clothes."

Mackenzie glanced at the driver, but he was talking into a Bluetooth headset and clearly paying no attention to the two of them.

"Do you like this work?" Mackenzie asked, gesturing at Emma's designer dress.

Emma hesitated for a long second. "Most of the time," she said. "I know I'm doing something useful and I know it matters. I'm part of something I believe in. When it all goes well, I love it."

"I can see the attraction," Mackenzie said. "But it's so odd when you think about it."

"Look," Emma said. "This is simple work tonight. All you have to do is believe you are the person who wears these clothes and goes to the Balmoral for drinks and dinner. If you believe it, everyone else will. If it helps, come up with a legend for yourself."

Mackenzie gave her a blank look.

"A back story," Emma explained. "Who are you?" She pointed at herself. "I'm Anna Case, I'm in charge of distribution for an oil company based in London. I'm in town for meetings with our partners." She gestured at Mackenzie. "Who are you?"

Mackenzie thought for a moment. "I'm . . . Catherine Merritt. Everyone calls me Cat. I run a . . . a . . ." Her face creased as she thought. "I run a property investment company. Gold Coast Homes. We've had a few very successful years."

"Perfect. I believe you. Now you just need to believe yourself."

Emma glanced out the window. The lights of the Balmoral Hotel were just ahead of them, catching the falling rain and turning it into jewels.

"Here we go. Get ready. It's showtime."

9

As they walked through the wide glass hotel doors, Emma clung to Mackenzie's arm and giggled. "That driver was insane! Did you see how he took that corner? I thought he'd kill us both."

Her accent was posh and careless. Just another rich girl out on the town.

Mackenzie gave her a look that was part puzzled, part amused, and for a second, Emma wondered if she'd play along. Maybe she simply couldn't do it. She was always so serious, so dour.

But then Mackenzie laughed too. Smiling changed her expression completely, brightening her heart-shaped face, crinkling those extraordinary blue eyes. With her hair lightened and in the sleek suit, she was transformed. Nobody who knew the detective in the too-small jacket would have recognized her.

"You're ridiculous," she said. "It was perfectly normal."

"You always say that," Emma complained. "You'd say it if the car was on fire. It's as if you don't value my opinions. Shall we have a drink before dinner?"

"I thought that was the whole point of coming here," Mackenzie said.

Emma smiled. This was going to work.

With their arms looped, they strolled casually across the lobby of the five-star hotel. Emma glanced around, absorbing the details, looking for problems, but it all seemed normal. The crystal chandeliers, the round table holding bouquets of hothouse flowers—all was as expected.

A reception desk was discreetly tucked in a corner, and above that, a mezzanine level overlooked it all. That part concerned her a little—the upper level was cast in shadow and anyone could be watching. But what would they see? Nothing unusual.

Both Emma and Mackenzie looked as if they belonged here.

Emma wore an effortlessly chic form-fitting dress of caramel silk, which contrasted perfectly with Mackenzie's dark blazer. To anyone passing they would have looked like a pair of well-heeled friends on a night out. Or perhaps sisters; Martha had made Mackenzie's hair the same shade as Emma's.

By now, Mackenzie was comfortable with the act, following Emma's lead as they chatted. She almost seemed to be enjoying the deception.

Back at the office, Emma had given her the basic information about how it would all work. She hadn't told her that the chunky gold watch on her left wrist held a hidden camera. Or that the bracelet on Mackenzie's wrist contained a tracker that also monitored her heart rate and breathing. Or that Emma wore a fine-bladed knife in a custom-made holster strapped to her right thigh.

There was no need for her to know those things. Not yet.

Tucked at one end of the lobby, the hotel bar had dark leather seats and muted lighting. About half the tables were occupied, but Emma could see no sign of Nick Orlov as they took a table with a good view of the restaurant and the hallway beyond.

Emma ordered a vodka martini; Mackenzie chose a whisky sour.

When the waiter was gone, Mackenzie leaned closer to Emma and spoke quietly. "I don't actually know what I'm meant to be doing at this stage."

"Just keep an eye out for anything odd. Anyone who shouldn't be here." Emma opened her small clutch bag and took out a compact, pretending to look at herself in the mirror as she studied the seats behind them. "You'll know it when you see it. It's just detective work, after all."

Mackenzie rested back in her seat and looked around, smiling as Emma made idle chitchat. The room was filled with the kinds of people you'd expect in an expensive hotel — middle-aged men in banker suits, toned women in heels, a loud group at the back who seemed to be celebrating some sort of business deal with magnums of champagne from oversized silver ice buckets.

Their drinks were just arriving when Nick Orlov walked in with a slim blonde at his side.

Emma was intrigued. Either Balakin was coming later, or the "V" in his calendar had been a woman.

"Thank you," Emma told the waitress as she set an iced glass on the table in front of her. Holding up a credit card in the name of Anna Case, she told Mackenzie, "This one's on me."

She paid, watching out of the corner of her eye as Orlov crossed the room with long strides.

The second the waitress had gone, she tapped Mackenzie's arm. The detective followed her gaze to the broad-shouldered Russian man and his date, who had taken a seat two tables away.

Mackenzie's eyebrows rose. "Girlfriend?" she whispered, picking up her glass.

Emma watched Orlov pull a chair out for the woman, who smiled prettily.

"I don't think so," she said. There was no visible affection between them. They seemed stiff, and the woman kept making short, almost nervous statements, which Orlov didn't always acknowledge.

"This is their third date," Emma guessed. "At the most."

Mackenzie gave her a baffled look.

"Can't you see it?" Emma asked. "They aren't casual enough

with each other to be in a long-term relationship. She's nervous—sitting straight, showing off a bit. He's curious but distant. No quick conversation. No 'Oh, Harry at work said the funniest thing . . .' the way you do when you're close and you already know a lot about each other."

Mackenzie shook her head. "This isn't detective work. This is sorcery."

"The most important part of what I do is understanding how people act when everything's fine," Emma explained. "It makes it easier to notice when it all goes wrong."

Mackenzie tilted her head at Orlov, who was motioning impatiently for the waitress. "Is anything wrong with them?"

Emma considered the two. "He's tense. See the muscles in his shoulders when he lifts his hand? He's all bound up with tension. She can tell he's not having a good time, but she doesn't know why."

"So, he's nervous but he hasn't told her what's going on." Mackenzie watched the couple over the top of her drink. "Why is he here at all?"

"That is a very good question," Emma said.

There was, she knew, only one way to get the answer.

Still, she bided her time, nursing her drink, until Orlov and his date both stood up.

"Good lord." Emma glanced at her watch. "It's after seven! We forgot all about our dinner booking."

"Do we have to?" Mackenzie asked, as the couple passed them. Orlov gave the two of them a quick, curious glance. "I'm enjoying the drinks."

"We really should." Emma stood. "I didn't have lunch."

They walked in the wake of their target, talking quietly. They were nearly to the restaurant when Orlov suddenly paused and half-turned. Emma rested her hand on Mackenzie's arm, slowing her.

"Just a second, my shoe's gone loose." She reached down to adjust the strap on her stiletto, tilting her head to watch Orlov.

He wasn't looking at them. He didn't even seem to have noticed them. He was looking above their heads.

Emma glanced up.

A thin, dark-haired man stood above them, on the mezzanine, watching Orlov with a fixed, almost preternaturally intense look.

Balakin.

Emma's heart stuttered, and she quickly glanced away.

"Is your shoe fixed?" Mackenzie asked as Emma straightened. Emma saw her gaze take in the Russian man above them before turning back to her.

"Yes, sorry about that."

Emma noticed Adam sitting on a leather chair, his attention apparently on his phone, a short distance from the Russian spy.

Orlov was still standing where he'd stopped. His date was watching him with bewilderment.

Keeping her movements easy, Emma linked arms with Mackenzie and began walking toward the restaurant. Behind them, she heard Orlov's date say, "What's wrong, Nick?"

Orlov's response was a curt "Nothing."

A second later, he and the blonde hurried past Emma and Mackenzie, almost rushing.

When Emma reached the restaurant doorway, she glanced back. Both Balakin and Adam were gone; she and Mackenzie were alone.

"Who was that?" Mackenzie asked, looking up at the empty balcony above them.

Emma shook her head. "I'll explain later."

Inside the elegant restaurant, classical music streamed quietly from hidden speakers and the air smelled tantalizingly of melted butter and roasting meats. As they stood in the entrance waiting to be seated, Emma couldn't stop thinking about the look on Orlov's face when he noticed Balakin watching him.

He'd been terrified.

There was no way Vladimir Balakin had been the V in Orlov's calendar. He hadn't expected to see him here. Hadn't wanted to ever see him again.

When the hostess returned to the desk after seating Orlov and his date, Emma spun a story about views and space and somehow convinced her that she and Mackenzie needed to sit at a table that just happened to have a clear view of Nick Orlov.

Mackenzie waited until they were alone before whispering, "Right. What's going on?"

Lowering her voice, Emma said, "The man you saw was a Russian spy. His name is Balakin."

Someone brought them water, and Emma ordered glasses of wine. They chose food with little thought, keeping their attention on their target. They could both see the tension in Orlov's body now. Anyone could. Every muscle was taut as a wire. He kept looking at the restaurant entrance, flexing and loosening his hands.

His date tried engaging him in conversation but got little back, until she gave up and began openly looking at her phone.

"Something's got him shook," Mackenzie observed.

They both fell silent as the waitress arrived with plates on which smoked trout curled like carnelian jewels atop delicate emerald leaves.

"Eat," Emma ordered when the waitress had gone, and stabbed a slice of fish with her fork. "Remember—we're having fun."

Slowly, Mackenzie picked up her fork.

"What's he scared of?" she whispered. "That spy?"

"I think so," Emma said. "And that's news. We didn't know he was afraid. We thought they might be friends."

Noticing the waitress watching them, she held up her glass to Mackenzie, and beamed at her. "Happy birthday, Cat!"

Mackenzie gave her a bewildered look and at that moment, Orlov stood and muttered something to his date before striding away.

Emma set her glass down abruptly.

"Stay here," she told Mackenzie, picking up her phone. "Eat the food. If it gets awkward, tell them I've had an urgent call."

Before the other woman could reply, Emma was following Orlov out of the restaurant into the hotel's wide marble-floored hallway. She noticed the way he glanced up at the empty mezzanine before taking a sharp right turn and disappearing into the men's room.

Emma stopped not far from the door and held her phone to her ear without calling anyone. From inside the men's room she heard a voice speaking in Russian, presumably Orlov on his phone.

"Why is he fucking following me?" he demanded. "I do exactly as he tells me, and yet I go out for the night and there he is. Watching me. What does he *want*?"

There was a pause, presumably as he listened to someone reply.

"This can't go on," he said. "I've done my part. Tell him to go away, please. Enough."

Seconds later, the door to the men's room swung open violently.

At that moment Emma lost her grip on her phone and let it fly from her fingers, crashing onto the thick carpet directly in front of Orlov's foot.

Instinctively he bent over to pick it up. Emma crouched down at the same time and their heads collided.

"Oh god, I'm so sorry." Emma laughed as she straightened and put her hand on her temple. "Ouch. Are you OK?"

"I'm fine." He stood, unsmiling, holding out her phone. "You dropped this."

As Emma took it from him, she met his gaze. His eyes were large and deep brown, and filled with worry.

She paused. "Wait. Aren't you Nick Orlov?"

Her accent was perfect Oxbridge, her eyes wide and innocent.

He'd been turning away when she spoke. With some reluctance, he turned back.

"Yes . . . ?"

"You don't remember me." She made a self-deprecating gesture. "Of course you don't. I'm Anna Case. We actually met at the oil futures conference in Oslo two years ago."

"I'm sorry . . . I don't recall." His eyes searched her face. He'd relaxed slightly, having identified her as not a threat.

"We met only briefly. I remember you because you gave the most amazing speech on fossil fuels and the changing public attitude. It was so prescient and wise—I've quoted that speech more than once."

The speech had been referenced in an article in Orlov's MI5 files. Emma had found the text online and read it during the long sleepless hours last night.

Orlov seemed nonplussed. "Thank you, that's very kind. You said your name is Anna Chase?"

"Case," she corrected, with an easy smile. "This is a silly question, I'm sure, but . . . are you here alone? I'd love to have a drink and talk through some of the changes that have happened since that conference."

"Alas, no." He gestured at the restaurant. "I'm with a friend."

"Of course you are." Emma blushed. "I shouldn't keep you. It's just . . . Well. It was such a coincidence to see you again." She held up her mobile. "Thanks for rescuing my phone."

She turned to walk away.

"Anna, wait."

She looked back. Orlov stepped closer.

"Perhaps you could give me your number? I'd love to talk to you again when I have more time." He was so tall he had to tilt his head to look down into her eyes, a move he used to good effect, standing just near enough that she could smell the clean scent of his cologne. "It's not often you find out you made an impact with a speech you thought to be routine."

"Oh, it wasn't routine at all," Emma enthused. "Not for me and my company, anyway."

At the mention of a company, a different kind of interest flared in his eyes. "Remind me who you're with?"

"Global One," she said. "Do you know it?"

"Of course. You're one of the biggest distribution companies in the country." He studied her with a different kind of interest—that of a business executive sensing multiple opportunities. "We really should meet."

"I'd love that," she said. "It's just, I'm only in town for a few days. I'm here for meetings."

"Well, then we cannot wait." He smiled, and she felt the full power of his charm.

He likes the ladies, Zach had said.

"Let's exchange numbers," he said, pulling out his own phone.

For a moment they stood close together, heads bowed over their devices as they exchanged numbers.

"Got it," Orlov said. "I'd like to see you while you're in town." His eyes searched her face almost hungrily.

"I'd love that," Emma smiled. "Let me know what time and I'll be there. I'm so pleased I ran into you tonight."

"As am I," Orlov said.

He lingered in the hallway while she walked back to her table, conscious of his eyes following her.

Emma glanced over to where his date sat alone, an empty cocktail glass in one hand, her expression bored.

He doesn't want her to see him walk in with another woman, Emma realized.

When she sat down, Mackenzie glanced at her, one eyebrow raised. "What happened?"

Emma picked up her wineglass and smiled. "The game is on."

10

Emma and Mackenzie continued the pretense of being friends on a pleasant night out until Orlov and his date left, leaving their coffees untouched in bone china cups.

This time it was Mackenzie who followed them to the hotel's heavy glass door, watching as a valet pulled up in Orlov's bright red Bentley.

"He and his date barely exchanged two words," she told Emma when she joined her outside a few minutes later, having paid the impressively steep bill with Anna Case's MI6 credit card. "I don't think their night went well."

"Maybe not, but mine did." Emma held up her phone. On its screen was a text from Nick Orlov.

"It was lovely to reconnect. Meet for coffee tomorrow?—
Best, Nick"

As a taxi pulled up, and the doorman strode over to open it for them, Mackenzie swore softly. "How the hell did you do that?"

Emma laughed.

The rain had stopped, and the night air was damp and there was a hint of winter ice in the breeze. Emma pulled her coat on over her dress, and cinched the belt around her waist before climbing into the backseat next to Mackenzie.

In the taxi she replied to Orlov's text, and they set a time and location to meet the next day.

Unlike the driver who had brought them to the Balmoral, this one wore no headphones, so neither of them spoke until the taxi deposited them at the car park where Emma had left the BMW.

When he'd gone, they stood shivering in the dark as the wind whipped around them.

"Can I give you a lift home?" Emma asked.

Mackenzie nodded. "I don't fancy freezing my tits off waiting for the bus, and I left my car at home today. Also, I want you to tell me everything."

As Emma navigated the dark streets she told her more about the encounter in the hotel hallway, and Nick Orlov's sudden, intense interest.

"He seemed to relax as soon as he thought he knew me," Emma said. "Especially when he thought I fancied him. It's as if he was relieved to have something to distract him from whatever's going on with Balakin."

Mackenzie studied her. "What will you do? Will you go out with him?"

"Of course." Emma kept her eyes on the road. "I'm going to get into his life. Find out all I can."

"You'll genuinely go on a date with him?" Mackenzie sounded incredulous.

Emma gave her a quick surprised glance. "Come on. You know how undercover works. You're on the drugs squad."

"Yeah, we don't do this kind of thing anymore. Not to the extent of going on a date with someone."

"Well, we do. It's an extremely useful way to find the truth." Emma's tone was crisp. "By the way, you better give me some directions."

Still frowning, Mackenzie cast a glance at the damp street ahead. "Left at the next light."

It was after eleven, and the residential streets were quiet. Soon, the sturdy stone terraced buildings of central Edinburgh faded and were replaced by the featureless brick structures that were the hallmark of a modern suburb.

When Mackenzie spoke again, her tone was cautious. "I don't mean to harp on about this but doesn't it bother you? To go out on a date with someone you don't have any romantic feelings for?"

"How is it different from swiping left or right?" Emma asked. "In some ways, it's more personal, what we do. After all, I know everything about Orlov. I've seen his house, I've seen his girlfriend. Last night I read a speech he gave in Norway that quite passionately called for the oil industry to adapt to climate change and use cleaner practices, so I also understand his work. There are some wives who don't know their husbands as well as I know Nick Orlov."

Mackenzie watched the road, her brow creased with thought. "I couldn't do it," she said, after a while. "It's too much to ask. It would make me feel like a prostitute. Turn right. I'm on the next intersection."

Emma flinched. She'd never been part of a honeytrap before and the idea of doing it made her feel a little queasy. But there was a lot at stake and she'd seen his interest kindle in that brief encounter at the Balmoral. It would be malpractice not to exploit his weakness to find out what the Russians were planning.

When they reached the house, Emma cut the engine. In the sudden silence they could hear the warm metal ticking as it cooled.

"Look," she said, "I don't like the idea, nobody does. But we don't have time to work Orlov in the usual way. We only have a few days. There's a lot on the line here, Mackenzie."

Suddenly, she was cross at her for making her feel uncomfortable about her work.

"Besides," she added, her tone cooling, "I've done worse than go on dates with men for my job. Much, much worse."

The other woman studied her with a look Emma didn't like. It was almost sympathetic.

"Well, respect to you," Mackenzie said, reaching for the car door. "I couldn't do it. See you tomorrow."

Emma watched her walk through the cold until she'd unlocked the door and disappeared inside.

On the drive back into the city, she fought to get Mackenzie's voice out of her mind.

As she'd told her earlier that night, so much of spying was believing. Believing you could become someone else. Believing people would accept you were who you said you were. Tonight, she'd believed she was Anna Case and Nick Orlov had believed it, too. That was the deal. That was the game.

The second you started doubting you were done. For just a moment there, Mackenzie had made her doubt.

She couldn't allow that.

Dating Nick Orlov would be simple undercover work. In the past she'd done similar work with women—befriending them, convincing them she really cared about them until they divulged their secrets. The heartbreak and betrayal they felt in her wake was no different than someone in a romantic relationship might experience. The methods were much the same.

It was the job. And the job was everything.

This thought cheered her, and when she reached the car park she messaged Ripley.

"Available for a debrief?"

His reply came back in seconds.

"Meet me in the bar at my hotel."

The Gleneagles Townhouse Hotel was only a short walk away through the quieting city center, but the wind off the Forth was biting, and she was breathless and red-cheeked when she arrived in the top-floor bar ten minutes later.

Emma hadn't been here before, and when she stepped out of the elevator, she looked around in bemusement. The room was dimly lit and almost ludicrously baroque in design, with marble columns and crystal chandeliers that shimmered in the shadows overhead.

Her boss sat on a coral banquette in the far corner looking morose, his black cigarette case unopened at his elbow.

"I ordered you a Lagavulin." Ripley pushed a heavy glass of amber liquid toward her. "Figured you'd need it. It's cold out there."

Emma lifted the glass and sniffed the whiskey, wrinkling her nose at the peaty scent. "I might as well drink a cigar."

Ripley shook his head. "Philistine. That's liquid gold."

It was after midnight, and the bar was mostly empty, aside from an American couple talking quietly to the bartender, and an older man who sat alone at a table drinking methodically. Nobody was near enough to overhear the two of them.

"How'd it go?" Ripley asked.

When Emma told him about Balakin, and the encounter with Orlov, he listened quietly, his expression brooding.

"There was one thing that was clear to me. Orlov is frightened of Balakin. More than that, actually," Emma corrected herself. "He's terrified. There's no way he knew Balakin would be there tonight. He seemed stunned."

"Interesting." Ripley turned the cigarette case over in his hands. Emma knew that it contained the number of Dunhill blues he'd allow himself to smoke in a day—he rationed them strictly—and a razor blade. Just in case. "So Orlov may not be cooperating with Balakin's plan voluntarily. You can use that. Where are you meeting him tomorrow?"

"A place near his office. We're meeting for coffee."

"Good."

Emma mentally contrasted his approving tone with Mackenzie's revulsion.

We are strange people, she thought, *to do this without regret.*

"Have you identified his date?" she asked.

"Zach tracked her down. Her name is Victoria Hardy-Smith. Age twenty-eight. Daughter of a Scottish banking executive. Socialite. Nobody we're interested in."

At that moment, the bartender turned up the volume on the pop song streaming from the sound system. The young American couple began dancing.

"Let's go outside." Ripley stood up. Taking his drink and his cigarettes, he headed to the glass doors at the edge of the room. Emma followed, grabbing her coat.

Outside, the Georgian roof terrace had a heavy stone balustrade; a row of statues at the edge like guardians, watching the city below. In the darkness, Edinburgh seemed to come alive, with gold and red lights and the rugged, uplit castle glowering from above.

Emma looked around for somewhere to sit, but the chairs and tables on the roof terrace had been stacked away. Ripley stood near the edge of the terrace and lit a cigarette, taking a long, relieved drag.

"The fact that it's illegal to smoke in a bar is a sign that I'm getting too old," he observed.

"Nonsense. You just know what you like." Emma tightened her coat belt. "Did anyone follow Orlov when he left the hotel?"

Ripley nodded. "He dropped Victoria at her house. There was no goodnight kiss. Then he went home."

"He texted me from the car. He must have sent it as soon as he dropped her off. Or even before," Emma said.

"He's eager." Ripley took a sip of whiskey. "That'll be useful tomorrow."

"There's something I forgot to tell you," Emma said, remembering. "He had a furious call with someone Russian. Someone who knows Balakin. Orlov was demanding to know why he was being followed. Who could that be?"

Ripley exhaled a stream of smoke before replying. "I don't know. The only other person we've seen the two of them with is . . ."

". . . the driver," Emma interrupted, remembering the man with the angular face whom she'd first seen on the airport tarmac. "I assumed he worked for Orlov."

"What if he doesn't?" Ripley suggested. "What if he works for Balakin?"

"We need to know who he is," Emma said. "He could be the one keeping Orlov in line."

"What time was that call?" Ripley asked.

"Just before eight o'clock."

"We'll try and trace it," he said, "but it's probably a burner."

He took another drag on the cigarette and fixed her with a steady look. "What are you thinking? That Orlov's being blackmailed?"

"There are a couple of possibilities," she said, slowly. "Orlov's vain. Maybe he stumbled into this plot thinking he was smart enough to handle it, and now he realizes he's dealing with the kinds of people who don't care how much money he has."

"Perhaps." Ripley looked out across the city. "He could also have been dragged into this. He's got dealings in Russia still. But why him? That's the part I don't understand."

"No, me neither," Emma said. "It doesn't fit. None of it fits."

"Agreed." His gaze met hers. "You've not done a honeytrap before. Are you up for it?"

It was unnerving how he always seemed to know when she had doubts. It bothered Emma that he could see through her like that.

"I am," she insisted. "It's not a problem."

He held her gaze steadily. "You can say no. You might have to do more than you're bargaining for. It won't be pleasant."

Emma didn't answer right away. She'd always done whatever

she was asked by the Agency. She believed in their work. She had risen through the ranks over the last two years, proving she was capable of every facet of this job. To have him question her now felt like failure. And yet he was right, she did have doubts.

But she wasn't going to discuss those now.

"I'll do whatever it takes." She emphasized each word.

Still, he watched her as if looking for something in her expression. Finally, when worry had just begun to send the faintest shiver down her spine, he nodded and tucked his cigarette case into the breast pocket of his coat.

"Well then. It starts tomorrow." He tucked his hands in his pockets and looked up at the dark sky above them. "Let's go back inside. It's bloody freezing out here."

THURSDAY

10 October

SPECIAL TO THE PRIME MINISTER
INFORMATION: PUBLIC COMMUNICATIONS G7
SECURITY LEVEL: HIGH
RISK LEVEL: HIGH

Personal Note from Lauren Cavendish:

This is the article I phoned you about last night. As you directed, we tried to stop it but the paper refused all changes. You need to be aware that Alex did not get <u>any of this</u> from my office. MI6 deny being the source, they believe it may have originated with the police. A high-priority internal investigation is underway to identify the source of the leak.

THE SCOTSMAN
Page One

IS DANGER LOOMING FOR THE G7?

BY ALEX LOUIS

With the G7 now four days away, rumors are rife in Whitehall that the government and security services are expecting trouble, and perhaps even violent disruption.

Intelligence sources tell me communication has been intercepted from unknown groups planning an attack designed to create chaos that could fully disrupt the gathering of world leaders. This attack, I'm told, could include what they're describing as "terroristic methods."

This information explains why security forces and police have ratcheted up security in advance of the gathering. Princes Street was closed to all vehicular traffic late last night, and police said it will remain shut to nonofficial vehicles until after the G7 next week. Police refused to say how many streets will be closed or whether more disruption could be expected.

Airport-style security measures are being put in place at local museums, and police said to expect them at any large gatherings over the next few days.

In general there is a sense of heightened nervousness throughout the Scottish capital, and even more so in London. No officials would agree to go on the record for this piece. The Home Secretary's office refused to comment.

The Prime Minister's Chief of Staff Lauren Cavendish said, "We absolutely refute the allegations in this article. Plans for the G7 are moving smoothly and all security measures in place are standard for major events."

However, a high-ranking source told me privately, "The PM's office is terrified that something is going to go wrong with the gathering. Any disruption would only exacerbate the sense that he's losing control." Within his own party the mood is heated. The hardliners can see their chance to get rid of him and bring in one of their own. It's not an opportunity they're likely to pass up.

11

On Thursday afternoon, with streets closed all over Edinburgh, traffic was lethal. Emma, running late for her coffee date with Nick Orlov, was forced to abandon the car on a side street and walk the rest of the way.

The restaurant he'd chosen—called Harry's Place—proved to be an unfussy spot with mismatched wooden tables and chairs. A bar dominated at one end of a room decorated with framed posters from classic films. It was a far cry from the five-star Balmoral Hotel.

Breathless, Emma paused just inside the door. The restaurant was small but popular, and every table was taken. Orlov was sitting at a table near a poster for the movie *Casablanca*. Instead of the designer suits he usually wore, he was dressed casually in khaki trousers and a button-down shirt. He stood up as she crossed the room.

"I'm so sorry I'm late," she told him, in Anna Case's Oxford-educated accent. "I think they've closed every street in Edinburgh."

"No worries at all," Orlov assured her. "To be honest, I wondered if you'd really come." This admission was followed with a disarming smile that looked almost shy.

"How could I not?" Emma asked. "Running into you last night was serendipitous."

"Serendipitous." Orlov repeated the word. "The perfect description."

Emma shook off her coat, beneath which she wore an outfit carefully chosen by Martha—jeans with a loose white blouse. Orlov's gaze swept her body approvingly as she draped the coat across the back of the chair and sat down.

"With someone like Nick Orlov, you need to look like money doesn't matter to you," Martha had said, settling Emma in front of a mirror in the long, empty office. "He's been dating spoiled brats and I don't think he's happy about it. You need to be refreshing. Smart. Different. Then, perhaps, he won't ask too many questions."

It was uncanny, Emma thought, how right she always was.

Martha had told her once that when Ripley discovered her, she'd been working in the film industry. She still had a natural talent for imagining a scene and then making the disguise fit the moment.

"What kind of coffee would you like?" Orlov asked, as she took a seat. "Or would you prefer a glass of wine? It's nearly Friday, after all."

She laughed and shook her head. "A cappuccino would be perfect."

He walked to the bar and ordered from a man in a black apron who was cleaning glasses and seemed to know him. The two exchanged a few sentences, and Emma watched as Orlov leaned against the bar, grinning broadly.

It was interesting seeing him so comfortable. If it weren't for his Russian accent, he might have been born and raised in this city.

There was little sign now of the worry she'd seen in his body language the day before. Instead he seemed cheerful as he strode back to sit down across from her.

"Coffee is on the way," he announced.

"Wonderful." Emma tilted her head at the room around them. "I like this place."

"It's good, isn't it?" he said. "Harry, the owner? He's a good man. He worked in restaurants for years as a cook–always working for someone else, until he decided to start his own place. He put all his money into this business, and he works hard. He should be rewarded."

"I must say, it's nothing like the Balmoral," she observed.

"Oh that." His nose wrinkled. "I don't like that place. Victoria likes expensive places. It was not my choice."

"Victoria," Emma lingered on the name. "Is she your girl-friend?"

The song streaming through the speakers ended, and in the brief silence he picked up a teaspoon and moved it over two inches before setting it down again.

"Victoria is an old friend," he said, carefully, as the new song began. "We've dated a little but it's not serious." When she didn't speak, he made an X on his chest. "Cross my heart."

Emma laughed. "Good to know."

She couldn't deny she was charmed by him. He was so obviously trying to win her over, and she liked the way his smile lifted his face, crinkling his large brown eyes at the corners.

"You are the person who interests me," Orlov said. "Not Victoria."

Their eyes held. The air between them crackled with a new tension.

At that moment, Harry walked up with two large mugs.

"Here you go," he announced.

Emma and Nick Orlov both fell silent.

"Two cappuccinos," Harry continued, brightly. "Can I convince you to have a slice of cake? The chocolate is to die for, or so I'm told. Can't touch it myself without gaining half a stone."

Emma let color rise to her cheeks. Orlov, still watching her, replied just a moment too late. "No thanks, Harry."

Harry looked from him to Emma and back again, amused un-derstanding dawning.

"Now then, I feel like I've blundered in at precisely the wrong moment. I think I'll go away and come back later."

Above his neat beard, Harry's blue eyes danced as he patted Orlov on the shoulder before turning to walk away.

When he'd returned to the bar, Emma stirred her coffee and gave a nervous laugh. "Well, that was mortifying."

"Harry loves to tease me." Orlov grinned. "Now, where were we? Oh yes, the Balmoral. Is that where you're staying while you're in town?"

"There's no way my company would pay for that," Emma said ruefully. "I was out with my friend Cat. She lives here in Edinburgh. She just came out of a bad breakup and wanted to let her hair down."

"Oh, breakups." Nick shook his head. "They mess you up."

Emma was struck by how fluent his English was. Yes, he'd lived in Scotland for over a decade, but it takes most people longer than that to absorb a new language to the point that they can express themselves as fluidly as a local. Her own mother had never fully mastered the nuances of the English language.

"I hope this doesn't sound insulting," she said, "but your English is incredible."

He held up his hands. "Not insulting. A compliment. I studied English in Russia, and then work brought me here many times before I decided to make it permanent. Besides, I'm a natural with languages. I speak Russian, German, Ukrainian . . ." He gave a shrug. "It's easy for me, for some reason."

Emma, who spoke those exact languages and several more, knew just what he meant.

"Good lord," she marveled. "And I can barely speak English."

"It runs in the family," Orlov demurred, modestly. "My mother spoke five languages. She was born in Ukraine, moved to Kazakhstan, and she taught German at a school."

"Is Kazakhstan where you grew up?" Emma asked.

He nodded. "I spent most of my childhood there."

"I've always wanted to see Kazakhstan," Emma confessed. Orlov gave her a doubtful look and she laughed. "I'm serious. It looks so wild and bleakly beautiful. Besides, I work with a lot of Kazakh companies, so I know a bit about the region."

"Which companies do you work with there?" he asked.

Emma paused to think. "Oh, let's see, Bolashak is one, and Arctic Group . . ."

"Boloshak is one of my partner companies!" Orlov's brow furrowed. "It's so strange I don't remember meeting you. Our paths must have crossed more than once, and you would be very hard to forget."

"Well, we definitely met in Norway, but you were thronged at the time," she said. "I was part of a large crowd of fans, all trying to ask you questions."

"I was a fool not to notice you." He held her gaze just a little too long. Emma didn't look away.

"What are you doing for dinner tonight?" he asked.

She shook her head, a slight smile playing at her lips. "I haven't thought about it."

"Come to my house. Let me cook for you. I want to get to know you better, Anna. There's no pressure. We'll just . . . eat. And talk. Please say yes."

His voice was almost pleading. Emma's smile widened. "Yes, of course I'll have dinner with you. That would be lovely."

"Good." He picked up his coffee. "I missed you the first time we met. I'm not making the same mistake twice."

.   .   .

Technically, beyond the most obvious security requirements, the Agency had no firm rules on dating, but Emma had rules. She had lots of rules.

When she'd first become a spy, she'd been in a relationship with a soldier from her unit in Germany, but the lies she was forced to tell him had gradually destroyed any trust between them. He hadn't been stupid, and he knew she wasn't telling him the truth about her sudden disappearances and long absences.

After that, she'd tried dating the normal way, through an app. But the men she met were so far from her world with their worries about cars and promotions and gym memberships, each time she quickly grew bored.

Her one attempt to date a fellow spy had ended disastrously when he was revealed to be a double agent selling out his country to Russia.

Since then, there'd been nobody. And that, she suspected, was how it would have to be. How could she trust anyone? How could anyone trust her?

Most of the spies she knew were single. Ripley and Adam were both divorced, and Emma thought she knew why.

Perhaps pretending to be someone's girlfriend would fill that gap, she thought with some irony as she drove slowly through the gridlocked city center, where temporary barricades blocked access to every street she needed to turn down. It was entirely possible that pretending to like Nick Orlov would be the closest she'd ever come to having a real relationship.

In fact, if she really thought about it, there was only one man she could imagine herself dating, and he was impossible.

As Emma pulled into the central Edinburgh car park at last, she tried to wipe the thought from her mind. She didn't let herself think about Michael Primalov these days. He was in the British government's protection program, and even spies weren't allowed to know where he was living. She hadn't seen him in a year.

Surely, she thought dryly, *there has to be someone out there who isn't either a traitor or in the witness protection program.*

When she walked into the office, Ripley was waiting with Adam at the long table, studying something on the wall screen.

"I'm worried," Emma announced, shrugging off her coat. "Something's not right."

"Really? I thought it went well." Ripley gestured at the screen where they would have observed her interactions with Orlov through the tiny camera hidden in the top button of her blouse.

"It went too well. I'm a complete stranger and he's telling me about his family, and I mean the whole truth about his family. I've read his files, and I know his mother really was a teacher who speaks five languages."

"He likes you," Adam said. "Take it as a win."

"Maybe," Emma said. "I thought it would be harder than this to win him over but either he's a complete innocent or he's playing me." She turned to Ripley. "Are we sure he's not a Russian agent?"

He held up his hands. "As sure as we can be."

Emma glanced at Adam. "What about Balakin? Did he do anything interesting last night?"

"He drank wine with the driver, who is clearly not a driver," Adam said. "Then they had dinner, and in between they stalked Nick Orlov." He shook his head. "It was the strangest thing, the way Balakin stood on that balcony, staring at him. It was like he was reminding him of something."

"Well, it scared Orlov to death." Emma glanced at Ripley. "Have we ID'd the driver yet?"

"Ah yes, you don't know." Ripley typed something, and an image of Balakin's companion opened on one of the wall screens. This photo had been taken on a sunny day in what looked like Heathrow Terminal 5. In the photo, the man held a phone to his ear and was looking at the departure board, his impatience evident in the tight lines of his jaw.

"Leonid Fridman," Ripley said. "He's no more a chauffeur than I am. He's with the FSB. Essentially, he's Balakin's henchman. He makes sure everyone toes the line, whatever that line might be."

Emma studied his face, the fair hair, his eyes like chips of stone. He had a scar on his chin—small but deep. It was the only imperfection she could see.

Emma stood up, her eyes on the screens, each of which displayed a different part of their investigation: Orlov's front gate, the North Seven entrance, Leonid Fridman, Vladimir Balakin. All the pieces in the puzzle. But how were they linked?

"So, two senior FSB officers are here before the G7, and they want something from Orlov, but what?" Emma murmured.

"This is what we need to know." Ripley stood up and walked over to a hard-sided case in the corner and took something out. When he returned, he handed Emma a small cardboard box. "There are three devices in here. I need you to plant them in Orlov's house tonight."

Emma opened the box and tilted it until three tiny electronic chips, each no bigger than the tip of a fingernail, slid into her palm.

As she held one up to examine it, Ripley continued. "These will pick up everything said in a room, and feed it to us. I'd like you to place one in his study, if he has one, another in the living room, and the third in his bedroom."

"That's a big ask," Adam objected. "If she's alone with him there's no one to distract him."

"I can handle it." Emma slid the devices back into the box.

"Good," Ripley said. "We haven't got the manpower anymore to provide backup. You're going to have to do this alone, and you must succeed. We have to get these devices into place if we're going to find out what Nick Orlov has that the Russians want so badly. We don't have time for mistakes."

12

After that meeting, there was nothing for Emma to do but wait. She should have slept, but she felt too restless, her thoughts whirling through everything she needed to remember that night, all the things she'd said to Orlov when they'd met, and how he'd reacted. She had to be the same person again that evening—the same voice, the same motions. The history she'd created for Anna Case had to be on the tip of her tongue, whatever he might ask. She had to be absolutely consistent, and this time they'd be alone together for hours.

Then of course, there were the big questions. What would Anna Case do if he invited her into his bed? What should Emma do? What if Orlov wasn't as naïve as he seemed? What if he was playing her? If that were the case, those high walls around Orlov's house would turn into a prison.

For a while she walked aimlessly down the cold streets, turning whenever she reached a barricade. Edinburgh was becoming increasingly impossible to traverse. Over and over she passed pairs of police patrolling, some of them armed, and for the first time Emma noticed a crop of television news vans sprouting in the car parks and on the streets. When she spotted a reporter holding a microphone stopping people to interview them, she turned sharply, finding herself near Greyfriars Kirkyard, on a bridge with a view of the city's jagged roofs.

She didn't know how long she'd been walking when she noticed she was cold, even in her coat. The ever-present wind blew her hair into her eyes as she followed a winding cobbled lane down to a row of tiny shops, where she bought a wool hat and gloves.

Stepping outside the shop, she pulled one glove off long enough to dial a number on her phone.

"Are you busy right now?" she asked. "Want to meet for coffee?" She paused to listen. "Great. No, I'll come to you."

When Emma arrived at the coffee shop called Café West, Mackenzie was standing outside. The elegant clothes she'd worn to the Balmoral were long gone, and she was back in her rumpled black raincoat. Her hair was still blonde, though, and the lighter tone suited her, Emma thought.

"I'm sorry to bother you," Emma said, when she neared her. "I'm sure you've got plenty to do."

"It's no bother," Mackenzie said. "I'm supposed to be your guide, after all."

She asked few questions, and Emma was grateful for that. She was starting to understand how smart Kate Mackenzie was. How intuitive. The less she asked, the more she understood.

Inside, the coffee shop was small and warm, with an array of vivid paintings on the wall. The only person working was a young man in a T-shirt, his arms covered in a complex array of tattoos.

Emma ordered a green tea—the last thing she needed right now was caffeine; she was wired already from nerves and insomnia.

Mackenzie raised an eyebrow and ordered black coffee.

They took the table at the back. It was a quiet time of day, and most of the tables around them were empty.

When they were settled, Emma sipped the bitter tea while Mackenzie watched her with those knowing blue eyes and said,

"Are you going to tell me what's going on or do you just want to talk about the weather?"

To her own surprise, Emma found herself telling her a bit of the truth. That Orlov was far too relaxed, and that didn't make sense. That she'd never had to seduce a target before, and she wasn't looking forward to it. That she believed in the work, but the methods sometimes were difficult.

Mackenzie listened patiently, without judgment, occasionally sipping her coffee.

When Emma finished, Mackenzie said simply, "What are you going to do?"

Emma held up her hands. "I'm going to do the job."

Mackenzie nodded, as if this was just what she'd expected. "You think you're in danger?"

Emma considered this seriously. "No," she said, after a moment. "The dangerous person is Balakin. Orlov I can handle."

"And there's no chance of this guy Balakin showing up, I guess?"

Emma hesitated. She remembered Orlov's voice the night before at the Balmoral Hotel: *"Why is he following me?"*

"It's unlikely," she said, after a moment, "but not impossible."

Mackenzie took another ruminative sip, and then said, "Do you want me to be there? I mean, outside. Just in case."

Emma opened her mouth to say no, don't be absurd, my guys have this covered. And heard herself say "Yes."

"OK, then," Mackenzie said. "I'll be there. You'll have your phone?"

Emma nodded.

"Then we should be golden."

It was so strange, but knowing this calm practical cop would be outside the gates eased Emma's nerves. Mackenzie was the kind of person you wanted to have your back—she wouldn't hesitate to run toward danger. She was utterly reliable.

It was odd how easily she'd slipped into having a partner. She'd never wanted one. Even as part of a team, she still operated mostly solo. The fewer people with you, the fewer chances there were for betrayal. She'd learned that lesson over and over.

And yet, she trusted Mackenzie.

Of course, she'd done her research. After that first day in Scotland, Ripley had sent Mackenzie's MI5 files. Although those had been brief, one thing had been clear. Throughout her career, Mackenzie's main problem had been her brutal honesty, and a refusal to compromise. Like politics, policework requires a certain instinct for when to stand up and when to stay seated. Mackenzie simply could not stay sitting down.

Emma was drawn irresistibly to that instinct to do the right thing. It was rare and precious.

She admired Ripley more than anyone she knew, but she was fully aware that he would, when needed, deceive her. Spying is lying, and they were both spies. She would lie to him for the same reason. In fact, she lied all the time. Her entire life was a lie.

But with Mackenzie, the veil of deception was lifted, and it felt freeing.

Maybe this was why she'd called her, and why they sat in the coffee shop for more than an hour, talking. Not just about Orlov but about other things. Life.

"So how did you get into this . . ." Mackenzie waved one hand expressively ". . . business?"

Emma thought for a moment before replying. "I guess you could say this is the family business. I do the same thing my dad did."

"Is he still in the . . . company?" Mackenzie asked.

"He's dead. He died before I was born." Emma left it at that. Mackenzie's view of spying was already dark and if she knew her father had been executed, that wouldn't help.

"I'm sorry," Mackenzie said. There was a pause before she added, "My mother died when I was thirteen."

Emma gave a slight nod of recognition, one half orphan to another. "Do you mind if I ask what happened?"

"Overdose." Mackenzie said. "She was a junkie. Which I believe is now a politically incorrect term for her many addictions."

Her tone was flat, but Emma could sense the conflicted emotions beneath the surface.

"That had to be hard," she said. "Thirteen's a terrible age."

"It was a shit show," Mackenzie said. "She died in the bathroom with a needle in her arm. I found her there when I got up to get ready for school. We were living in Glasgow. My parents were divorced, so I called my dad and told him Mum had hurt herself." She shrugged. "You can imagine the rest."

Emma could imagine very clearly: the frightened child, the cold corpse, the confused and angry father, the police, the emergency services . . .

Her heart ached for that girl whose life would never be the same again, but she knew better than to express that sympathy. Mackenzie wouldn't welcome it.

"What happened after that?" she asked instead. "Did you live with your dad?"

Mackenzie gave a short laugh. "Yeah, for about six months. My stepmother hated me. She had a toddler of her own and she was too emotionally immature to know how to love someone else's child. She convinced my dad to send me away." She met Emma's gaze with sardonic blue eyes. "She said it would be *better* for me. After all I'd been through."

She took a drink of coffee and looked around at the empty tables. "Turns out she was right. I went to live with my grandmother in Yorkshire, and she basically saved my life. I didn't make it easy for her, mind you. I got into all kinds of trouble that first year — drinking, petty crime, shoplifting . . . the usual. I got caught, of course. And then I was put in a police program for troubled youth." She gave a faint smile. "I hated it at first, and then one day, I didn't. I just got it. I understood what the police were doing."

Seeing Emma's doubtful expression, Mackenzie laughed. "OK, it wasn't that straightforward, but I really connected to the cops who ran that kids' program. They understood me. Actually, no—it was more than that." She paused, her forehead crinkling with the memory. "They forgave me, if that makes sense. They seemed to think I wasn't a terrible person. And I guess I needed someone to tell me that."

Her face was so expressive in that moment, she suddenly looked quite beautiful. Her eyes bright, her heart-shaped face illuminated from within.

"So you became one of them," Emma prompted.

"Yep." Mackenzie stirred her cold coffee. "I finished school, got decent marks, and signed up to be a cop myself. I was with West Yorkshire PD for five years before moving to Scotland and becoming a detective."

That explained why her accent was that curious mix of Scottish and English, a perfect meld of the two sounds.

"Why did you leave Yorkshire?" Emma asked.

"Why does a young woman do anything? Because I fell in love with someone, and he wasn't about to leave Edinburgh, so up here I came." Mackenzie gave a wry smile. "I was wrong about him but I was right about Edinburgh; it's a beautiful place to live and it's always been kind to me. Well, until lately, anyway." Dropping the teaspoon, she sighed. "You know, I always thought I was a cop for life. Now I'm not so sure." She glanced at Emma. "What about you? Do you have any doubts about your choices?"

"Constantly," Emma said, without hesitation. "But I know it's the right job for me. Just because it's not easy doesn't mean it's wrong." She angled forward holding Mackenzie's gaze. "I know why you find it hard to understand my work. But you must see that what I'm doing is important enough to merit taking these sorts of risks. Making these kinds of hard decisions. You can see that, can't you?"

Mackenzie studied her for a long moment. Emma didn't know

why it mattered so much, but for some reason she needed her to agree.

"I do see that," Mackenzie said, finally. "But not everyone can make those sacrifices."

"No, but I can," Emma said firmly. "I'm good at this. And it's what I always wanted to do."

It was the truth. She'd wanted to be a spy ever since she was a child. There was no other career for her.

"What does the rest of your family think about that? You said it was the family business," Mackenzie said.

"It was my father's business," Emma clarified. "My mother is not in the company. And she doesn't know that I am. She can't know. I love her too much to tell her."

Her expression softening, Mackenzie gave a slow thoughtful nod. "You don't tell the truth to anyone, do you, though?"

"I tell some people. I mean, I'm telling *you* more than I should," Emma pointed out. "I've told one person everything. But he'll never tell anyone."

"Because he's dead?" Mackenzie guessed.

"Because he's trustworthy." Emma met her gaze. "Like you."

A look of understanding passed between them, and then Mackenzie picked up her coffee mug. "If we're staying, I'm getting more caffeine."

By the time Emma left the café, shadows had begun creeping across the damp pavement, and that nervous, jittery feeling she'd had all day was gone. She felt centered and ready for whatever was coming as she pulled the black knit hat over her hair and threaded her fingers into the warm gloves.

She was due to meet Martha at five o'clock to prepare for her date with Nick Orlov, and she walked up the hill toward her car with long, confident steps, her mind already looking ahead. When she turned the corner, she almost didn't notice the man in the distance.

He was slim, with thick, dark hair, and moved with a runner's walk—a kind of bouncing, muscular stride.

In the end, that was what drew her attention. It was such a distinctive way of walking. She'd once known someone who looked just like him. With that same dark hair.

Something clicked in Emma's chest. Her breath quickened.

But it couldn't be him, she told herself. There were thousands of athletic dark-haired men in the world.

Still, when she reached the BMW she didn't stop. She kept following him, her steps fast and light on the wet paving stones, sticking to the shadows.

The man never looked back, his attention focused entirely on the road ahead, in a way that felt achingly familiar to Emma.

It can't be him, she reminded herself. *It can't be.*

At last, the man reached a corner, and turned. As he did, the early evening sun, its fading beams apricot and gold, caught his face.

Emma drew a sharp breath.

It was a face she knew very well. And now fate had brought them together again.

13

Michael Primalov had been Emma's first major assignment when she joined the Agency. He was the English son of two former Russian spies now in the protection of the British government. The Russians sent a team to kill Michael as revenge. Emma was sent to save him. It had turned into a night she could never forget.

Because of multiple incidents happening at once, the Agency had been spread too thin to offer backup, and she'd had to handle it all on her own. Over the course of twelve hours, Emma had been shot, and forced to kill a Russian assassin in order to keep Michael safe. By the end of the night it felt as if they'd walked through fire together. The experience had bonded them more tightly than she'd expected. She'd formed a connection to him she couldn't really explain, and one she'd never completely got over.

He was the person she'd mentioned to Mackenzie, the one she'd told everything to. Michael even knew her real name.

As soon as they'd reached safety, though, he'd been swept into protective custody where he would live for years, if not the rest of his life. He'd been given a new home and a new identity. The law forbade anyone from knowing what that identity was—even spies could not know where he lived.

Emma had never seen him again. Until now. Because Michael Primalov was right in front of her, walking down a Scottish street, into an autumn sunset that had begun to set the sky aflame.

It was such an extraordinary situation that she found she simply didn't know what to do. She didn't believe in coincidences ordinarily, and yet here she was right in the middle of one. It was as if fate had decided today was a good day to torment her.

The rules on this sort of thing were very clear. She could not interact. Michael remained at risk of assassination, and any contact would be dangerous to both of them. Emma's duty was to walk away before he could ever see her. Before he ever knew their paths had crossed.

And yet, she stood stock still, watching him go about his life.

How many times had she imagined this moment? It had been a fantasy—the idea that she might see him again someday, and throw questions at him just to hear him answer in that pragmatic and thoughtful way he had.

Even as she thought it, she shook her head. This was impossible. Nobody could know where he was. She had to turn around and forget that this moment had ever happened.

Ahead of her, Michael was disappearing into the blinding light of the sunset.

The sounds of the city faded to silence, until she could hear nothing except her own breath moving through her lungs. *In. Out. In. Out.*

She had to leave. She had to do it now. Martha was expecting her. She was meeting Nick Orlov soon.

Nevertheless, Emma began to walk toward the sun.

Once the decision had been made, she treated the situation as if it were an assignment, staying close enough that she didn't lose track of Michael, but far enough away that, if he looked back, he wouldn't notice her. But she knew he wouldn't look back. He never did.

She moved slowly then faster, stopping to let him get further ahead, before picking up the hunt a minute later. When Michael crossed a street and went into a shop, Emma lingered in the shadow of a parked van, waiting patiently until he emerged carrying a small shopping bag.

He hadn't changed in the year that had passed since that night. His dark curly hair was still slightly out of control, and in a jacket and neat trousers, he had the sartorial look of a overworked young professor. It occurred to Emma that, given the hour, he might be coming home from work.

He'd once been a doctor specializing in cancer, and she wondered if those protecting him had found a job for him in a hospital again. She hoped so. She'd had a chance to see how good he was with patients, and the world needed more physicians like him. He was born to be a doctor in the same way she'd been born to be a spy.

At the next corner, Michael turned onto a tree-lined residential street; it would be hard to stay out of sight there. As she paused to watch, he walked past three doors before turning in to a small, terraced house. It looked like a postwar build, very plain but sturdy. The bright blue door was the only touch of color. The vivid shade was almost an act of rebellion against the plain backdrop of the building, and somehow Emma knew it was his home. That blue door was very Michael. She wasn't at all surprised when he tucked the bag under his arm, pulled out a key and unlocked it before stepping inside.

She held her breath as the door closed behind him. And then he was gone from her life once again.

Emma exhaled slowly.

Well, that's it, she told herself. *You found him and you saw that he was healthy and alive. Now get out of here.*

But her feet wouldn't follow that order. She stood staring at that door until the sun slipped below the skyline, and the shadows took over.

With every passing moment she questioned her own decisions.

This wasn't something she'd have done a year ago. Nor in the months after Michael was taken into protection. This was new.

But she didn't need anyone to tell her why this was happening. It had been a year of betrayal and lies and death.

No, she understood perfectly well why she was behaving irrationally, but she couldn't seem to stop herself. This felt like fate. Except she didn't believe in fate. Did she?

She'd just been talking to Mackenzie, who reminded her so much of Michael. And now she was standing outside Michael's house.

Like Mackenzie, Michael had found her world unbearable, and yet he'd seen good in her. Good that she herself had recently lost sight of. Sometimes, as she was falling asleep, she heard Michael's voice in her head repeating the last words he'd ever said to her.

"You are extraordinary."

But was she extraordinary? She didn't think so. She was just an ordinary spy playing a rough game, and she missed seeing the good in people. Mackenzie and Michael both let her do that again. See the good around her.

The cold had begun to creep from the ground into her blood when the vibration of her telephone roused her. She pulled off one glove to check the secure message from Martha.

"Is everything OK? Your date with O is in an hour."

Emma's heart stuttered. Somehow, she'd been standing here for more than half an hour. Had she completely lost her mind?

This had to end.

She spun on her heel so quickly she startled an elderly woman passing her. "Sorry," Emma muttered, and ran back down the street, passing the corner shop where Michael had stopped for groceries, and then racing up the hill to the BMW.

In the driver's seat she ripped off her gloves and messaged Martha quickly before shifting into gear.

On my way.

As she drove back toward the city center, she lectured herself sternly.

"What's wrong with you? Are you having some kind of nervous breakdown? Because now isn't the fucking time. First you have to save the world, then you can go completely mad. That's the correct order of things."

She was genuinely angry with herself. This wasn't who she was. She had to get her focus back.

One thing was certain—she'd never tell Ripley what happened today. He could never know she'd seen Michael. Not least because he had the power to have Michael moved.

By the time she walked into the long office space after fighting her way through the traffic, she was calm again. She had a job to do, and she was going to do it well.

Ripley was nowhere to be seen and that, at least, was a blessing. Zach was busy at the computers and didn't even look up as she crossed the room.

If Martha wondered what had happened, she knew better than to ask, instead leading Emma straight to a seat in front of a lighted mirror, picking up a brush.

"There's actually not much to do to you after yesterday so it's a good day to be late," she said, as she began to smooth her hair. "Just a bit of polish and you'll be right as rain."

Emma met her eyes in the mirror. "Thank you."

Martha nodded. "I've checked traffic. You'll be about ten minutes delayed by the time we're done and you get to Orlov's house. I suggest you tell him you've been in meetings all day and the last one ran late. We'll put you in a blazer and good flat shoes, and you can say you didn't have time to change. It works in our favor. We want him to see you as busy and self-sufficient. Nothing like those other women he's been seeing." Setting down the brush, she picked up a pot of powder. "It'll prove you're no boring gold-digger."

Despite herself, Emma laughed. "Thanks, I think." She

glanced over to where Zach sat alone, headphones perched on his head as he typed furiously. "Where's Ripley?"

"He and Adam are following Balakin." She met Emma's gaze. "Balakin's pilot filed a flight plan an hour ago. He's going back to Moscow tonight."

As Martha turned away to look through the rack of clothes, Emma stared at her own face in the mirror. If Balakin was leaving the country, then whatever he'd come here to do—at the Russian embassy, at Orlov's house, at the Balmoral Hotel—was finished. But what was it?

The fact that they were no closer to knowing what was planned than they had been three days ago sent a chill through her.

If Balakin was going, then tonight mattered more than ever. She had to find out exactly what they were planning. And then she had to stop them.

14

An hour later, Emma emerged from a taxi and walked up to Nick Orlov's forbidding front gates. In a black wool coat and sturdy, knee-high boots, she was the picture of a career woman at the end of a working day.

As she approached the intercom, her phone vibrated. She pulled it from her pocket to find a text message from Mackenzie.

"Nice coat."

Emma smiled as she put the phone away and pushed the button on the intercom. The infrared light on the camera above her head glowed in the darkness. There was a brief silence before she heard a metallic click, and a small pedestrian gate to her right swung open.

Emma stepped inside, and at last saw what Nick Orlov had been hiding behind those high walls. A path bounded by artful low lighting curved between mounds of topiary shrubs toward a three-story stone manor house. It was the same house she'd found on the property website, but a much improved version, with tall gables made of sturdy, rough-hewn stones, and fronted by a modern curved driveway and a beautifully manicured garden dotted with trees. Further to her left she could see a brightly lit garage with two cars parked in front of it—one was Orlov's red sports car. The other was the dark Land Rover with a YR73 license plate. It was the same one Emma had seen at the airport the night Balakin arrived. The same vehicle that had driven him out of Orlov's gates two days ago and taken him to the Balmoral Hotel. That car had been rented several days ago from a local agency by Leonid Fridman.

Emma's steps slowed. If the Land Rover was here, then Fridman must be here, too. Balakin might be heading back to Russia, but it appeared he had left his henchman behind. And now he was waiting for her.

She squared her shoulders and kept going. The camera hidden in her coat's top button would capture whatever happened next and broadcast it onto one of the wall screens in the long, cold office. She had another camera in a button on her blazer.

The three bugs she was to plant in Nick Orlov's house were hidden in the heel of her sturdy left boot, and a knife was tucked inside the right.

It's all about the details, she told herself, as she headed down the walkway toward the house, tense and ready.

As she approached the front steps she heard raised voices, one of them clearly belonging to Nick Orlov. Both voices were shouting in Russian. Before Emma could make out any words, the front door swung open with such force it hit the wall behind it with an ugly thud.

Leonid Fridman stepped out into the glow of the security light. Turning back to look inside, he said, "You know what you have to do. Just *do it*. You know what will happen if you don't."

Hidden in the shadows, Emma studied him with interest. He was about thirty-five years old and medium build, with dark blond hair cut short. He hadn't seen her yet, and she stopped walking just as Nick Orlov stepped into the doorway, his sculpted face twisted with anger.

"I do not take orders from you," he growled. "Why don't you go back to Russia with him and leave me in peace?"

Fridman gave him a look of withering contempt. "Because you are a fool." His voice was low and laced with malice. "And so I must stay to make you do the job you agreed to do."

Turning on his heel, he strode down the walkway to the parked Land Rover, his face set with fury. Still, he hadn't noticed Emma, half hidden in the darkness.

Clearly, his visit had nothing to do with her. He was here as an enforcer, to make Nick Orlov do whatever Balakin had planned for him.

Whatever their plan, Orlov wanted nothing at all to do with it. Standing in the doorway, he was pale, tense lines carved into his forehead as he watched the gates open and the SUV roar out into the night.

As if he sensed her eyes on him, his gaze swung to her, and he forced a tight smile.

"Anna, I must apologize for my rudeness. There was a disagreement."

Emma climbed the steps to join him. "Who was that?"

Orlov looked over to where the Land Rover was disappearing through the gates. "A colleague. Nobody important."

"Was that Russian you were speaking?" she asked.

"Yes." For a long moment he stared after the car, then with some effort, he seemed to gather himself. Forcing a faint smile, he motioned at the door. "Please, enough of this unpleasantness. You will freeze. Come inside."

Emma followed him into a warm entrance hall with soaring ceilings and a few well-chosen paintings on the walls. She could see that the Edwardian building had been beautifully restored, the oak floors polished to a sheen, and stained-glass windows glowing around the door.

"Your house is gorgeous," Emma exclaimed, as she followed Orlov down a wide hallway. "These floors look original."

"They are." Orlov glanced down. "I restored them by hand."

Emma looked at him. "*You* did that?"

Hearing the disbelief in her voice, he smiled. "It is not common knowledge, but I am capable of hard work. Now, I don't know about you, but I need a drink. I've made some cocktails. Do you like gin?"

As he led the way through the entrance hall and shut the door, he said all the right things, but it seemed to Emma that his mind was elsewhere. She hadn't had to make an excuse for being late—he hadn't noticed what time it was. He hadn't even taken her coat.

She removed it, draping it over a tall-backed chair with the button-camera facing the living room. The house really was beautifully done, furnished with a mix of leather sofas and chairs upholstered in dark gray fabric. A cowskin rug lay across the floor in front of the wood-burning stove, where a fire burned merrily.

Emma, who had spent a considerable amount of time studying oligarchs, was struck by the décor. Most rich Russians' houses were filled with over-the-top Louis XV furniture and ostentatious modern art, chosen primarily because of its high price tag. This was different. It had the understated elegance of an upscale country retreat.

Unaware of her scrutiny, Orlov headed straight toward a tray of drinks atop an antique cabinet.

"Gin and tonic?" He lifted a glass from the tray and held it out to her.

"Thank you." Emma took it from him.

The ice in the glass had melted, and she wondered how long he'd been arguing with Fridman before she arrived.

Picking up his own drink, Orlov drained it. When it was empty, he set it down and inhaled slowly.

Emma watched this with a slight frown. He was clearly shaken by his encounter with Balakin's enforcer.

"Look," she said, hesitantly, "I feel like I arrived at a bad moment. That argument out there—I couldn't understand what you were saying, but it looked intense. Are you OK?"

Orlov met her gaze. The color was slowly returning to his cheeks as the alcohol banished the pallor that fear had left on his face.

"I'm sorry you saw that," he said. He gave a helpless gesture. "This wasn't how I'd envisioned the evening starting."

"Please don't worry about that," Emma said. "I just hope the argument wasn't about anything serious."

"It was nothing," he insisted. "Just a little disagreement among colleagues."

"Why was he so angry?" Emma pressed.

She was making him uncomfortable, but Anna Case wouldn't give up easily after seeing something like that when she first arrived. She would insist on answers.

"It's hard to explain." Nick reached for the cut glass pitcher and poured himself another drink. "I agreed to work with him on a project, and it was a mistake. Now he thinks he owns me. His company is much bigger than mine, so . . . it's difficult. There are things I don't want to do." He stopped, correcting himself. "I *very much* do not want to do them. He says he understands, and then he comes into my house making threats."

As he said the last word his hand tightened around his glass with such force Emma was surprised it didn't break.

"Making *threats*?" She frowned. "Nick, this is serious. You should call the police."

When Orlov looked up at her, for a second she saw something vulnerable in his expression—an urge to talk as real and clear as the fire blazing behind him. But then, abruptly, his eyes shuttered. When he spoke again, his voice held a forced lightness.

"Please, it's fine. Ignore me. A bad day, nothing more." He forced a smile. "Now, I'm supposed to be cooking you dinner. Come."

Picking up her glass, Emma followed him through oak doors into a modern kitchen, where the white walls soared twenty feet high and long ceiling windows looked up at the night sky.

He'd obviously started cooking earlier—vegetables were chopped and ready on a cutting board. A pan rested on a large stove. In front of a row of glass doors, a sturdy oak table had been set for two.

Orlov reached for the knife and resumed chopping carrots. "Now, this is what I wanted to be doing this evening." As he worked, he glanced at Emma's virtually untouched glass. "You don't like the cocktail?"

"It's delicious," Emma said, taking a sip. "What are you cooking?"

"Haggis, with black pudding," he said.

There was a pause.

"Yum," Emma said, unconvincingly.

Orlov threw back his head and roared with laughter.

"I can't believe you don't enjoy our delicious Scottish cuisine," he said, when he'd recovered. "Who wouldn't love sheep stomach and blood pudding?"

Emma raised her hand. "Me. I wouldn't."

"Southern softie." He was still chuckling, the tension from the argument now fully dissipated. "Well, I should have made that, but I didn't. We're having lamb sautéed with fresh spinach." Turning on the stove, he drizzled a small amount of olive oil into the pan. "It's one of my favorites."

"Now, that really does sound amazing," she said.

They made light conversation and Emma watched him work, his hands making quick assured movements.

"You're so good at this," she observed. "I can barely heat milk in a microwave."

That, at least, was true. She didn't cook at all.

"Ah, but you're a modern woman. Too busy for housework. That's a good thing, as far as I'm concerned. I think women should be in charge of everything. Now, me, I'm a natural housewife. When I'm not working, I want to be doing things here. It relaxes me. I'm like an old man, pottering around the kitchen, trying out recipes from Nigella Lawson."

This was so unexpected, Emma laughed.

"What?" Nick feigned indignation. "She is our greatest cook. Why do you laugh? Do you prefer Jamie Oliver?"

"No!" She held up her hands. "I'm just impressed by your knowledge of British TV chefs."

"Everyone has hobbies," he said, and threw her a wink. He turned to the stove and dropped a filet of lamb into the pan to sear it.

"Well, you're truly one of us if you've got a favorite chef." Emma leaned casually against the marble counter. "How long have you lived in the UK, anyway?"

Nick added the vegetables to another pan before he answered. The air in the room had begun to fill with the rich scent of cooking meat.

"It's been fourteen years," he said, wiping his hands on a towel. "No. Fifteen. I lose count."

"Do you still do work back in Russia? I'm only asking because of the man earlier," she explained, with innocent curiosity. "Who was he, again?"

Orlov turned his back to her and stirred the vegetables. "Just someone I work with."

"At North Seven?"

"No." Orlov set the wooden spoon down and turned to face her. "He is someone I was working with on something else. Another project. I was recommended to him by a friend who knew me in Russia. The project turned out not to be what I expected, but he cannot accept that I don't want any part of it. It is illegal and I think immoral." He spoke rapidly and with heat, before picking up the spoon again. "It's a problem, but I am handling it."

Emma picked up her drink and took a sip, her mind working.

If he was telling the truth, then he'd never planned to be a part of the plot Balakin was cooking up. Someone had dragged him into this, and now, whether he fully understood it or not, he was trapped. You didn't walk away from Vladimir Balakin. You left when he pushed you away, or worse.

"Well, I'm glad it's all under control," she said, keeping her voice light. "Actually, there's something I wanted to show you." She turned to reach for her bag and then paused as if surprised. "Oh, I must have left my bag in the other room. Stay here, I'll go get it."

Orlov, who was turning the lamb in the hot pan, barely looked up as she ran into the living room. Glancing over her shoulder to make sure he hadn't followed, she sat on the arm of the sofa and crossed her left boot onto her right leg, twisting the heel to reveal the small hiding place inside.

The fire still burned in the hearth. In the next room she could hear Orlov clattering at the stove.

Working quickly, she plucked the three tiny devices, and then swung the heel back until it locked in place.

Standing, Emma surveyed the room. It had three armchairs and two sofas. One of the leather chairs, deep and inviting, was slightly more worn than the others, as if it were used regularly. Next to it was a table with a lamp.

Reaching into her bag, she lifted out a small pot of what appeared to be lip balm. She unscrewed the top and dipped her finger into the soft, rubbery adhesive inside.

Before she could replace the lid, a bang from the kitchen made her jump, and she froze, her eyes on the oak door.

There was a brief silence. Then the cooking sounds resumed.

Emma dashed to the lamp and quickly swiped her finger against the base of the bulb leaving a smear of adhesive on the black plastic. With her other hand, she pushed one of the listening bugs against that small smudge of glue.

Against the dark background, the small device was virtually invisible.

Dropping the other two bugs and the tiny pot of adhesive into the pocket of her blazer, she half ran across the room to the kitchen, slowing her steps at the last minute and strolling in casually with her phone in her hand. "I wondered if you saw this article in the FT about 'High Energy Oil Companies'?" she said, scrolling to the piece, which she'd saved earlier, and turning the phone for him to see. "You get a big mention."

Wiping his hands on a towel, Orlov glanced at it with a quick smile. "I did see that. A generous description. Our press office was very pleased."

"You must be used to that sort of thing, I guess." Emma added a hint of envy to her voice. "My office would kill for headlines like that."

"I wouldn't say you get used to it," he said, modestly. "It's hard work to keep reminding people about what you're trying to do. And harder to get them to believe that you want to produce clean oil. All companies say they want to do that, but only a few really mean it."

He glanced at his watch. "Please, excuse me for just a moment. I need to put the lamb in the oven."

As he began to open cupboards and pull out pots, Emma said sweetly, "Could you point me in the direction of the loo?"

"Of course. It's down that hallway there." Nick indicated a door at the end of the kitchen.

A few seconds later, Emma found herself alone in a short hallway with three doors. Moving fast, she opened the first one—a small bathroom, beautifully decorated with paneling and paintings of Scottish flowers.

The next door proved to be just a utility closet, and Emma closed it quickly.

The third door opened into the house's main entrance hall. Here Emma paused. If Orlov came looking for her, she'd have no good excuse for being here. But this could be her best chance to look around the house alone.

She decided to keep going. Aside from the entrance to the living room, there were just two other doors here.

Emma opened the first door to find a coat closet. Swearing softly, she turned to the last door. It opened easily at her touch to reveal a large study.

"Bingo," Emma whispered, closing the door behind her.

The room was so quiet she could hear the radiator near the window tick. She might as well have been completely alone in the house.

Emma switched on the lights. Like the other rooms she'd seen in Nick Orlov's house, the office was decorated in a traditional style. A brass lamp with a green shade stood at the edge of the leather blotter on the desktop. Bookcases lined one wall and a fireplace dominated another. At the center of it sat a large, sturdy desk.

Quickly, Emma crossed the room. Reaching into her pocket, she pulled out the second of the listening devices and the pot of adhesive. As she had done in the living room, she dipped her index finger into the pot and swiped the glue near the base of the lightbulb.

When she put the bug in place, the tiny square of metal stuck firmly.

Emma exhaled. Just one more to go.

Still, she didn't get up. They'd been desperate to know more about Nick Orlov, and suddenly she had full access to his office. She couldn't pass this opportunity up.

The desk was made of oak, with drawers on either side of the foot well. Sitting in Orlov's chair, she opened the top drawer. It held nothing but a few pens and envelopes, so she closed it quietly and tried the left side. The top drawer was mostly empty, the bottom drawer, though, was more hopeful. Emma pulled out the stack of papers it held and placed them on the desktop, where she flipped through them quickly. But they proved to be only bills related to the house and an article about North Seven.

Putting it all back in place, she moved on to the right top drawer.

Something thudded against the wood as she opened it. Peering inside, she saw a gleaming black SIG Sauer handgun.

Pulling her sleeve down over her hand, she picked up the gun and took a picture of it, which she sent straight to Ripley.

Strike one, she thought, as she put the weapon away. There's no way that weapon was legal. British law simply wouldn't allow it.

She opened the last drawer. This seemed to be the place where he put most of his paperwork. Files and stacks of papers had been shoved in, in no discernible order.

Emma knew she'd been gone too long now, but Orlov was distracted and she wasn't ready to give up. Hurriedly she flipped through the files, scanning them for anything useful; most were mundane receipts and bills, and she was putting them back, disappointed, when a single sheet slipped free and fell to the floor.

Emma picked it up and paused. It was a note, in Russian. It said, "You know what you have to do." It was unsigned. Underneath those words was a photo of a dark-haired boy, about ten years old, sitting on a sofa. He was looking at the camera lens, his eyes wide. Emma had never seen this child before, but there was no doubt in her mind that he was afraid.

Afraid of what? Is this what Balakin held over Orlov's head? Was this Orlov's son?

She took a quick picture and sent it to Ripley and Zach.

She was out of time. Hurriedly, she put the note back in the drawer and closed it. She stood and crossed the room to the door. After a quick glance to make sure everything looked as it had when she arrived, she turned out the light and stepped out of the study.

Orlov stood in the hallway watching her with a face like thunder.

"What the hell are you doing in my office?" he demanded.

15

S tartled, Emma took a half-step back as Orlov glared, his face lined with suspicion. He seemed to have forgotten the tea towel he held in his hand, and its jaunty blue stripes fluttered incongruously as he pointed at her.

"What is going on here?" he demanded. "Answer me, Anna."

Emma gave a helpless laugh. "This is so embarrassing. Your house is so beautiful I was dying to see more of it so I took a little nose around. That's all."

She kept her tone light but Orlov's expression did not change.

"Is that the truth?" he asked, making it clear he didn't believe her.

"Yes, of course it's the truth!" Emma flushed. "I just wanted to see your house. That's all."

She could see Nick starting to doubt himself, but he still pressed for more. "Why didn't you just ask if you wanted to see the place? Why sneak about like this?"

"It's just . . . I guess we get on so well I forgot you don't really know me." In Anna's light, upper-class accent Emma made herself sound mortified. "You see, I do this sort of thing all the time, any of my friends could tell you I'm the nosiest person. I just assume nobody will mind if I look around. But now I've upset you, and that's the last thing I wanted. I promise I haven't touched anything—I would never do that." Suddenly, Emma's voice broke, and she took a quick breath. "I'm so sorry I've upset you, Nick. I really am."

As she spoke, her throat tightened, and heat rushed to her face; she was nearly in tears.

It had always struck her as odd that she could do this—summon emotion when she needed to. But my god, it was handy.

Gradually, the coldness faded from Orlov's expression.

"I'm not angry," he said, slowly. "I was just surprised. I didn't realize you were . . ." His voice trailed off. "Actually, I've got an idea. Let me turn off the stove and I'll show you around. Dinner will keep."

The tension in Emma's chest eased.

"Are you sure you're not cross?" she asked, following him back across the living room to the kitchen. "I would never invade your privacy or anything like that. And I honestly really want to know who your decorator is."

Orlov laughed as he switched off the stove, and the tension between them was gone as quickly as it had arrived.

"I'm flattered that you like the house so much," he said. "The decorator was me, for the record."

"No!" Emma was genuinely surprised. "Honestly, Nick, you're so unpredictable I don't know what to make of you."

She was using his name more freely now, signaling to him that she liked him. She could sense his response. His eyes lingered on her.

As she followed him back into the hallway and up the stairs, she kept up a stream of chatter about her love of Scottish architecture as she glanced around, quickly absorbing the details of the rooms and the layout of the old building.

The house, like Orlov himself, was not what she'd expected. From the front, with its high gates, security cameras, and barred entry, it had all the trappings of a billionaire's mansion. But inside, this was a comfortable family home. Upstairs there were four bedrooms, each substantial and decorated in a sophisticated masculine style. It wasn't ostentatious or over the top, there were no marble statues or wall-sized pieces of modern art. In fact, what art there was was modest—impressionistic landscapes of the Isle of Skye, and moody paintings of the North Sea—rather than the usual expensive pieces, chosen purely for their price.

No, this was the house of an ordinary, successful single man.

And yet, she'd seen the look on Orlov's face when he spotted her coming out of his office. He'd been afraid.

Something was scaring the hell out of him. Making him paranoid. Making him suspicious even of a young woman he believed he'd met eight months ago.

Maybe he wasn't an oligarch, but somehow he had stumbled into their world and made some sort of devil's deal with Balakin. There was no way that could end well. And Orlov knew it.

Emma had to find out what was going on before it was too late for him.

The last room on the hallway was the master bedroom. Orlov walked in first and switched on the lights, pausing near the bed.

Like the others, this was a handsome room with thick gray carpet and a carved oak bed frame. The heavy curtains had been left open and the autumn darkness outside pressed hard against the window panes.

A leather sofa and chair clustered around a small table, and Emma stopped there, half a room from where Orlov still stood beside the bed. Their eyes met and a new tension crackled in the air between them. It was as if the very presence of the bed changed the dynamic, filling the space with some new possibility.

Reaching out, Emma ran her hand nervously along the edge of a tartan throw the gray-green of heather leaves. Orlov watched her stroke the soft wool as if hypnotized. While he was distracted, she opened the tiny pot of adhesive in her pocket with her other hand.

"Are you really your own decorator?" she asked. "Would you please do my flat next?"

Leaning against the wall next to the dresser, Orlov chuckled, still watching her. "How much would you pay?"

Languidly, she touched the marble top of the small table next to her, leaving a minute trace of adhesive on the underside.

"I don't think I could even afford this table," she said, with a smile. "Much less you."

She let her eyes linger on Orlov's lips, and saw the pulse in his neck quicken as she reached into her pocket again and found the last tiny listening device.

"But if I could afford it," she continued, "I'd buy everything in this room."

She did it right in front of him. He never looked down. Never noticed the tiny silver chip between her thumb and index finger. His eyes were fixed on hers as she pressed the device firmly into the smear of adhesive.

Releasing her hold on the table, Emma gave a teasing smile. "Well, I suppose I should let you cook me supper."

"I guess you should." Smiling, he walked over to join her. She could see no suspicion at all in his expression as his gaze lingered on her lips.

This was too easy. He was too gullible.

"So you have no staff at all?" Emma pressed, as they walked back downstairs. "Not even a cleaner?"

It would seem an odd question to direct at many people, but most wealthy Russian expats had cleaners, cooks, and gardeners. Many also had chauffeurs, nannies, and security guards. It was one way they proved their wealth to each other, like feudal lords of the manor.

Nick shook his head, his expression suddenly serious. "I don't like having people in my house. And besides, I know how to use a Hoover. And, as you can see, I'm a fantastic cook."

She was struck again by how Scottish he sounded. That last line had been said with pure Scottish flair.

Her phone vibrated as they reached the kitchen, and she glanced at the screen while Nick's back was turned. It was a secure message from Zach.

"3X5X5"

The listening devices were all working perfectly.

Back in the kitchen, Emma stood by the stove while Nick finished cooking the lamb and served it up on rustic plates. The conversation flowed easily. He seemed to enjoy having her near, and quite unexpectedly she found that she liked talking to him.

The dish Nick made was a kind of lamb stew with smoky Moroccan influences, topped with a scattering of ruby pomegranate seeds. He served it with sautéed spinach and chilled white wine, which he poured into her glass with a flourish.

"Nick, this is delicious!" Emma exclaimed when they were seated at the table. "Absolutely perfect."

"It's nothing," he demurred. "A simple meal." But he looked pleased.

While they ate, Emma directed the conversation back to his work and other safe subjects, giving him time to relax. She asked about his family, his history. His answers, which came quickly and without apparent planning, all matched the information held in government files. And more than that—they were interesting replies.

Nick Orlov appeared to be a thoughtful man, deeply concerned about things most wealthy people never think twice about—the environment, the future, fairness. Emma found herself engaging in the conversation genuinely, asking questions and anticipating his answers eagerly. He was funny and charming.

They'd thought they'd been wrong about him, that somehow they'd missed a Russian spy hiding in Edinburgh pretending to be a business executive, but she was increasingly confident they'd been right about him all along. And if they were right from the start, and he really was an ordinary man, then what the hell was she doing here? And why had Vladamir Balakin spent twenty-four hours in his house?

When the meal was over, she helped him clear the table, and he poured them both more wine, which they carried into the comfortable living room.

The fire had burned down while they'd been in the kitchen, but Nick quickly built it back into a warming blaze. Classical music—Bach, Emma thought—streamed softly from hidden speakers.

Emma sat on the leather sofa while Nick, showing, she thought, some appreciation for the fact that this was their first date, took the deep leather chair where he sat, a glass in his hand, and studied her with open interest.

"So tell me," Nick said. "Who is Anna Case?"

Emma smiled. "She's sitting right in front of you."

He waved one hand. "I meant, tell me about yourself. How did you get into the oil business?"

"I've always been interested in it, I suppose," Emma said. "My father worked in banking and I learned about business from him when I was young. I studied commodities at Cambridge and went straight into work after that."

All of this was part of the legend—or invented history—the Agency had made for Anna Case at the very beginning of this investigation. If he'd researched any of it, he would find it to be true. Records at Cambridge would show an Anna Case as a student during those years, and the social media profiles Zach had built for her would reflect it as well, including a Facebook page featuring pictures of Emma on holiday and holding a puppy, which she found disturbingly convincing.

The company Anna ostensibly worked for was run by an old friend of Ripley's, who was set to back up her invented history entirely if anyone phoned to ask about her.

There would be no holes in her story. It would satisfy anyone who didn't know how hard they should look.

"It's not a particularly romantic area of study, is it?" Nick asked.

Emma's eyebrows rose. "You mean, for a girl?" Her tone told him what she thought of that.

He held up his hands. "I withdraw the question. I suppose what I mean is, there's something about you that seems not right for this business. I've been in oil my entire life and the people in it tend to be more . . ." He searched for the right word.

"Boring?" Emma suggested, amused.

"Well, yes." He laughed. "Something like that. It can be a very dry industry."

"But can't you see that it's changing?" Emma let her voice grow warm and enthusiastic. She reminded him of all the things Anna loved about the changing business and greener energy, stopping after a while with a look of chagrin. "Now I *am* boring you, aren't I?"

"Not at all. You're not wrong about any of it." He paused. "I researched you, you know."

"Did you?" She took a sip of wine.

"You've risen through the ranks at GlobalOne quickly, they clearly value you. But they're not giving you enough of a platform. Nobody I work with has heard of you."

Emma's heart rate accelerated just a little, but she kept her expression interested and steady as he studied her.

"To be honest, I'd hire you if I could," he said, unexpectedly. "My company would know how to build your career properly. You've got incredible potential."

"Would that be a good idea?" Emma gestured at the room around them. "Under the circumstances?"

It was provocative but useful, sending the clear message that if he was interested in a relationship, she was open to it.

Their eyes locked again. Again, she saw the instant physical reaction as his breaths shortened.

"Probably not," he conceded.

It was time to go. She'd done what she needed to do here. The trap was baited and set, and the devices were in place. And she didn't want to find herself taking things with Nick too far, too fast.

Emma glanced at her watch. "Oh my gosh. Nick, did you know it was after eleven? I'm afraid I really have to go. I've got a meeting first thing tomorrow morning."

He looked gratifyingly disappointed. "Oh, must you go?"

"I wish I didn't have to," Emma said, standing regretfully and setting her wine down on a side table.

"I understand." He stood and joined her. "But it's been wonderful getting to know you better."

They walked toward the entrance hall, so close to each other that their hands nearly touched.

"It's been such a lovely evening. I've enjoyed it immensely," she told him, reaching for her coat which still lay across the back of the chair, where its button camera had been capturing images of the room all evening.

He took it from her and held it as she slipped her arms into the sleeves.

"What are you doing Saturday night?" he asked, his hands lingering on her shoulders. "We could go to dinner?"

"I'd love that," she said.

Emma turned and found her face inches from his.

She moved to hug him, but at the last second, he turned his head. Their lips met.

He pulled her close, his arms firm around her back, his lips soft and questioning against hers. Emma's lips parted and his tongue touched hers.

It was the oddest sensation, kissing him. His lips tasted faintly of wine, and his hands were firm against her back, pulling her to him. Her mind reminded her that she wasn't Anna Case, but her body softened against his, and her lips responded to his kiss.

When they straightened, Emma was breathless and surprised to find that some part of her wanted him to kiss her again.

Nick's face was flushed, his eyes bright.

"Are you sure you have to go?" he murmured, his hands still resting on her waist.

Emma gave a regretful smile. "My first meeting's at half seven."

"At least I'll see you at dinner Saturday," he said. "Seven o'clock?"

"Perfect." Emma reached for the door handle, but it didn't budge when she attempted to turn it.

"Wait, I have to unlock it." Nick pulled the curtain next to the door back and pressed his thumb against a small device hidden there. Emma had a second to take in the sleek, boxy design before the curtain fell again.

The device gave a subtle beep and the door released, letting in a rush of cold air.

"Goodnight." Emma gave him one last lingering smile before stepping outside.

When the door closed behind her, she took a deep breath, and exhaled slowly, shaking Anna Case from her shoulders.

As she walked out of the gate a minute later, she texted Ripley:

"We need to talk."

16

"The biometric lock was small; state of the art," Emma revealed, as she sat with Ripley an hour later. "It was the only thing in his house that felt out of place. Everything else was normal."

Ripley had given her the address of a pub called The Queen's Arms, just off George's Street in central Edinburgh. It was midnight and the place was rammed. When Emma walked in, she'd seen no sign of her boss, so she'd ordered herself a vodka on the rocks and then wandered through the crowd.

The pub was made up of interconnected rooms, most of them lined with bookcases, which gave it the air of an alcoholic library. The air smelled quite deliciously of ale, books, and polished wood. When she'd spotted Ripley, Emma had fought a smile; he was sitting in a corner with a glass of whisky, seemingly absorbed in the thick volume in his hand. The title, visible on the spine, was *The Decline of the West*, by Oswald Spengler.

He glanced up at her and closed the book. "Oh, there you are."

"How is it?" she asked, nodding at the book's dusty jacket as she pulled out a chair.

"A bit slow. I must say. Spengler does drone on." Ripley returned the book to the shelf behind him before turning his attention to her. "So, it went well?"

"Better than I expected." Emma filled him in on the evening, and her sense that Orlov was completely out of place in their world. She'd had time to think about it now, and that had only raised more questions in her mind about Orlov, and the entire investigation.

"He completely accepted that I just wanted to see his house," she said, about the moment outside Orlov's study. "I think he has a real crush on Anna Case."

"That could be useful," Ripley observed. "But make no mistake, Orlov is no fool—the locks, the refusal to hire any staff, the high walls . . . he's worried about something."

"Yes, actually, there's more." Emma told him what she'd noticed as she'd walked through the darkened grounds to the gate when she'd left that night; how the trees around her had glimmered with the glowing red eyes of night-vision CCTV cameras hidden in the branches. "It's as if he's been preparing for a long time for something bad to happen."

Ripley nodded vaguely. "Yes, I suppose he has."

When he said no more than that, Emma gave him a puzzled look. His attention seemed fixed on a group of twentysomethings drinking shots at a nearby table but she had a feeling he wasn't really seeing them. In his right hand, he turned the slim cigarette case over and over between his fingers.

"Is something wrong?" she asked.

Ripley set the case down carefully. "There's been a leak."

It was such a change of direction; Emma took a second to catch up. "Of information? From *our team*?"

They were surrounded by people but everyone nearby was too busy with their own conversations to pay any attention to the two of them. This was why Ripley liked meeting in busy bars—they were anonymous here. Still, she lowered her voice and leaned closer.

"Are you sure?"

"It wasn't us." Ripley's voice was firm, but she could see the worry in his face. "It couldn't be us. But I don't know who it was, and that's a problem."

"Is there going to be press?" Emma asked.

He lifted his head, his expression dark. "There already is."

Emma didn't know what to say. It was hard enough to do their jobs in absolute anonymity, their work unknown even to the people who paid their salaries. If the press got involved—even if word simply got out about the danger facing the G7—there could be panic; there would definitely be political ramifications. It would be disastrous.

"What are we going to do?" she asked.

"Andrew's handling it," Ripley said. "But we're on the edge here, Emma. We're off the books. If word gets back to London about what we're doing . . ."

He didn't finish the sentence. He didn't have to. They both knew even a whisper of political scandal would be the end of The Agency.

He took a sip of whisky and set the glass down. "Enough of that. Let's talk about tonight. So Leonid Fridman was there when you arrived? And he was threatening Orlov?"

Emma nodded. "Orlov was furious. He said Fridman was someone he worked with, who thought he was his boss. But nobody is his boss, he made that very clear."

"If he thinks Fridman's not his boss, then he's a dead man," Ripley said, bluntly.

Emma thought of Nick Orlov, the color of fury high in his cheeks, sweeping her inside and closing the door like he was lowering a portcullis against an attacker.

"He doesn't believe that," she said. "He still thinks he can handle it."

"Then perhaps he is a fool after all," Ripley said.

Emma paused. "He wants to see me Saturday for dinner. I'll use that. He almost trusts me."

A burst of wild laughter erupted at the table next to them, but neither of them spared it a glance.

"Good. Shame it's not tomorrow night, but Saturday will have to do." Ripley paused, his expression suddenly grave. "I've asked you before, but I'm going to ask you again. Are you sure about this? It's not too late to pull out. We can find another way."

They both knew she might have to sleep with Nick Orlov. In fact, she almost definitely would. Everything she'd seen tonight told her Orlov was extremely self-protective. He wouldn't trust her until she'd proven herself. Until their relationship had somehow bonded them. And she had no time to do that any other way—no time to befriend him and convince him she was who she said she was.

"I'm sure," she said. "I can do it."

The confidence in her voice belied the twist in her belly, and Ripley continued to hold her gaze, his expression inscrutable, as if he knew that. "It's not for everyone, this sort of thing. People refuse to do it all the time. Good people. Talented, experienced people. There's no shame in saying no."

"You've done it though, haven't you?" Emma pushed back. "When there was no other way?"

"Once or twice," he conceded, after a pause. "I can't say I recommend it."

Emma picked up her glass and took a long drink. The vodka uncurled her tightened nerves. "Look, I don't *want* to do it," she said, when she set the glass down. "There's something awful about it—for me and for him. But there's no time for the usual methods. We need this information fast."

When his brooding expression didn't change, she found herself bristling.

"I honestly think if I were a man, we wouldn't be having this conversation. Would you warn Adam not to do this?"

Ripley tapped his fingertips against his glass of whisky, the sound lost in the noise around them.

"You are not the first young intelligence officer I've worked with, Emma. I'm not singling you out. I don't consider you incompetent. I simply know things that you do not. Operations like this one change you. If you do this, it *will* change you in little dangerous ways."

"I can handle it," Emma insisted, stubbornly, although nerves had begun to swirl inside her.

Ripley studied her from beneath lowered eyebrows.

"Yes," he said, after a moment. "I suppose you can handle it."

Somewhere in the bar, someone turned up the volume on the music, and a blast of guitar made Emma twitch. The crowd whooped, and then the music turned down again. It was getting warm.

"If I could offer some advice," said Ripley, who looked cool and calm, "the best way I've found to handle this sort of thing is to believe it's true. Convince yourself for as long as you must that your feelings for him are real. In that sense, it's like acting. In fact, sometimes it can become true."

As he said those last words, his long, worn face suddenly appeared unutterably weary and regretful. But it must have been a trick of the light as, a second later his normal enigmatic expression returned.

"When you meet Orlov again, move things forward. Confide in him, give him some secrets he will appreciate — about you or your family. Some loss you've suffered. If you feel it, he'll feel it. This will bring him closer to you. You're trusting him, so he may trust you. Trust is contagious."

He picked up his glass and drained the last of the whisky.

Without warning, Emma found herself considering telling Ripley about Michael Primalov. That she'd seen him. That she knew where he lived. That she'd thought about him when Orlov kissed her by the door. But she knew better, and so all she said was "I'll try that."

She was certain Ripley didn't approve of her decision. He

didn't think she could handle this. As she made her way down the dark street toward her own hotel a short time later, Emma told herself she'd prove him wrong. She would be fine.

She was still convincing herself of this when her phone rang. It was Mackenzie.

"Don't you ever sleep?" Emma asked, by way of hello.

"That's a bit rich coming from you." In Mackenzie's tart Scottish accent this was unexpectedly funny, and Emma laughed.

It felt good to laugh. It was increasingly a relief to talk to Mackenzie.

"How did it go, anyway?" Mackenzie asked. "You fairly flew out of that house."

"Yeah, it went fine," she said. "Thanks for being there. I'm meeting him for dinner Saturday."

"So you really are in, then."

Still on edge after her conversation with Ripley, Emma thought she could sense the same disapproval in Mackenzie's voice that had been in her boss's expression earlier that night.

"Yes," she said, coldly. "That's the job and I'm doing it. I wish people would stop treating me like a *child*."

"Oh, hang on, I wasnae questioning you." Surprise made Mackenzie's accent thicker. "I'm just trying to understand how you work. I'm on your side."

I'm on your side. Why did that simple sentence make Emma feel so much better?

"I'm doing whatever I have to do to stop an attack," Emma said. "That's it. That's all I'm doing."

"You're doing it well," Mackenzie told her, gently. "I'm in awe."

Emma took a breath. Let it out. "Thank you."

"Do you want me there again? Wherever you're meeting him next time?" Mackenzie asked. "I'm happy to do it."

But Emma couldn't bear the idea of her watching the seduction play out. Seeing her contorting her morals into a twisted logic no sane person would understand.

"No, that's OK," she said. "You take some time off. I'll call you if I need you."

"As you wish. But I'm free if you need a hand," Mackenzie said.

When the call ended, Emma continued down the dark street, her head bowed against the strong wind blowing in from the north.

I can handle this, she told herself, but those words echoed hollowly inside her head.

SPECIAL TO THE PRIME MINISTER

EYES ONLY

SECURITY LEVEL: TOP SECRET

RISK LEVEL: HIGH

Private communication

From: Andrew Field, Chief Officer,
Secret Intelligence Service

The investigation into the leak of classified information to the Scottish press has uncovered no evidence that the leak came from our operation. My team has had no interaction with any media, and checks of comms devices found no messages to those individuals or organizations. As you directed, we have also searched the devices of select staff inside your own office, and found many communications with outside individuals, but none related to this operation or containing relevant information. We have also investigated The Agency, and found no evidence of their involvement. I believe it is clear that the source of the information is inside the police. Several officers worked closely with us on this project. With your permission,

I can authorize a further investigation to identify which of these officers is the source. As you know, there are some technicalities about the legal side of this sort of investigation as our office has no oversight of the police. But given the time and the risk level, if you approve further action I will make sure it is taken. In particular, our focus will be on Graham Brodie and a detective, Katherine Mackenzie. I await your authorization to proceed.

17

In the quiet of an early Friday morning, Emma parked the BMW down the street from the last place where she'd seen Michael Primalov, and began to wait.

It wasn't yet seven and the black night sky, which had mocked her through one sleepless hour after another, was only beginning to show hints of gray dawn. The city still teetered on the edge of day.

No one passed as she sat, but even if they had they wouldn't have noticed Emma—her black wool hat and dark jacket rendered her nearly invisible in the shadows of the car.

She didn't think she'd need to wait long, and she was right about that.

She understood Michael Primalov. She'd studied him. He was a creature of habit. So when his front door opened at seven o'clock precisely and he stepped out in a gray hoodie and worn black-and-white running shoes, she was unsurprised.

What did catch her off guard was the way her heart jumped at the sight of his familiar face—unchanged, undamaged.

She watched as he locked the door and dropped the key into his pocket before stepping out onto the pavement, his movements loose and relaxed. He never spotted her of course, even when he stopped next to the car to pull out his phone and choose music for his run.

It amazed her that, after everything that had happened to him, Michael still lacked the natural wariness she'd always had—that wall of protection she'd built around herself as a child and never allowed to weaken. In all her life, she didn't think she'd ever stepped out of a building without checking the street first. That instinct seemed to be burned into her DNA, and perhaps it was. After all, her father had been a spy.

By contrast, Michael's parents were scientists. Scientists who had betrayed the Russian government by sharing secrets with Britain, yes. But they were never spies. They'd done what they'd done because they believed it would keep the world safe. Keep their son safe. But they didn't have the natural duplicity she sometimes thought she'd been born with.

Emma rolled down the window and a blast of cool air flowed in as she called his name softly.

"Michael."

He paused, his brow creasing as he looked at the empty pavement around him, before turning to the parked cars. She didn't know what kind of reaction she'd expected, but when their eyes met, he froze, mid-step, and stared, all expression draining from his face.

He was frightened.

When he spoke, his voice was uneven. "Emma? My god. What . . . what are you . . . ?"

"I'm so sorry to surprise you like this," she said, quietly. "Nothing is wrong. Everyone is safe. But . . . please get in."

Still he hesitated, and Emma, with a stab of guilt, thought she understood why.

She remembered the night she'd rescued Michael Primalov as one of the best nights of her life. She'd withstood every attack, every threat. She'd survived everything Russia had thrown at her, and she'd saved an innocent man. But for Michael Primalov that night had been an extended nightmare. And she had been the one responsible.

She could see the effort it took for him to decide to open the door. She sat still as he reached uncertainly for the handle, and climbed reluctantly in, before starting the engine and pulling out into the street.

"We're not going far," she explained, before he could ask. "Just to a street where we're unlikely to see anyone you know."

Up ahead the road was clear. The only person she could see was a woman in a blue coat walking a large golden retriever, and she didn't glance at them as they drove by. Emma was certain the government wouldn't still be watching Michael's house after all these months in hiding—not on an intense level. There would be security cameras on his door and inside, but they didn't have the manpower for full-time security for every family they took into protection.

As she turned onto a side street she could feel Michael's eyes on her face, noticing her blond highlights, her tired eyes.

"Everything really is fine," she said.

"If everything's fine why are you here?" he asked.

"I just . . ." Emma paused. Why *was* she here? There were a hundred places she could be that made more sense than this. "I'm here for something else, but I saw you yesterday. Walking down the street."

She knew it made no sense, but it was all she could think of to say.

"You saw me." His tone was empty. In his lap his hands were clenched and nervous.

This wasn't going the way Emma had hoped at all.

Despite all her training and the years she'd spent learning not to let it happen, heat rose to her face.

She and Michael had connected on their one night together in a way she'd never experienced before or since. She'd been certain he'd want to see her again. But now it was clear that feeling had been one-sided.

Spotting a parking space near a busy road, she pulled into it quickly and cut the engine. Unsnapping her seatbelt, she turned to face him.

Michael looked just as she remembered—his large brown eyes filled with caution, his wiry frame tense.

"I'm sorry," she kept her voice steady and low. "I shouldn't have surprised you like this. I didn't mean to scare you. It really was simply by chance that I saw you yesterday. I didn't know they'd moved you here. I should have let it go—I shouldn't have any involvement with you. But under the circumstances . . ." She paused, seeking the right words. "I guess it felt like fate."

"I thought you didn't believe in fate," he said, but for the first time a smile curved the corners of his lips.

"I don't." She held up her hands. "And yet—"

"Maybe fate believes in you," he said.

More relaxed now. Michael studied her seriously. "How are you, Emma? You look tired."

"I *am* tired. I can't seem to sleep. I just lie there thinking. And then I get up." She didn't know why she was telling him this. "Anyway, I've been better, but I've been worse, too. How about you?"

"Well." He paused. "I'm safe. And that was the point of everything, wasn't it?"

He tried to keep his tone light but Emma heard the hint of bleakness beneath his words.

"What about work?" she pressed. "Did they get you something in a hospital?"

"Almost," he said. "For the last three months I've been training as a paramedic for the local ambulance service."

There was no emotion in his voice, but regret tightened its grip on Emma's heart all the same.

Michael Primalov, before the night he first met Emma Make-peace, had been a brilliant doctor, specializing in pediatric cancer. When he'd been forced into hiding he'd had to give up everything—his career, his friends, a lifetime of experiences and connections. All that was lost when the government stepped in to protect his family.

It seemed to Emma he'd lost everything except his life. She struggled to find the words to say this, but he must have seen the sympathy in her expression because he grew defensive.

"They did their best for me. They say I can't work as a doctor yet because they have to get the paperwork transferred into my new name first. And that, as everyone tells me, over and over, takes time." He paused, a nerve working in his cheek. "It'll happen," he said, as if trying to convince himself it was true.

"It will," Emma promised. "If you're going to be here a long time, they want you to be happy. They can do it, it's just a lot of work."

A silence fell until Michael said, suddenly, "I'm glad to see you, you know. I'm glad you're alive. But what I don't understand is—coincidences aside, honestly, why are you here?"

Emma looked out at the Scottish sky, which had begun turning an extraordinary gray-blue—a dreamy wash of color very different than the London skies she knew so well.

"I'm not sure," she said. "I guess . . . I've worried so many times that you might be unhappy. That I ruined your life. I just didn't want to think that was true. And this was my chance to find out."

When she glanced back at Michael, she saw the bafflement in his eyes.

"You are so strange." He shook his head. "You are the toughest, bravest person I've ever met. And yet I genuinely believe you were worried I was angry. Is that really why you're here?"

"Partly," she admitted.

"Partly?" His brow creased. "Well, I'm not angry. I know you saved my life. I'm grateful, and I always will be. So what's the other part?"

Emma knew she should make a joke, a distraction, something light and charming, turning the conversation away from her job as a spy, but she couldn't seem to do that. The lock inside her that kept everything she knew forever encased in steel felt dangerously loose around Michael Primalov.

"I had a bad year," she confessed. "Someone I worked with, someone I trusted, lied to me—to all of us. I didn't see it. I just . . . couldn't see it." Her voice was thin and oddly high pitched, and she made herself slow down. "That shook me. It was the first time I felt . . ."

Her voice trailed off and Michael finished the sentence for her, ". . . human."

Emma blinked at him, surprised and a little hurt by that. "That's not what I meant."

"But don't you see? This is what happens to us humans." Michael's tone was gentle. "Sometimes we get things wrong and life kicks us in the arse. It feels worse for you because you're used to being in control. But then fate takes that control away and you realize how helpless you are."

She wondered if he was still talking about her, or himself, but it didn't matter, because he wasn't wrong–she didn't allow herself to make mistakes. There was no space in her world for error. But in the last year, things had gone wrong too often, and it had rattled her. Maybe that was why she felt so odd about Nick Orlov.

"OK then, yes," she said. "I got my arse kicked, and since then things haven't been right. Now I'm doing something at work. Something I can't tell you about. It's important. It could save lives. But I don't want to do it. And I haven't told anyone I don't want to do it. I *can't* tell them. They need me."

"Right." Michael looked concerned. "You can't tell me more than that?"

Emma made an exasperated gesture. "It's not *murder*, Michael. I'm not physically harming anyone. It's deception, but it feels . . . wrong."

A car rumbled by, its headlights bright against the gray. Neither of them spoke until it had turned a corner. When it had gone, the quiet settled on them again, as thick as a blanket.

When Michael spoke, he sounded thoughtful. "Well, if you don't want to do something it's not because it's dangerous. That wouldn't bother you at all." He thought for a moment. "Whatever it is, it compromises you, doesn't it? Whatever they've asked of you—it's too personal. Or it feels that way."

Emma felt suddenly breathless. In all her life she'd never met anyone who understood her the way Michael Primalov did. He had a fine intelligence and intuition. She'd always thought that if he weren't so trusting he might have been a useful spy. But you can't train that suspicion and duplicity into someone. You have to be born with it. As she had been.

"The thing I have to do—other people do it all the time," she said, carefully. "But you're right, it is personal. The ultimate lie. And I just think . . ." She paused, looking out the window, thinking of Ripley's grave expression the night before. And the way, despite everything she'd said, it had shaken her. "I think it might change me, if I do this. Make me somehow . . . less."

Michael's response was instant. "I don't believe anything could lessen you, Emma. You are too strong for that. I've seen you fight with a bullet in your shoulder. I've seen what you're capable of." But it wasn't that kind of strength she was talking about, and he knew it. "OK, look at it this way." He held up his hand. "As a doctor, I had to deal with life and death on a daily basis. The life and death of children. You saw them. You know what I mean."

Emma nodded. She'd never forgotten that hospital ward. Those small faces and frail bodies.

"When I couldn't save them—when medicine wasn't enough— I had to tell their families that their child wouldn't survive. I watched my words crush them." He held her gaze. "I had to learn how to not let that destroy me. Because if I were destroyed I couldn't help anyone. And they needed me. I had to think of the people I was saving. Not the ones I knew I would lose."

The world outside the car windows seemed to fade away. Goosebumps rose on the backs of Emma's arms and she leaned toward him, listening intently.

"That's what you have to do," Michael continued. "Your world is life or death, just like mine. Everything is at stake every time you get out of bed. In that sort of situation, it's easy to doubt yourself, easy to lose faith. But you have to keep your focus. Whatever it is you have to do, will it save lives?"

"Yes," Emma whispered without hesitation.

"Then those lives are what matters. Think of the people you're saving. Keep them always in your mind." He reached for her hand, his fingers warm against hers. "And you can do anything."

18

Emma and Michael sat talking as the city awoke around them, until she finally started the car and drove back to his neighborhood, parking around the corner from his house.

"This is your stop," she said, with a smile.

He turned to look at her. The color had returned to his cheeks and his dark curls tumbled over his forehead. She had to stop herself from brushing them back.

His hair was so distinctive, she thought. Too distinctive.

"You should cut your hair," she told him, abruptly. "Cut it short, or shave it off."

"Again?" He grew instantly serious. "Your people made me do that when we first moved here, to change my appearance. But it's been a year since everything happened and I thought . . ."

"I know," Emma said. "Look, I can't tell you everything, but there are a lot of Russians in town right now. Important Russians. There's almost no chance you'll encounter them. But then there was almost no chance you'd encounter me. So, cut your hair. And perhaps wear sunglasses, just for a week or so. But don't worry. You'll be fine."

He nodded, that worried look still creasing his brow. "I'll be fine," he agreed.

They both knew he had to go. People were walking by the car now, on their way to the shops or the park. The quiet that had enveloped them earlier was gone now. Still, he kept watching her.

"It was good to see you alive," he said.

"And you," Emma said, meaning it. "Really good."

"Shall we do it again next year?" he suggested. "Same time?"

"It's in the diary." She smiled at him, unable to stop herself.

And then, at last, Michael opened the door and stepped outside.

Emma started the engine, but instead of driving away, she rolled the window down.

Michael leaned in.

"I really will come back next year," she told him. "It's a promise. Look for me."

"I'm counting on it," he said.

.   .   .

He hadn't gone five steps when Emma's phone buzzed. It was a message from Ripley.

"Come home. Mother needs you."

It was an emergency code. Something was happening.

Emma swore and shoved the car into gear, gunning the engine.

In increasingly impossible traffic, it took nearly half an hour for her to get to the city center. When she finally arrived, the usual car park was full, and she had to circle it three times before a spot opened. By then, she was fuming.

"It's easier to park in *London*," she muttered, as she unbuckled her seatbelt.

Part of the problem was that one entire row of parking spaces was now occupied by television news vans and satellite vehicles. As Emma raced down Princes Street, a woman in high heels and a skintight pencil skirt clutching a microphone stepped out in front of her.

"Would you like to comment about the G7?" she asked, in a bright Australian accent.

"No," Emma retorted shortly, and hurried away.

She could sense the change in the air. The huge machine of the G7 was in motion now. If the press was here, the politicians would be right behind them.

By the time she burst from the elevator into the Distinctive Exports Ltd. offices, she was breathless.

The long room, with its exposed wires and rough cement walls, was mostly empty. Ripley and Martha were standing at the table of computers, listening to voices speaking in Russian.

"What's happening?" she asked.

Ripley, his craggy face so shadowed with fatigue she wondered if he'd slept at all, glanced up at her.

"We've caught something on the listening devices you planted last night. A phone call with someone—we believe it was Leonid Fridman. We can't hear his side of things, but it sounds like they want Orlov to do something. Listen."

He hit a button and Nick Orlov's voice, cool and angry, filled the air.

"I told you I was finished," he said in Russian. "I don't know why this is so hard for you to understand."

There was a pause as he listened to a voice they couldn't hear.

"So that's your plan, you sick bastard?" He laughed, a bitter, unfunny sound. "You threaten my family and you think I'll join you. No, you listen to me." His voice rose. "I won't help you. And I won't talk to Blake. Nothing will make me help you." He paused to listen, and then shouted, "If you injure one hair on his head I will kill you, do you understand me?"

Ripley hit the button again and the voice disappeared. "After that he hung up," he said.

"When did this call happen?" Emma asked.

"Last night, about an hour after you left his house," Ripley said.

Emma thought about Orlov's words: *If you touch one hair on his head . . .*

"Was there anything else?" she asked. "Did he talk to anyone after that?"

Ripley shook his head. "He took that call in his bedroom, and then the microphone in the office picked up sounds of him typing on the computer. But nothing appeared in his email."

He slid a paper across to her. "This is a transcript of the conversation. The call came in about thirty minutes ago."

Emma picked it up, reading Orlov's words again. "Who was he talking about? The part about not hurting his family. Are his parents alive?"

"No," Ripley said. "They're both dead."

"He was talking about a boy," Martha interjected. "He said not to touch a hair on *his* head. Does Orlov have a son?"

"There's nothing in his files about children." Ripley glanced at Emma. "Did he mention anything to you?"

Suddenly, Emma remembered the photo in Orlov's office. The boy with fear in his eyes.

"He's never said anything," she said. "But I sent you a picture last night from his house of a boy—I found it in his office."

"Yes, we got that." Ripley considered this. "I didn't think much of it because if he had a son, we should know. MI5 would have been able to find out. And we don't know when that photo might have been taken. It could be a ten-year-old image."

"It was the only picture in the office," Emma told him. "I suppose if it's not his son, it could be a nephew or a godson, someone he cares about."

"It just doesn't seem likely. No, there's something we're missing." Ripley didn't hide his exasperation. "Over and over again, we find we don't know enough. Ignorance is death and right now we're fools. This operation is a disaster." He fixed Emma with a glare. "Remind me: When are you seeing Orlov again?"

"Tomorrow night, for dinner."

"Too late." He smashed his fist down on the table hard enough to make the computers jump. "We have to move faster. We have to get closer. It's all taking too long."

He stalked to the window and lit a cigarette and stood looking out at the gray city, smoking viciously.

Giving Emma an expressive look, Martha stood and walked quietly to the section of the room filled with clothes and lights that had become her own, leaving the two of them to work this through.

Emma wasn't certain where Ripley's dark mood had come from but the first hint had emerged last night in the pub when he'd told her about the leak. She didn't dare question him about that now, but clearly something was very wrong.

It was best, in such circumstances, to leave him alone.

Quietly, she sat down at the computer and rewound the audio file until she found the section she wanted, and listened again to Orlov speaking in Russian.

Glancing at Ripley's censorious back clad in black worsted wool, she cleared her throat. "I'm certain Orlov mentions someone named Blake. Is Zach around? He could search the files . . ."

Ripley swung around to face her. "Zach and Adam are working together to get eyes into North Seven's offices. They should be back in a couple of hours." He seemed calmer now.

Emma decided to press her luck. "Is everything OK?"

His narrow gray eyes fixed her with a look of judgment. "Hardly."

"Well, of course, but I mean, beyond the usual mess." She regretted asking now but felt that she'd committed to the cause and couldn't back down. "The things we talked about yesterday . . ."

At that moment, his phone began to ring and he picked it up with obvious relief.

"Ripley."

He listened for a moment and then said, "Hold on. I'm logging in now."

He set the phone down and began to type; after a second, the screen showing North Seven went black. Through the speakers came the chaotic, concussive sound of microphones rubbing against fabric.

Emma angled forward, her eyes on the black screen. "What's happening?"

"Zach knocked out the internet in the North Seven office building an hour ago." Ripley tamped out his cigarette. "He and Adam are going inside now, as repairers."

Through the speakers, Emma heard Zach's muffled voice. "We just need to find the fault. It shouldn't take a few minutes." A woman replied, "Oh, thank God you got here so quickly. It's killing us. Nothing works."

This was followed by the sound of walking, rubber-soled shoes squeaking on a polished floor, the woman giving general directions.

"James, check that line there." It was Adam's voice. Emma guessed "James" must be Zach.

They heard the sound of metal rattling—a ladder, Emma thought—and a few seconds later Zach's face appeared on the wall screen, his brown eyes enormous as he leaned forward to adjust the tiny camera.

When he moved, suddenly they had a perfectly clear view of the entire North Seven front lobby. Emma could see Adam standing at the foot of the ladder, watching as Zach climbed down to join him.

"Good," Ripley murmured to himself, his gaze on the screen.

Adam turned to the slim, blond receptionist who sat behind a comma-shaped desk at the center of the lobby. A security guard stood next to her.

"Tha' line is workin' perfectly." Adam had adopted a Glaswegian accent, thick as syrup. "Ha' you got a main office somewhere, where the lines all link?"

The guard and the receptionist exchanged mystified glances. "I guess he means Nick's office," the receptionist suggested.

The guard looked doubtful. "Mr. Orlov doesn't like anyone going in there."

"Aye, we'll only be a second," Adam assured him. "You can stay with us. We just need to check the interface between the circuits."

There was a pause. "You better let him," the receptionist advised the guard. "Nobody can get anything done without the internet."

The guard heaved a sigh and motioned for the two men to follow. "This way."

On the screen, Adam and Zach, both wearing dark blue polo shirts with "RAFT Digital Solutions" written in white, picked up the ladder and followed the guard to a set of doors, which he opened with his pass.

Adam carried the ladder through, and Zach followed with a black tool case.

Zach didn't usually work undercover, and it was odd seeing him without his usual blazer and T-shirt. Wisely, he spoke little, leaving Adam to do the talking.

"It's a tricky one," Adam told the guard, cheerfully. "A very complicated system."

"Mm-hmm," said the guard.

The doors closed and the two men disappeared from screen, but their voices still came clearly through the speakers.

"We've just got to find where the fault occurred," Adam continued. "That's the key."

"Well, I need you to be fast," the guard said. "The boss doesn't like strangers in the building." There was a pause when they could hear footsteps and jangling metal. And then the guard said, "We're going in this room."

"Great," enthused Adam. "We'll set up here. I think it will be on this wall."

Emma heard the clang of the ladder rattling, followed by quiet that seemed to last too long.

Ripley picked up his cigarette case and whispered, "Come on, come on . . ."

Suddenly, Emma heard Nick Orlov's voice growl, "What the hell is going on here? Angus, who are these people?"

At that moment, the image of the reception lobby disappeared on the screen, replaced by an office paneled in oak and Zach's worried face as he straightened the lens before sliding down the ladder to the floor.

Now they had a clear view of an executive office, with an imposing desk and a table with six black leather chairs surrounding it. Next to it stood the guard sturdy, his face purpling, and Nick Orlov.

"I'm sorry, sir," the guard sputtered. "The internet went out in the whole building. These two are from the supplier."

"I can see that." Orlov glared at him. "What the hell are they doing in my office?"

As the men spoke, Zach knelt beside his workbox and pulled out a small keyboard, which he opened.

"The conjunction box, sir," Adam interjected. "It's on this wall." He tapped the wall behind him. "That's where the problem is."

"A conjunction box." Orlov fixed him with a steely glare. "That's a new one on me. There should be nothing of the sort in this office. When you set up this system I made it very clear that I wanted no equipment of that kind in this office."

"I beg your pardon," Adam said. "But it's actually on the other side of this wall. Unfortunately, the easiest access point is on that wire there."

He pointed up, and Nick turned to look directly at the camera, his expression so intent, Emma found herself holding her breath.

"I never noticed that wire before," Orlov said.

At that moment, Zach stood up and announced, "It's working."

All three men turned to look at him with expressions of blank surprise.

"The internet," he explained. "It's working. You're back online."

The guard glanced at Orlov, who threw up his hands.

"Well, wonderful," he said. "Now *get out.*"

Adam grabbed the ladder, while Zach hastily stuffed tools back into his box and the two of them followed the guard out into the hallway.

"We should check the line on the other side of the wall," Adam said, keeping up the act.

"I don't think that will be necessary," the guard said. "We'll call you if we need you."

They continued to talk but Emma's attention was fixed on the feed from Orlov's office. The executive stood alone in the middle of the room staring at nothing, his face set in lines of absolute despair.

Unexpectedly, this made her chest tighten. He seemed so hopeless.

"Look at him," she said, as Orlov didn't move. "That is not a man who wants to be in the middle of a plot to assassinate any-one."

"He looks shattered," Ripley agreed.

As if he'd heard them, Orlov pulled his phone from his pocket and dialed a number.

Ripley spun to Zach's computer and checked something. "It's the burner. There's no call going out on his registered phone."

"I won't meet you," Orlov growled into the phone. "There's no point. Stop calling me. Stop calling my business."

There was a pause. His face reddened.

"Listen to me: I want no part of this. None. I'm out, do you hear me? *Out.*"

In a spontaneous move of absolute fury and frustration he hurled the phone at the wall. It shattered into pieces.

For a long second, nobody spoke. Then Ripley turned to Emma, his mouth tight.

"He's ready. You need to be absolutely prepared, because when you meet him tomorrow, you need to bring him in."

SATURDAY

12 October

SPECIAL TO THE PRIME MINISTER
INFORMATION: PUBLIC COMMUNICATIONS G7
SECURITY LEVEL: LOW
RISK LEVEL: LOW

*Below, please find today's round-up of press in advance of G7
Summit in Edinburgh.*

BBC TODAY PROGRAM TRANSCRIPT,
12 OCTOBER, 07:13 HOURS

JULIAN CASEL: Well, it's just two days until the Gathering of
Seven leading democratic nations begins in Edinburgh, and the
city is bristling with security and not a little bit of excitement as
they prepare for the first leaders to arrive. Our Sarah Lams is on
the ground covering it for us. Sarah?

SARAH LAMS: Yes, Julian, the excitement and to a certain extent
the worries are growing here, as the clock ticks down to Monday.
Security is very tight here in Edinburgh, if you listen you can hear
the clanging of metal fencing being fixed into place virtually

around the spot where I'm standing near Edinburgh Castle. It's increasingly difficult to navigate the city, with so many roads closed, and others roadblocked to all but residents.

But it's all worthwhile, the government says, as a safe and effective G7 is critical to all the member governments going forward. The decisions made here on Monday and Tuesday will impact global relations and economies for the coming months.

Russia is clearly aware of this, as it has continued to launch jibes at the gathering. In a post on its social media account, the Russian government today wished the G7 "A glorious waste of time. Nothing that happens there will matter." Another post was more cryptic, telling the G7 leaders to "be careful in Edinburgh, you never know what might happen there."

The US government issued a statement calling that post "irresponsible and childish."

Although security is undeniably intense, the government in Whitehall has denied reports of threats against the gathering, and insists everything being done is "routine activity to keep all participants safe." We will find out on Monday, what this G7 will bring.

19

"I'll pick you up at your hotel at 6:30. Be ready for anything.
Bring your passport."

The text from Orlov arrived just before noon. Emma held the
phone out for Mackenzie, who set down her coffee to take it.

"Passport? Where's he taking you?" Mackenzie asked, handing
the phone back.

Emma shook her head. "I have no idea."

The two of them were at a coffee shop called The Hideout.
Mackenzie had chosen it and because it was tucked away down a
narrow cobblestone passage well away from the G7 chaos, Emma
had approved it.

Mackenzie had shown up in a worn black leather jacket and
jeans, her brown hair pulled back, and her heart-shaped face
clean of makeup.

Her bright blue eyes searched Emma's face. "Are you going to
go?"

Emma thought of Ripley slamming his fist down onto the table
the day before; of Orlov hurling his phone at the wall—the sense
that everyone was growing desperate.

"I have to," she said. "I've got to find out what Orlov knows."

"But he could take you anywhere," Mackenzie objected. "Forgive me, I'm sure you know what you're doing but in my business we'd call this absolutely fucking batshit crazy."

"We call it that in mine, too." Emma picked up her coffee. It had gone cold, but she drank it anyway—her mouth had suddenly gone dry.

She hadn't counted on Orlov doing something so unexpected but she couldn't back out. Too much was at stake, and she was too close now. Ripley was right—if she played her cards right tonight, she could bring Nick Orlov in.

Think of the people you're saving. Keep them always in your mind . . .

"Look, this is why I wanted to meet," she said, setting the cup down. "I need a favor."

"Name it." Mackenzie said it without hesitation, and Emma could have hugged her.

"Nick Orlov had a call yesterday where he was threatened. In it he mentioned someone named Blake—said he wouldn't meet him. He was really pissed off about this person. And Blake isn't a Russian name."

"No, Blake will be one of ours." Mackenzie's expression sharpened. "Do you know if it's a first name or a surname? It can be either around here."

Emma shook her head. "All he said was 'I won't meet with Blake.'"

"And you want me to figure out who it is," Mackenzie said. "That's not much to go on."

Emma leaned forward, her voice suddenly urgent. "We're in trouble, Kate. The G7 starts Monday and we're not much closer to understanding what's going to happen. If this Blake person has anything to do with it, we need to find out who he is and stop him. I'm going to be too busy with Orlov, and the rest of my team is being pulled in about fifty directions right now. You know this city better than anyone."

Mackenzie pulled out a small notebook and wrote something down. "Leave it with me. I've got some ideas."

Emma touched her arm. "Thank you."

"Don't thank me, just be careful tonight." Mackenzie gave her a direct look. "I'd really appreciate it if you'd stay alive."

When Emma left the coffee shop, she walked straight back to the office, moving fast. By now, all the main streets were lined in temporary metal barricades that turned the center of Edinburgh into a kind of glittering prison.

In the office, she took Orlov's message straight to where Ripley and Adam sat with Zach at the long table. Ripley read it, his expression curiously blank, before handing the phone to Adam, who gave a low whistle.

"That's not good," he said.

Adam turned to Zach. "Look through Orlov's email. Is there anything in there about travel? We need to know what he's planning."

Zach typed quickly and Orlov's outbox appeared on his monitor. Emma watched over his shoulder as, with almost dizzying speed, he opened and closed email after email, until he turned to Ripley.

"There's nothing in the last twenty-four hours about travel. No air tickets purchased. I'll check the recordings from Orlov's house for key words," Zach said. "See if he's made any calls from there that we missed."

"Dammit," Ripley swore softly. "I'll see if I can find anything out from Andrew, but we're not meant to be pursuing Orlov so he's not meant to help us."

"I can handle this," Emma said, although nobody was paying much attention to her. "I'm not afraid of Nick Orlov."

Adam looked doubtful. "You'll have no backup. We can't put a wire on you because you'll be out of range. And we have no idea where he might take you. What if he flies you to Moscow?"

Emma's brow furrowed. "Why on earth would he do that? Russia isn't a place he misses. You've seen his files—he's barely gone there in the last fifteen years. No, I think he's going to take me to Paris for some sort of fancy dinner with lots of champagne. It's a classic billionaire move."

While they'd talked, Martha had arrived, and now she joined them, giving Emma a questioning glance. Emma held out her phone to show her the text from Orlov.

"Oh, that's so *romantic*," Martha exclaimed. "He fancies the pants off of you."

"That's what I'm trying to tell them," Emma said. "I think Nick Orlov just wants to impress Anna Case and get away from Vladimir Balakin and his plots. We know he's a womanizer and he gets a buzz from seducing someone new." She turned to Ripley. "This could be the break we're looking for."

Ripley glanced at Adam, who shrugged. "She's got a point. It all comes down to how much risk you want to take."

Ripley rested his long fingers on the table and stared at the array of screens on the wall in front of him, then he turned to Emma.

"I trust your judgment. The Anna Case passport should work at the border but remember we're off the books here. While you're out of the country you're not an intelligence officer. You're Anna Case—a nobody."

Emma's pulse quickened.

"Understood," she said. "I'll be careful."

Ripley picked up his phone and began to dial as he spoke. "Martha, find something suitable for Emma to wear tonight. Assume she's right and it's a posh dinner. Zach, if you can think of anything she can take to make communication easier . . ."

"On it," Zach said, jumping to his feet.

Emma and Martha walked to the racks at the end of the long room, their footsteps echoing off the bare walls. Emma was suddenly aware of the chill in the unheated room, and she pulled her coat tighter around her.

"Now then," the disguise specialist said, touching her chin with one carmine fingernail. "I think we need to make you very sexy."

Always a flamboyant dresser, Martha had toned down her look while they were in Scotland, and today she wore an ankle-length skirt with biker boots, and a gilet, lined in fake fur. She and Ripley had a connection Emma didn't fully understand. She'd sometimes privately wondered if they were sleeping together. If they were, neither of them would ever say a word.

"Is he OK?" Emma asked quietly, tilting her head to the other end of the room, where Ripley was talking to Adam.

Martha made a vague gesture. "He's stressed, but he's fine." She gave Emma a considering look. "How about you? You look exhausted."

Emma glanced at her own face in the lighted mirror and saw what Martha could see — her blue eyes were underscored by shadows and she looked thinner; her cheekbones had sharpened.

"Yeah," she said, smoothing her hair back. "This project is taking it out of all of us right now."

"Don't worry, I can fix this." Martha picked up a bottle of foundation and poured a small amount on the back of her hand, reaching for a makeup brush. "But, without knowing where he's going to take you, it's hard to know how you should look. Should you wear a posh dress? An expensive suit? What do you think? You know Orlov better now—what's he really like? What's he looking for?"

As Martha swept makeup onto her face, Emma thought about Nick chatting with the owner of the restaurant near his office, looking like a normal Scottish man. And later, standing by the stove with a tea towel flung over one shoulder, laughing at something she'd said.

"He doesn't like anything obvious. He finds designer fashion tawdry, so I wouldn't go too low-cut," Emma said. "He's the kind of guy who prefers his local boozer to a posh wine bar. Did I tell you he decorated his house himself? He's worth a billion pounds and he doesn't even have a regular cleaner." She paused. "He can be very charming but he's easily bored."

As the words came out of her mouth, she realized with a jolt that she liked Nick Orlov. She'd been so busy processing her fears and doubts she simply hadn't had time to think about it. But it was true. She did like him.

That was why she knew he wasn't going to take her anywhere dangerous—he wasn't planning to harm her. He just wanted to seduce her.

And she could use that to get him to talk.

20

At six o'clock that evening, Emma stepped out of her hotel lobby to find Nick Orlov waiting for her next to the sleek red Bentley sports car. His eyes swept Emma's body, defined in a waist-cinching dress of a pale gray silk, with appreciation. She and Martha had gone for a classic Grace Kelly look—her hair was up, and she wore a wrap of white cashmere across her shoulders. Her only jewelry was a pair of simple diamond drop earrings and a matching bracelet.

("Lose those and I'll murder you," Martha had warned, as she'd handed the earrings to Emma. "They're such good fakes.")

"My god, Anna," Nick said appreciatively as she approached. "You look fantastic."

"You do too," she told him. And it was true, he did look good. The perfectly cut suit in a dark gray fabric had an expensive sheen to it and suited his long build and broad shoulders.

"Nonsense," he said, but he smiled as he opened the passenger door for her.

Emma watched him as he got behind the wheel and started the car. The engine engaged with an expensive, throaty purr. Nothing in his expression said he'd been threatened today. It was as if he were a different Nick Orlov from the one who'd thrown his phone across his office that morning. As he navigated the car out into traffic, his hands were steady on the wheel, his shoulders were loose, and the lines of his face betrayed no tension. If anything, he seemed more relaxed than he had the last time they met, as if a weight had been lifted off him.

Emma couldn't figure it out. Either he was incredibly skilled at hiding his emotions, or he'd simply decided that Balakin and his people were no threat.

"This is all so mysterious. Won't you give me some hint about where we're going?" she asked, as they turned onto a main road.

Orlov shook his head playfully. "Surely you don't want to ruin the surprise?"

"Yes I do," she replied without missing a beat.

He laughed. "Well, I'm not telling you a thing."

Emma hid her frustration. Despite its efforts, the Agency had been able to find out very little about Orlov's plans. Andrew Field had warned them that Orlov had chartered a private jet. But chartered jets were very hard to trace—unlike commercial jets, passenger names aren't shared with government agencies until the plane lands at its destination.

There were four chartered jets scheduled to fly from Edinburgh Airport this evening. According to the flight plans, one was going to London, one to Paris, one to Istanbul, and one to Rome. They didn't know which of these was Orlov's.

Istanbul would be a serious problem. The Turkish government had a testy relationship with Britain for a variety of reasons and a close relationship with Russia. That was the one that worried Ripley the most.

Regardless of the destination, Emma could carry no weapon—she'd have to pass through a metal detector and it would be impossible to explain so much as a knife. All she had was a tracker in her phone, and another inside the heel of her right shoe.

That will make it easier to find my body, she told herself, grimly, and then immediately suppressed the thought.

Orlov made light conversation as he drove. He seemed to enjoy teasing her, pointing out city sights as if she was a tourist he was showing around.

She wondered what he would think if he knew that right at this moment, Zach was disabling his home security system. By the time she and Orlov reached the airport, a team would be inside the stone mansion, searching it floor by floor.

The G7 started on Monday, so this operation was ending, one way or another. The gloves were off. Tonight was Emma's last chance to get some truth from Nick Orlov, but right now he seemed completely out of touch with the world he was in and the danger that surrounded him.

She looked at the road ahead, illuminated in the white glow of headlights. "I don't want to suggest I'm figuring this out, but we appear to be headed to the airport."

He barked a laugh. "Has anyone ever told you that you lack patience?"

"They have, in fact," she said. "And I would still love to know the plan."

"The plan is . . . wait and see." He continued to smile to himself as they turned onto the motorway and joined the stream of cars flowing out of the city, taillights forming rivers of glowing red.

Emma studied him with open curiosity.

"You're quite cheerful today," she observed.

"For a good reason. Do you remember that guy—the one at my house?" he glanced at her. "The one I was shouting at when you arrived?"

Emma nodded, thinking of Leonid Fridman's furious angular face; the threatening tone in his voice.

"Well, I got rid of him for good."

"Oh, really?" Emma tilted her head. "How did you do that?"

"I just made it clear I wasn't working with him anymore. You might say I quit." Orlov gave a short, contented chuckle and lifted both hands from the wheel. "I'm free of him forever."

Emma's heart sank.

No, you're not free, she thought. *You've just painted a giant target on your own back.*

But all she said was, "That's fantastic. I'm glad you sorted it all out."

And as the Bentley turned into a private entrance at Edinburgh airport and a guard rushed over to check Orlov's name from a list of expected travelers, Emma felt the first cold tendrils of doubt creep around her heart. But it was too late now. Everything was in play.

Following a brief conversation with the security guard, Nick Orlov pulled into a space near the terminal building. All the cars parked around them were luxury brands—Emma noted gleaming black Bentleys, a voluptuous Rolls-Royce, and a low-slung sunflower-yellow Bugatti, and she found herself wondering if anyone in her team was keeping an eye on this airport entrance.

When they got out of the car, Nick lifted a small black suitcase from the boot.

"Hey, that's not fair," Emma objected. "You told me not to pack anything."

He gave her a Cheshire cat smile. "I packed for both of us."

They walked through a side entrance of the airport into a space designed to look more polished than the usual modern airport, with faux oak paneling, black leather chairs, and artful up-lighting.

Nick headed straight to the front desk and handed his passport to a woman in a blue uniform with a small matching hat.

"Ah, Mr. Orlov." The woman smiled. "Your plane is fueled and ready." She turned to Emma. "May I please see your passport?"

Emma handed over Anna Case's falsified documents. Although she didn't show it, all her muscles had tensed.

MI6 made all the Agency's paperwork, and everything should pass inspection. But nobody had anticipated her going abroad, and it was always possible someone hadn't properly coded the biometric chip. Or that there was no chip at all.

Emma kept her expression neutral as she watched the false passport slide through a digital reader attached to the keyboard.

As the woman stared at the screen, a slight frown appeared on her face. She seemed to be reading something long and complex.

Emma's heart began to pound. She made herself stand still, hands loose at her sides. She didn't fidget, didn't shift her balance, didn't do any of the things that nervous people do, but her palms had begun to sweat.

Orlov tapped his fingers impatiently against the tall black desk, glancing over the woman's shoulder at the double doors behind her.

Finally, the woman looked up at Emma.

"You're all set," she said, and held out the passport.

Was there something new in her expression? Some caution that hadn't been there before?

But she was letting her through, and that was all that mattered.

Emma smiled and took the document back. "Thanks."

When they were well away from the desk, she rubbed her hands against the fabric of her dress.

The glass doors slid open as they approached, and a blast of cold air hit them with the sharp, astringent scent of jet fuel.

Outside, a white electric cart stood waiting, the driver already behind the wheel.

"Hi, Tom," Orlov said, putting the case in the back.

"Nice to see you again, Mr. Orlov," the driver replied.

Nick waited for Emma to climb into the backseat and got in behind her. The driver released the brake, and the cart headed out silently toward a row of small jets, lined up like white birds on the black tarmac.

It was already getting dark as the cart jolted down the long line of private planes with a collective value, Emma thought, of billions, before pulling up in front of a Dassault Falcon. The stairs had been unfolded and the lights inside glowed invitingly.

Emma drew her phone from her bag and held it up to take a

picture of the plane. "Is that the one?" She filled her voice with excitement. Any photo she took would automatically appear on Zach's screens in the office.

"That's it," Nick said.

Emma kept her phone in her hand. A listening app in it would broadcast her words back to the office.

"Is this yours?" Emma asked, raising her voice to be heard as a commercial jet roared down the main runway.

"I wish," Nick said, with a grin. "I'm just renting it for the day."

They climbed the five steps into the plane, and instantly the noise of the world receded. Inside, beige leather armchairs were arranged in rows of two, each with a window. Small tables bolted to the floor held little lamps which emitted a subtle glow. It all conveyed the impression of a particularly narrow upscale cocktail bar.

"This is a long way from Ryanair," Emma said.

"Take a seat," Nick told her, and headed to the cockpit where she heard him say, "Alastair, how are you? Are we all set?" sounding far more Scottish than Russian.

Emma sank down on a smooth leather seat, setting her handbag on the table, but keeping her phone in her hand. Within seconds, a young woman appeared from the back in a dark blue blazer and cap.

"Can I bring you a glass of champagne?" she asked, with a bright smile. "We have Taittinger, Laurent Perrier, and Veuve Clicquot today."

"How lovely," Emma said. "A glass of any of them would be wonderful."

"I agree." Nick walked back to join her. "Thanks, Helen. Two glasses of Taittinger, and bring some of those nuts I love, won't you?"

"You've got it, Mr. Orlov."

Nick sat in the chair next to Emma and smiled at her.

"OK," she said. "I'm impressed."

His smile widened. "That's all I wanted to hear."

There was a whirr and a thump as the stairs were raised and the door closed. Seconds later, the engines started with a smooth whine.

The waitress returned and set two glasses down on the table, along with a bone china bowl of amber nuts and crisps.

"Enjoy."

The plane began to move toward the runway.

"Now," Nick said, picking up his glass, "I can tell you the plan. We're going to dinner. In Rome."

"In *Rome?*" Emma's voice rose.

Nick laughed with childlike glee. "Now *that's* the expression I was hoping for. You didn't expect Rome?"

"No, I thought London, or maybe Paris at the outside," Emma admitted. "But not Rome. I am genuinely surprised."

"Good." He gave a satisfied nod. "I like surprises. And I like seeing you surprised. You look even more beautiful then."

Without warning, he leaned over and pressed his lips softly against hers. Emma's breath caught, but she made herself lean into the kiss, letting him pull her closer. She could taste the crisp champagne on his tongue, feel the warmth of his hands against her back.

Before he lifted his head, he whispered, "I have more surprises planned."

Before Emma could respond, Helen returned, her smile undimmed.

"My understanding is that you've asked for dinner not to be served during the flight?"

"That's correct." He gave Emma a pleased look. "We're dining in Rome. At La Pergola."

Emma knew about La Pergola. It was popular with oligarchs for its over-the-top decor. It had three Michelin stars and was located inside the Waldorf Astoria. Tables were almost impossible to get.

Nick Orlov was celebrating.

"That sounds incredible," she said, raising her glass. "Thank you so much for this amazing surprise."

He clinked his glass against hers.

Helen said, "Seatbelts on, please, we're cleared for takeoff."

Emma secured her seatbelt. As she did, her phone vibrated and she glanced at the screen. A message appeared.

"Leonid Fridman and Vladimir Balakin both flew to Rome this afternoon. Be careful."

A second later the message disappeared. Emma knew there would be no record of it on the device. If she hadn't looked down in the second it appeared, she'd never have known it was there. Some part of her wished she'd never seen it.

The plane began to race down the runway, the force of it pushing her back against her seat.

"Hold on to your champagne!" Nick said, laughing.

Emma forced a smile but said nothing.

They were flying into a trap.

21

At nine o'clock on a Saturday night, Rome felt incredibly alive. Cars sped down the narrow streets, horns blaring, crowds wandered from bar to bar in the teeming city center, while groups sauntered from restaurant to city square, talking and laughing. Music blared from doorways and cars and the backs of Vespas. It felt like a university town, a big city, and a playground all rolled into one, and it smelled of rich food and petrol exhaust. Beneath it all lay the soft green river scent of the Tiber, which flowed silently through the night.

When Emma and Nick stepped out of the car that had ferried them from the airport though, it was into a verdant green hush. The Waldorf Astoria Rome is set up on a hillside, surrounded by peaceful parkland, shielded by mature trees and fiercely protective doormen.

"Mr. Orlov." The small man in dark livery swept Nick's bag from the driver's hand and ushered the two of them past the waiting valets to the heavy glass door. "Signora. Welcome. How was your flight?"

It was all so seamless, Emma thought, the lives of the very wealthy. The plane journey had been smooth and fast. At the airport there had been no queues or delays, they'd simply stepped out of the jet, handed their passports to an official who stamped them, and they were done. A driver had been waiting for them in the VIP waiting room when they emerged, and he'd whisked them to a car parked in a gated area near the door.

The whole process, from disembarking to getting into the car, had taken no more than ten minutes.

As they entered the grand lobby with soaring marble columns and a flotilla of staff armed with electronic tablets, Emma looked around for any sign of Balakin or Leonid Fridman, but there was no evidence of them in the serene lobby. Instead, everything was calm perfection. The air smelled faintly of jasmine from the huge floral arrangements that overflowed a round mahogany table, and piano music streamed at a volume just low enough to make it difficult to identify the tune. Everywhere staff in crisp, dark uniforms bustled without ever becoming obtrusive.

It would be difficult, Emma thought, for the two Russians to try anything here. Difficult, but not impossible.

How could they find out where Nick was staying in Rome? The Agency, with all its resources, hadn't been able to track that information down. If she and Nick left first thing in the morning, they should be safe. All the same, her nerves were taut as she gazed languidly around the ornate space, seeking anything out of place.

Nick put one hand possessively in the small of her back and murmured, "Shall we go and have a drink?"

Emma smiled at him. "I'd like to freshen up first. I'll meet you by the lifts."

One of the receptionists directed her down a long, lavishly decorated corridor to an empty ladies' room bigger than Emma's London flat.

Her heels clicked against the tiles as she checked each cubicle before pulling out her phone and calling the office. Zach answered on the first ring.

"You good?" he asked.

"I'm golden," she said. "What's the situation?"

"Balakin and Fridman arrived in Rome two hours ago." The

pause that followed gave Emma a split-second warning before he said, "Balakin has taken a suite at the Waldorf Astoria."

Emma swore softly. "This is a setup, Zach. It's got to be."

"Emma, Ripley here." Her boss's familiar voice interrupted. "What is Orlov's plan for the night?"

"Dinner at La Pergola, and then he's booked us a room upstairs— I haven't seen it yet. The plane is scheduled to take us back at nine A.M."

"Is the room in his name?"

"Everyone calls him Mr. Orlov."

Ripley paused for a little too long before asking, "What's his mood like?"

"Effervescent," Emma replied, still thinking about that pause. "He told me he's got rid of the people who were threatening him and now the problem is magically resolved, as far as he's concerned. What about Fridman? Do we know where he went when he got to Rome?"

"Negative. The Italian *Carbinieri* have been informed that he's in the country but . . ."

He didn't have to finish the sentence. Everyone was busy, and legally speaking, Fridman hadn't done anything wrong. They knew he was Balakin's muscle, and they knew he had threatened Orlov, but they had nothing to take to other intelligence agencies except suspicion.

From the hallway outside the door, Emma heard the sound of footsteps and high Italian voices. She paused to listen and then said quickly, "I've got to go, someone's coming."

By the time two women in perilously high heels and long silk dresses walked in, she was standing at the sink, applying lipstick. They passed her with polite smiles.

Emma studied her face in the mirror. Her expression was bland, but her blue eyes looked intensely focused.

Fridman had been Balakin's right-hand man for the last three years. There was no real evidence of what his job was, but it didn't take a genius to read between the lines: he took care of Balakin's problems.

Nick Orlov had stopped playing by the rules, and the odds were that he knew a great deal about what Balakin was planning. That made him a problem.

If they were all here in the same hotel at the same time, something bad was going to happen.

Emma put the lipstick away and smoothed her hair. Squaring her shoulders, she headed down the marble hallway with its endless display of Renaissance paintings to where Nick Orlov stood waiting near the elevators.

"All ready," Emma said, brightly.

Orlov's eyes swept across her body with such eagerness she thought she could feel the heat.

"You look perfect."

"Thank you." She smiled up at him.

Regardless of what might happen tonight, she still had a job to do.

Resting a hand in the small of her back, he guided her to the lifts, pressing the button for the eighth floor.

"You seem to know this place well," Emma remarked.

He shrugged. "My work often brings me to Rome, and this is my base when I'm in town." He smiled. "I'm a creature of habit, I suppose. I like knowing what I'm going to get."

Emma murmured a polite reply, but her thoughts were elsewhere. Everything was falling into place. If Orlov always stayed in the same hotel, Balakin would know that. He would know every hotel Orlov preferred, and he would also know which private jet he rented when he wanted to impress someone. Vladimir Balakin was a division chief in one of the most feared intelligence services in the world. He would have known everything about Orlov from day one.

When the two of them stepped out of the elevator, the famous restaurant was still in full swing despite the hour. The air smelled richly of butter and spun sugar, and Emma's mouth began to water. She hadn't eaten anything since that morning.

La Pergola is tastefully designed with cream linens and beige chairs. This was one of the most famous restaurants in the world, and as they were escorted across the long room to their table, Emma heard snippets of conversations in six languages, but she saw no sign of anyone who worried her. Still, she memorized those faces she did see. A plump man in a tuxedo with a crooked bow tie. A gorgeous blond woman in a yellow silk dress with a vivid blue scarf flung across her shoulders, speaking in Polish. Three young men in suits of varying shades of gray and dark blue, clustered over a small table, speaking French.

There were too many, passing too quickly. There must have been sixty patrons in the restaurant and bar, and at least twenty-five staff. It was too much to absorb. But there was no sign of Vladimir Balakin's thin face and blazing black eyes.

She was almost relieved when the waiter led them through glass doors to a broad stretch of balcony and seated them at a table near the banister. It was much warmer in Rome than it had been in Scotland, although a cool breeze gently ruffled the white linen tablecloth, but any chill was quickly dispelled by slim heaters arranged between the tables.

Even if it had been freezing, it would have been worth it for that view. The hotel was perched on a hill near Vatican City, and now all of Rome seemed to stretch out before them, in a carpet of light and shade.

Emma's gasp was real. "That view is stunning. Is that the Vatican there?" She pointed at the domed roof below them. "And my God, is that the Colosseum in the distance?"

"Now you understand why I come here." Orlov held out his hands. "The view feeds my soul while the chefs feed my body."

"It is an extraordinary place," Emma met his gaze. "Thank you for this. What a wonderful gift."

He lifted her hand from the white tablecloth and raised it to his lips. "Anything for you, Anna."

He'd been flirty and affectionate on the flight, but she'd managed to avoid more intimate contact. In fact, he seemed happy to wait. Contented with the progress he was making in his seduction, which was a relief for Emma. It gave her time to plan.

The waiter approached with menus, but Orlov intercepted him, and spoke quietly, gesturing occasionally at Emma. The waiter nodded, gave Nick a conspiratorial smile, and retreated.

"I hope you don't mind," Nick explained when he'd retreated toward the kitchen. "I don't want us to be interrupted. I've ordered the taster menu—there's bound to be something you love there. And of course"—he lifted one hand as the sommelier approached holding a bottle of Dom Perignon—"champagne."

As the drinks were poured, Emma observed her date silently. He was relaxed and happy, talking to the La Pergola staff like they were old friends, oblivious to the danger he was in. It was absurd. Views go both ways—anyone out in the gardens would have a clear shot at him right now, and she wouldn't be able to do one thing about it.

It was time for a more direct approach, but she needed to find the right time.

"Shall we toast?" Nick raised his glass. "To a beautiful night."

Emma played along, sipping the chilled champagne, cooing over the tiny tray of canapés designed to look like flowers.

Finally, during a quiet moment she said, "Oh, I've been meaning to ask. Do you know a man named Vladimir Balakin?"

Orlov, who had been raising his glass to his lips, froze so suddenly a drop of liquid spilled from his glass and tumbled to the table, spoiling the crisp white tablecloth. He set the glass down carefully, dabbing at the cloth with his napkin.

"That is a very strange question," he said, keeping his gaze diverted. "How do you know this name?"

"The night we met at the Balmoral Hotel," Emma kept her voice light. "I was with my friend—it was her birthday, remember?"

Nick nodded slowly.

"Well, in the bar, before dinner, I got to chatting with the man at the table next to us. He said his name was Vladimir Balakin, and I had the strangest feeling he knew you."

"Why was that?" Nick's baritone voice sounded strained, and he watched her closely.

"You walked in with your date, and he stopped talking mid-sentence, and just . . . I don't know . . . watched you in a very odd way. I asked if anything was wrong and he said, 'No. I just saw a friend.'"

The last word made Nick twitch. He picked up his glass and drained it, motioning to the waiter to refill his glass.

"So, is he your friend?" Emma pressed. "He seemed very odd, I have to say. Almost unpleasantly intense."

"He's not my friend." He said it with contempt. "He's someone who knows my family, back in Russia. Or at least, he knows who they are and where they are, and he has tried . . ." He stopped speaking with visible effort, but then seemed to change his mind and spoke rapidly. "He has made my life very difficult lately. Threatening me and my family, trying to make me do things I don't want to do. To work with him." He leaned forward until she could smell the champagne on his breath. "He is a Russian spy and you must never trust him. *Never.*"

The passion in his voice was unmistakable. This was Emma's chance to get him to really confide in her. But at that precise moment, a waiter arrived with two small plates of golden sea bass fillets. Emma and Nick fell silent as the plates were arranged in front of them with the precision of a clockmaker putting the finishing touches to a precious timepiece.

When he'd finally gone, Emma leaned forward. "Are you a spy?" she asked, lowering her voice to a whisper. "Do you work for Russia?"

She made her tone breathless and arch, but it was clear this was no joke to him. His lip curled. "I want nothing to do with that world. I have never been a spy. But now I am forced to help them."

"How are they forcing you? Have they hurt your family?" Emma asked.

"Not yet. No, not yet." His tone was stiff and tetchy; he wasn't enjoying this line of conversation. She decided to press harder.

"But you seemed so happy today," she pointed out. "You said you were free. That the trouble was behind you."

Again, Nick picked up his glass and drained it as if it were whisky instead of champagne. When a waiter stepped over to fill the glass, he waved him away with an impatient flip of his wrist.

The waiter cast a worried look at the exquisitely cooked sea bass cooling untouched on the table.

"I have quit everything. I told Balakin's man today that I would do no more for him. I want nothing to do with their plans. I never did. They used me and my home, and I will not let that happen again." Nick shook his head slowly. "Never again."

"But what about your family in Russia?" Emma asked. "Who did they threaten?"

There was a long silence. Nick clutched the empty champagne glass.

"I have a son in Russia," he said, finally. "Not with my wife, with someone else. An affair. I have helped raise him. No one knew about him, but Balakin did, that bastard. Somehow he knew. He threatened to take him away, and I don't know what would happen to him." He murmured a word in Russian. "*Убийство*."

Murder.

This explained the picture in his office and the recorded conversation—Orlov had a son MI6 knew nothing about. It could have been the existence of this child that had destroyed his marriage and sent his ex-wife back to Russia.

As her mind fit the puzzle pieces into place, Emma kept her expression compassionate and open.

"What will you do?" she asked.

Orlov looked near to tears.

"I did my best to save him," he told her, brokenly. "But I can't be caught up in this. I can't. My life . . . they want my *whole life*."

Instinctively, Emma reached out and took his hand; his fingers gripped hers.

This was the moment.

"Nick," she said, urgently. "What is the plan? What did they want you to help with? What are they going to do?"

The look he gave her then was anguished. She could feel his need to talk as clearly as she could feel the cool breeze shifting her hair.

His fingers tightened around hers, "I have—"

"I am sorry to disturb." A voice with a heavy Italian accent interrupted them, and they both looked up to find the head waiter standing by their table, a stiff smile on his face, his black apron perfectly smooth. "Is there a problem with your fish course?"

Emma opened her mouth to reply but Nick Orlov spoke before she could.

"There's nothing wrong with the bloody fish," he snapped. "Can we be left in peace for five minutes?"

The waiter's face turned the color of his crisp shirt. "I beg your pardon. Of course."

He withdrew quickly, but when Emma turned back to Nick, his face was closed. He pulled his hand away from hers and reached for his wineglass.

"I'm sorry," he said, his voice stiff. "I don't want to drag you any further into this mess. We're supposed to be having fun tonight. Just forget I said anything."

"You're not dragging me into anything," Emma began, but Nick cut her off.

"Enough misery. Let's have a lovely evening."

Emma knew if she pressed too hard it would only make things worse.

"Of course," she said. "But I have to say, it sounds like you need someone to talk to."

"What I need is a good lawyer." Nick held up his empty glass to get the attention of the wine waiter. "And a gun."

22

As one exquisite course after another arrived on gleaming china, the conversation retreated to safer ground. Nick's mood improved markedly after a second £700 bottle of vintage champagne was ordered and poured.

Emma made light conversation, trying to maneuver him back to where he'd been in that moment before the waiter interrupted them. Nick wanted to talk, she was certain of that, but all his instincts were screaming at him to stay silent. Somehow, she had to overcome the barricade he'd erected. She believed her best chance would come when they were alone, and so she waited impatiently for the meal to end.

When at last the final dish of chocolates arrived on a polished olive branch with the color and smoothness of sterling silver, Nick signed the bill with a sweep of his pen.

"Shall we?" He rose unsteadily.

Emma had nursed her glass throughout the evening, even knocking it over at one point to avoid having to consume too much, which meant Nick had consumed the vast majority of the champagne, and she felt coldly sober as they crossed the dining room toward the door.

It was after midnight. All evening, she'd kept an eye out but she'd seen nothing that worried her. If Balakin and Fridman were here, they were staying out of sight.

She'd seen no faces that looked familiar from Balakin's MI6 files. And the staff hadn't put a foot wrong. It would have been difficult to place someone in this sort of restaurant. Five-star restaurants were incredibly particular about their staff, and everyone right down to the dishwashers would have been vetted as thoroughly as any spy service.

But Balakin would not give up easily. If Orlov had resisted blackmail, then he'd left the Russian spy chief with few options. He'd want Nick Orlov gone.

She and Orlov had been one of the last tables seated that evening and as they left, the restaurant was mostly empty. The head waiter walked over to shake Nick's hand as they left, smiling broadly. All was forgiven about the sea bass, it seemed.

When the two of them reached the elevators, they were alone.

Nick put his arm heavily across her shoulders as they waited for the lift to arrive. "You look beautiful," he whispered, his breath hot and damp against her cheek.

There was no question what he expected when they reached the bedroom.

Resisting the urge to pull away, Emma made herself lean against him.

"Thank you so much for this wonderful surprise," she whispered.

He smiled, with sudden eagerness. "The night is only beginning."

His Russian accent was thicker when he was drunk, and he was clumsier. His hands were heavy as he pulled her toward him, his lips touching the curve of her neck just as the lift doors slid open. A recorded female voice said "Going down" in Italian. Orlov pulled back.

"Soon," he said, with heavy promise. They stepped into the elevator and he punched the button for the fifth floor.

The recorded voice spoke again as the doors closed and it was, Emma realized, the first time anyone or anything had spoken to them in Italian since the plane landed. English was the lingua franca of the very wealthy to the point where she could have been forgiven for forgetting what country she was in.

Money was its own country.

Nick kept his arm on her shoulder, his gaze on the numbers ticking down beside the door. Emma smoothed her expression as she angled her body so that she would be the first out when they reached the fifth floor.

The elevator juddered to a stop, and the doors slid open.

Emma stepped out quickly, leaving Nick to hurry after her as she checked the landing, but no danger waited for them there. They were alone in a hushed and shadowed hallway.

"You're eager." Nick grinned, misconstruing her haste. He took her hand, nuzzling her cheek. "Me too. Let's go."

The building seemed designed to suppress sound. Emma could hear nothing as they walked except their breathing; the thick carpeting absorbed the sounds of their footsteps. She didn't like the quiet.

On the walls, baroque paintings were mounted every few feet. In the glow of the light sconces, the pale painted faces seemed to leer and grimace, thrusting out of the black backgrounds like ghouls.

Orlov stopped in front of room 509 and fumbled with a key card as he pulled it from the breast pocket of his jacket. Holding it up, he gave her a coy glance. "I can't wait to get you inside."

He swiped the card against the reader. The light on the lock turned green, and he reached for the brass handle.

Later, Emma couldn't say exactly what warned her. Was there a faint sound from inside the room, so quiet her mind took a moment to register it? Or perhaps it was simply her instincts, always on high alert that told her something was wrong? Either way, as Nick Orlov pushed the door open, Emma lunged for him, shoving him hard. He fell, his head cracking against the wall just as the gun was fired from inside the darkened room. Emma barely heard the deadened *putt* sound of the silencer.

Everything seemed to move in slow motion. She watched the puff of plaster dust as the projectile passed through the wall behind her right shoulder. She saw Nick, not yet understanding what had happened, struggling to stand up again.

"Stay *down*," Emma hissed, pushing him back and crouched beside him, her silk skirts swirling around her.

"What's happening?" Orlov asked, bewildered.

Emma whispered a one word answer. "Balakin."

His face turned ashen but there was no time for more explanation. Quickly, Emma slipped off her heels and left them on the corridor floor. She kept her eyes on the door to her left. It was still cracked open, but all she could see through the opening was darkness.

"Stay here," she whispered to Nick. "I'm going in."

"What the hell are you talking about?" Nick was bewildered. "You can't."

She gave him a steady look. "I'll be fine. It's not me they want to kill."

All evidence of Anna Case was gone from her voice now. The time for pretense was over.

For the first time, Emma saw understanding dawn behind Nick Orlov's eyes.

"Who are you?" he breathed, with something like fear.

As his words faded into silence, in the deep quiet of the corridor she caught a faint *shush* of movement from inside room 509.

Turning back to Orlov, she whispered urgently, "Stay here. Don't try to help me."

A split second later, the door flew open. Emma had time to see the black barrel of the gun elongated by the silencer, and the dark eyes of the man holding it, and then she was flying toward him, low and fast. She connected with his knees with ruthless force.

Leonid Fridman fired as he fell. Emma felt the recoil from the weapon travel through his body, an involuntary twitch, as the bullet bored a hole in the perfect plasterwork of the ceiling.

Fridman landed on his back, with Emma on top of him, but he recovered fast and swung the gun up, trying to get an angle to shoot her.

Emma grabbed his arm with her left hand and punched him in the face with her right.

"Let go," she demanded, in a whisper, conscious of all the rooms around them, all the innocent people sleeping.

Swearing, Fridman twisted his arm free and swung the gun toward her head. By then, though, she was in motion again, leaping to her feet, landing with one foot planted firmly on his wrist.

"Drop it," she ordered, her voice rising.

He swore in Russian and with unexpected speed and force swung a bruising blow behind her knees. Emma went down instantly, landing on Fridman's chest with all her weight. She immediately rolled onto the arm holding the gun, immobilizing it.

He tried to punch her again with his left hand, but the angle was wrong and his fist glanced off her shoulder, striking her temple. He grabbed a handful of her hair and gripped it hard, twisting her neck, shoving her face into the thick, soft carpet. She dug her feet into the carpet, twisting around to free herself.

"Let her go!" Orlov appeared in the doorway, and both Emma and Fridman paused to look up.

Fridman tried to lift the gun but Emma still lay on his right arm. Swearing furiously, he punched her again, frustration clear in his taut face.

"Get off!" he demanded.

Emma contorted her body until her legs were free and aimed a knee at his crotch. The Russian man flinched away and, as he moved, he fired the gun again.

This time Emma felt the force of the recoil through her entire body. With deadly silence the bullet hit the wall, sending a chunk of plaster flying. Orlov dived back out the door.

Emma fought to hold down Fridman's arm, but he was strong and she was tiring. This couldn't go on—all he needed was one lucky shot.

But Fridman was panting too. The fight was taking it out of him as well.

"Who are you?" he demanded, in heavily accented English. "MI6?"

"I'm nobody," she said, gritting her teeth as she fought to hold his gun-hand down. "Just helping a friend."

"You fight like MI6," he said.

Suddenly he rolled his body with tremendous force, lifting her off the ground. Emma clung to his wrist with her left hand while swinging her right elbow at his face with all the force she could muster.

This time he didn't have the chance to dodge the blow. There was a sharp stab of pain as her elbow made contact with his face, and a sickening crunch.

Fridman gave a juddering gasp. His fingers convulsed, releasing the gun at last.

Emma snatched the pistol and rolled off his arm, coming up onto her feet with her rumpled silk skirt flying around her. She pointed the weapon at his head.

Through the blood pouring down his face, Fridman's black eyes glared at her with loathing.

"His Majesty says hello," Emma said.

"You bitch." Fridman lunged, his body flying from the floor with extraordinary speed.

Gripping the gun with both hands, Emma swung it at his face, connecting with the side of his head. In the quiet, elegant room, the crack of metal against bone sounded deafening.

Leonid Fridman fell like a stone.

23

"Is he dead?"

Nick Orlov stood in the doorway, staring at the unconscious blood-covered man on the floor of his hotel room. The hand covering his mouth trembled as Emma strode over to him, pulling him inside and closing the door.

Reaching past his shoulder, she switched on the lights. The subtle glow illuminated a spacious room, walls covered in taupe silk wallpaper that caught the light and glimmered. The king-sized bed had been turned down invitingly, the curtains pulled across the tall windows.

Every item in the room had been skillfully chosen and beautifully arranged. The only thing out of place was the bloody body on the floor.

Crouching next to Fridman, Emma set the gun down and picked up his thin wrist. His skin felt warm. She put a hand over his mouth and noted the steady passage of his breath.

"He's alive." She remained beside the unconscious man for a few seconds more, thinking through their situation.

When she stood up, she picked up the gun and popped out the bullet cartridge, checking it with a quick professional glance. Fridman had fired three times. There were thirteen bullets left.

Lucky thirteen.

"We haven't got long. He's not alone." She snapped the cartridge back in place. "Do you have your passport?"

As if in a daze, Orlov stared at her.

"*Nick,*" she said, firmly. "Your passport."

After a second, his right hand floated down to his chest and touched the pocket of his jacket.

"It's here." His voice was strangely flat.

He was in shock. But there was no time for him to adjust to the reality of the situation. They had to move.

"Good," she said. "Your phone and your wallet, have you got those?"

He nodded slowly, his focus still on Fridman, who lay unmoving.

"Right, then. Let's go." Emma headed for the door, but Orlov didn't budge.

"I don't understand." He raised his gaze to meet hers. "I told them I was out. I wasn't going to do what they wanted. He said he understood—"

"I'll explain everything on the way." Emma cut him off, her tone sharp. "Nick, we can't stay here."

But her words seemed to have no impact on Orlov, who stood unmoving and pointed an accusing finger at her. "And you. You're a spy?"

Emma fought to quell the impatience rising inside her as she spoke quickly.

"I work for the British government. I'm here to protect you. That's all you need to know right now."

Nick opened his mouth to speak again but she stopped him, grabbing him by the shoulder with her free hand and shaking him hard.

"Nick, listen to me. If we don't leave now we're going to die. Someone is going to come looking for Fridman and if they find us here we don't stand a chance. Do you understand what I'm saying?" She searched his face, still set in lines of horror. "We have to get out of here and we have to do it now."

Whether it was being shaken or the intensity of her voice that did it, Nick took a stumbling step to one side, allowing Emma to reach past him and switch off the lights before opening the door.

The corridor was hushed and empty, the row of doors on either side closed tight. Emma's shoes and bag lay where she'd dropped them outside the door. Her pale cashmere throw was stretched out across the dark carpet, like a wraith.

She stepped out first, looking in both directions before motioning for Nick to follow. He did so cautiously, his shoulders hunched around his ears, as if expecting a blow.

"Where should we go?" he whispered.

Emma snatched her things from the floor as the door to room 509 closed silently behind them and locked with a muffled click.

"Not the lift," she said. "They'll be watching it. The stairs."

Barefoot, clutching her shoes in one hand, the gun hidden in the soft folds of the wrap, and her bag hanging over her shoulder, she headed down the hallway. Nick Orlov followed. He was breathing heavily, his hands twitching occasionally, but he was in motion. That was progress.

"You think he's not alone?" Orlov said it suddenly, as if her earlier words had just sunk in.

"I'm certain he's not alone."

The decisiveness in her tone left him no room for more questions, and he fell silent again.

Emma, who knew better than most how long it takes for adrenaline and fear to allow you to think normally again, left him in peace until she spotted the subtle sign for the staircase.

She stopped him with one hand. "I'll go first."

This time, he didn't question her, but dropped back as she threw the door open and jumped into the lighted stairwell, racing to the banister rail to check up and down the stairs as she listened for any sign of life.

It was utterly silent.

"It's clear," she said, turning back to Nick.

He followed her obediently as she headed down.

"What are we going to do when we get downstairs?" he asked. "My driver isn't booked until tomorrow."

"Your driver is being watched; we couldn't use him if we wanted to. But we do need a car." She glanced at him. "You know this place better than me—is there a side door?"

She watched him try to organize his sluggish thoughts.

"Yes, it opens onto a patio. I've had drinks there," he said.

"That's how we're getting out," she said.

As they wound their way down the stairs, she thought through her plan. It was all up to her now. There was no one to call for help—Ripley had made that clear. No MI6 backup, no helicopters coming to their rescue. They were on their own.

When they reached the ground floor, she cracked the door to peer out.

Down here, the hotel was lit up like day—the velvet chairs were neatly aligned, the cushions perfectly arranged—but it was empty. The lobby was down the hallway to her left, and Emma could hear faint voices from that direction, but there was no one within sight.

Closing the door again, she made sure the gun was wrapped in the soft wool of her wrap before turning to Orlov. "Here's the plan. We've had too much to drink and we've just had a row. I want to leave and you want me to stay. We'll go straight to the patio doors and outside. If anyone spots us, ignore them, and beg me to stay. I'll run out, and you follow. Got it?"

Nick stared at her dully.

"Nick," she leaned toward him, touching his arm. "Focus. Have you got it?"

"Yes." His voice was hoarse.

She turned to open the door when he spoke again. "You've got blood on your dress."

Emma looked at him in surprise, and then down at the dress of silvery silk. He was right. A dark streak of Leonid Fridman's blood was smeared across her ribs on the right side.

Swearing softly, she threw the pashmina across her shoulders, arranging it to cover the incriminating stain.

"Better?" she asked him.

"Yes."

He studied her with caution. A small amount of color had returned to his face, and he was starting to look a little more like himself.

"Who are you?" he asked for a second time that night.

Emma shook her head. "Later. First, we have to get out of here. Which direction to the doors? Right or left?"

There was a pause. "Right," he said.

She opened the door and stepped out. The marble floor was ice beneath her bare feet, cold and slick, as she turned immediately right without sparing a glance for the lobby to their left.

She walked with a jerking, unsteady gait, weaving slightly.

Nick hurried after her but she didn't look at him, her attention fully focused on the glass doors she could see further down the long hallway. She ignored the towering paintings, the huge vases filled with exquisite floral arrangements six feet tall, and the velvet chairs.

The building, with its hundreds of guests, was dangerously quiet. Emma couldn't even hear the voices she'd noticed earlier from the lobby. Nobody seemed to be around, and Emma hurried her pace, half-running now.

But then, a slightly built man in his twenties wearing a dark suit turned the corner and began walking toward them.

Emma's stomach clenched.

She saw the white rectangle of the name tag on his lapel.

He worked here. A night receptionist.

She saw the precise moment when he saw the two of them; the

frown crinkling his smooth skin as he noticed her lack of shoes, her tangled hair.

She really hoped he wouldn't spot the blood.

Shifting the shoes in her left hand so they caught the light, she turned to Orlov and spoke loud enough for the man to hear.

"I just want some air, there's no reason for you to come with me. I told you I just had too much wine, and to be perfectly honest, I don't believe a word you said about Clara. I think you *do* fancy her. And I'm just . . ." Her voice broke; hot tears scalded her eyes. "I'm just hurt and I need to think. Can't you see that?"

Being able to cry on cue is a vastly underrated skill.

Orlov looked from her to the man, who had slowed his steps. "You're wrong about Clara. It's nothing."

They were nearly to the hotel worker, but he seemed suddenly eager to avoid meeting the eyes of the intoxicated British guests. They passed without exchanging a glance.

"Just five minutes of fresh air, that's all I'm asking," Emma said, continuing the act as they turned toward the door.

She reached for the handle, praying they weren't locked.

The door swung open as if on oiled hinges, and Emma ran out onto the dark patio, so relieved she almost laughed. But she knew better than to celebrate too early—they weren't safe yet.

"This way," she hissed to Orlov, motioning for him to follow.

It was much colder outside than it had been on the restaurant balcony with patio heaters all around them. Emma's feet turned to ice, and she paused to slip her high-heeled shoes back on again. A chilly breeze sent her skirt billowing around her as they headed toward the main entrance, which glowed like a disco ball ahead of them. Emma clutched the pashmina tightly, trying to hide the red slash of blood and the gun at the same time.

"We need to get to the valet stand by the front door." Emma explained as they walked. "When we're there, I need you to distract the valet for one minute."

His brow furrowed. "How do I do that?"

"You're rich, drunk, and entitled. Tell him to get you a cocktail. Bump into something and knock it over."

Orlov curled his lip with distaste but didn't argue.

As they neared the bright lights at the front of the hotel, Emma spotted the valet huddling inside a small booth tucked behind a topiary shrub. There was no one else outside.

"Right," she told Orlov. "It's showtime."

As they entered the glow of the lights, she pushed him away. "I saw you with her," she said, with fury. "I know what you've been doing."

By now, Orlov had seen her work and he recovered quickly.

"Darling, don't be an idiot. I hardly know her," he said.

"Liar!" Emma stormed past him to the little hut where the portly middle-aged man was endeavoring to appear not to be watching them while also absorbing this public display like oxygen.

"Make him leave me alone," Emma demanded, a tremor in her voice. "He's a cheat."

The man emerged from the structure with slow reluctance.

"What's going on here?" He spoke in a thick, Italian accent, his small eyes moving from Emma to Nick.

Emma pointed a finger at Nick. "He's a cheater."

"My wife is mistaken," Nick insisted. "She's had too much to drink and it's making her emotional."

Draping an arm across the smaller man's shoulders, he led him toward the glass doors. "You know how women are. They get worked up about things. I just wanted to have another drink, you see? But she thought I was flirting with that pretty blond bartender—do you know her? The bartender, I mean?"

As he talked, Emma dashed into the empty valet stand. There was almost nothing in there—the barstool on which he'd been sitting, a small space heater on the floor that let out a stream of warmth, an electronic tablet on a stand. On the far wall, a metal locker stood open to reveal rows of car keys.

Emma snatched a set of keys at random and tucked it into the small clutch bag that held her passport.

When the valet turned his head to see where she was, she was standing innocently behind them.

He glanced down at her dress for a second, a puzzled expression on his face, and Emma quickly turned away, hoping he hadn't seen the blood.

"I've had enough," she announced, angrily. "I'm leaving."

Whirling, she stormed down the paved drive, the click of her high-heeled shoes loud in the quiet.

Behind her she heard Orlov heave a sigh. "I better go talk to her."

The valet snickered. "Good luck."

When Emma heard amusement in his voice, relief coursed through her. He couldn't have realized the stain on her dress was blood. He must have thought she'd spilled a drink.

She kept walking fast as if fueled by anger as she followed the long curved drive down a steep hill.

Orlov caught up with her just as they reached a parting in the trees, and Emma's breath caught. All of Rome was spread out beneath them, in a carpet of light. At the edge of it, the familiar dome of St. Peter's Basilica glowed with the delicacy of a Christmas tree ornament.

"It's so beautiful," Emma said, softly.

A moment passed before Nick spoke. "I've always loved this city but I doubt I'll ever see it the same after tonight."

His face was pale with exhaustion and drink; he looked ten years older than he had earlier that evening. He held his shoulders tight, his jaw clenched—every muscle contorted with fear and confusion.

He wasn't a bad guy, she thought. He'd been dragged into a

world he didn't understand. It's impossible to know what real fear will do to you until you're in the middle of something terrible. Only then do you find out what you're capable of.

Emma's instincts were always to fight. Orlov was smart and successful, and his instincts had been to manage the situation. But he couldn't begin to manage Vladimir Balakin. The Russian spy chief was in a different class altogether. He was cold-blooded and relentless, armed with endless creative methods to hurt you until at last you were so defeated you did what he wanted. He'd destroyed richer, smarter men than Nick Orlov.

Perhaps the lesson Nick had learned tonight was that he wasn't as smart as he thought he was.

"You shouldn't let this change you," Emma said. "This situation wasn't your fault."

Nick gave her a cold, untrusting look. "I don't want your advice. I want to know who you are and where we're going."

In reply, Emma held up her hand. The set of stolen keys glittered in Rome's light.

"Right now, we're going to go find our car."

24

t turned out finding the car wasn't as easy as it sounded. The hotel grounds sprawled over several acres, and first they had to figure out where the valets parked the vehicles.

The first car lot they found was too small to be the one they wanted.

"Staff parking," Emma guessed. "Valet parking must be nearby."

Nick didn't reply. He didn't trust her and he didn't mind if she knew it. If they were going to get out of this situation, she needed to regain his trust.

Her phone buzzed. Emma glanced quickly at the screen and saw Mackenzie's name flashing.

Not now, Kate, she thought, and sent the call to voicemail.

As they made their way down the curved drive, with the city at their feet, she gave a small sigh.

"OK," she said. "Here's what you want to know."

Nick's head snapped up.

"My name is Emma Makepeace, I work for the British government. I invented Anna Case to get close to you in order to find out what you were planning with Vladimir Balakin."

Nick Orlov gave a short, humorless laugh. "So you think I am behind this plot?"

"Of course not. But you know what Balakin's planning and you can help us stop it." Seeing his expression, she held up her hand. "Before you say no, please consider what just happened upstairs. If you're not playing by Balakin's rules anymore, then he wants you out of the game altogether." She stopped walking and turned to face him. "You're in a trap, Nick. Let me get you out of it."

"So the person who has lied to me from the moment we met is now telling me I should trust her? Don't do me any favors, whoever you are."

"It's not a favor," Emma fired back. "It's my job."

"And seducing me? Was that your job too?" he demanded.

"If that's what it took, yes." Her tone was harsh but heat rose to her face, and she was glad of the darkness as she held up her hand. "Look, I get it. But let's hash this out later. Assuming there *is* a later."

He made a noncommittal gesture, but when she resumed walking, he did the same. For a while neither of them spoke and the click of Emma's heels was the only sound, aside from the soft rumble of traffic from the streets below.

Finally Orlov spoke again, "So there's no Anna Case?"

"Not as far as I'm aware," Emma said.

"We didn't meet at a conference in Oslo?"

"I've read the speech you gave there," she said. "Which was genuinely good, and I mean that. But I wasn't at that conference."

Her attention turned to the grounds around them. She thought it was odd they hadn't passed a car yet. It was late, but one in the morning on a Saturday night in a lively city like Rome wasn't really late at all. She glanced over her shoulder.

Nothing. Just darkness and light.

Orlov was still trying to understand what had happened. "But I remember meeting you there. I remember our conversation. The dress you wore."

"False memory," Emma said, absently. "I told you enough details about our meeting in Oslo, and eventually you accepted it as real. I gave you the basics, you filled in the details. It's a psychological trick. Scientists call it cryptomnesia. It's surprisingly easy to do."

Through a long row of cypress trees ahead, she thought she'd spotted light gleaming against metal.

"There," she said, pointing at the shadows.

She hastened her pace, stumbling a bit on the gravel as they followed a narrow drive around and into a car park, where cars were parked in long rows.

"What car are we looking for?" Orlov asked.

"I have no idea." Emma examined the keys in her hand. A paper tag attached to it held the car registration number. "The license number starts FL397. So we're looking for that."

She held the key fob above her head and pushed on the unlock button, hoping for flashing headlights, but she saw nothing but darkness.

"It's too dark to really see the plates," Orlov complained, bending over a red Alpha Romeo.

"Use your phone light. I'll try the next aisle," Emma told him. She squeezed between a black Mercedes and a BMW to get to the next group of cars. Again, she held the fob and switched the locks on and off, turning in each direction, scanning the license plates with increasing impatience as the minutes ticked by.

"Nothing with FL on this row," Orlov called.

"I've done this aisle," she said. "I'm trying the next one over."

Emma raced to the next line of cars, cursing her heels as she skidded on a pebble, wrenching her ankle. Standing in the middle of the long row, she held her hand out and pressed the unlock button again.

This time a car midway down the row lit up.

"Found it!" she called, already running toward it. She could hear Orlov following. By the time he reached her, she was ripping off her shoes and throwing them into the back of the glossy black Porsche. The interior lights glowed in the dark night like a satellite.

"Get in," she ordered, climbing behind the wheel.

Inside, the car was pristine. The black leather gleamed like liquid, and there wasn't a speck of dust on the floor. It had that delicious new leather and plastic smell.

"Nice choice," Orlov remarked, as the engine started with a guttural growl.

Emma placed the gun in the small space between the driver's seat and the central console, and rested her small bag on top of it, hiding it from view. Then she pulled out her phone and examined the route to Ciampino, Rome's airport for private jets. It was a remarkably straight journey; only four turns to make before she'd be on the ring road, which would take them to the airport. But it was a long way—it would take more than forty-five minutes, even at this hour.

When she'd committed the turns to memory (*right, left, right*), she dropped the phone in her lap and began backing the Porsche out of the long row of gleaming cars.

"I'm going to need you to do something," she told Nick without looking at him. "Call your pilot and tell him to get the plane ready to fly back to Edinburgh."

"I can't," he said, instantly. "It's not my plane. It's rented. The pilot's not booked to fly us back until tomorrow morning."

"I know," she said. "But you can change your time of departure—they work for you. Call him."

Still, he hesitated. "What do I tell him? It's the middle of the night."

The car's tires crunched on gravel until they turned onto the hotel's wide paved drive. Emma shifted into third gear.

"Tell him there's been an emergency and you have to get home straightaway."

"But . . ." he began to argue.

"I don't care what you tell him," she snapped, braking as they reached the hotel exit, and the city's constant flow of traffic appeared ahead. She turned to look at Orlov. "I think you still don't understand what's going on. We're in a lot of trouble here, Nick. Your life is on the line. If Fridman or Balakin get to you before you get on that plane, it's over. Even with me here. Do you understand? People will die. Call the pilot. Pay him money. Give him an incentive. Just get us out of here."

Nick pulled out his phone and dialed. Emma focused on remembering the names of the streets she needed to take. When they stopped at a red light, she checked the map again—they were on track.

"Alastair, it's Nick Orlov here. I'm afraid there's been an emergency at home and I have to get back now. How long will it take you to get to the airport and get the jet ready?" He listened for a second. "I'm sorry it has to be now. I can't wait until morning."

Even over the sound of the Porsche's engine, Emma heard the voice at the other end of the line rise in protest.

"I know it's late but I have no choice." Nick's voice tensed, and she could see him fighting to stay calm. "Look, I'll sweeten it for you. A bonus of ten thousand, how does that sound?"

The voice said something quiet. Nick clenched his hands and took a pained angry breath.

"Fine. Twenty," he said, brusquely. "How long before you can get there?"

When the call ended, he shoved the phone away in disgust. "Twenty thousand pounds to go to the airport early. Pure greed."

Emma ignored this. "When will the plane be ready?" she asked.

"He said two hours."

"*Two?*" Her voice rose.

"He said he has to file a flight plan and get it approved, fuel up, and get a takeoff and landing slot." Nick sounded bitter. "And earn twenty thousand pounds."

Two hours, Emma thought. *Too long.*

Fridman would survive the blow to the head. When he came to, he'd call Balakin. They'd check the hotel and the airport. All of this, Emma estimated, would take about an hour.

Balakin would be able to get them into the airport; he traveled in private jets all the time. She and Orlov would find no safety there. And yet, there was no other way to get home.

Without taking her eyes from the road, Emma retrieved her phone and dialed Ripley's number, pressing the phone to her ear with her right hand and driving with the left.

He answered so quickly she didn't believe he could possibly have been sleeping.

"What's happening?"

"Leonid Fridman attacked us in Nick Orlov's room," Emma spoke quickly. "I disabled him and took his gun. I also liberated a Porsche Boxster with German license plates and we are en route to the airport now."

"Is Fridman dead?" Ripley asked curtly.

"Negative. Orlov's pilot has agreed to fly us back, but he says it will take two hours to get approval to take off."

"I know someone in the Italian secret service," Ripley said. "I'll see if we can speed this up. Get close to the airport but don't drive inside until you hear from me."

The line went dead. Emma dropped the phone back in her lap.

A motorway entrance ramp loomed ahead, and Emma turned onto it with relief. It was a straight shot from here to Ciampino.

She could feel Orlov watching her, hear his unasked questions.

"We're on it," she said, pushing the accelerator to the floor. The Porsche raced onto the motorway with a roar of power. "Everything's going to be fine."

She'd have given anything to believe that was the truth.

The two of them retreated into their own thoughts as Emma

navigated the Roman roads. The motorway was less busy than the streets in the city had been, and Emma let herself relax a little. If Ripley could just get them out of here sooner, they'd stand a chance. But, if Balakin had time to rouse and activate more of his operatives to come after them, she and Orlov wouldn't make it. She couldn't fight a war with thirteen bullets, and the Italian police wouldn't know who the good guys were in a shootout.

Their only hope was a quick, quiet escape.

But they'd only been on the motorway for five minutes when flashing blue lights appeared behind them. Emma glanced in the mirror, her grip on the wheel tightening.

"Police," she said, quietly.

"Pulling us over?" Orlov began to turn, but she grabbed his arm. "Don't look back. Eyes straight ahead."

He stared stiffly out the windshield. "Are they following us?"

"I can't tell yet. We'll know in one minute."

In the rearview mirror, the police car scattered droplets of blue light across the half-empty road as it raced silently toward them. Emma's mouth went dry, as she signaled and moved into the slow lane, lifting her foot carefully off the accelerator.

The police car was on them in seconds. For a brief, shattering moment it was right behind them, silent and blinding. Then, as they watched, it rushed by, speeding into the darkness ahead.

Emma let out a long breath through pursed lips and glanced at Orlov, who looked pale, one hand gripping the dashboard.

"Christ," he said. "That was close."

They never found out where that police car had been going; they passed few other vehicles before the first signs for the airport appeared, and Emma realized she had a new problem: what were they to do until she heard back from Ripley?

At the next exit, she signaled and turned off onto a side road, where she pulled into a gas station. It was closed; all the lights were turned off.

She drove around behind the small building, and backed into a shadowy corner and cut the engine.

Orlov looked around, clearly puzzled. "What are we doing?"

Suddenly aware of how tired she was, Emma slid down in the leather seat and closed her eyes.

"Waiting," she said.

25

Twenty minutes later, Emma's phone rang and she snatched it up.

"Makepeace."

"It's arranged." Ripley's voice was crisp. "Enter the airport through gate number nine. Use the name Anna Case. Nick Orlov's name will not be listed but nobody will ask. You are both cleared with security. Leave the car where they tell you and message me the registration number—it will be collected and returned to the owner."

Emma didn't ask who "they" were.

"And Fridman?" she said.

"Police and Italian intelligence have been to Orlov's room. Fridman's gone." Ripley's tone was flat.

Emma swore so suddenly and viciously Orlov jumped and stared at her as Ripley continued steadily.

"Security at the airport is on alert. His photo has been distributed, and Balakin is to be kept out if he attempts to enter. The VIP section at Ciampino Airport, at this moment, is empty." He paused. "It's probably the safest place for you to be right now. Get there as fast as you can."

"Copy that." Emma switched on the ignition and the Porsche roared to life.

Ripley's last words were a warning. "All eyes, Emma."

Emma drove back down the tangle of streets and filled Orlov in. As she spoke, he stared through the windshield at the bleak hinterland of warehouses and car parks that surround every airport in the world.

"So we're running away"—Nick's voice was leaden—"before Balakin and his friends kill me."

"Staying alive is the general idea," Emma conceded.

"What's to stop them killing me when I get home?" he asked.

Emma glanced at him. "We'll talk about that on the plane."

"Great," he said, a tetchy note in his voice.

Emma didn't want to get into it now, her hands were full enough with the effort of trying to find gate number nine in a stolen car. It was after two in the morning, but lorries and vans still traveled the streets around the airport perimeter. In an airport it is always day.

As she drove, Emma kept her eyes on the rearview mirror. By now, there'd been time enough for Leonid Fridman to seek help from Balakin. Or to get himself to the airport and lie in wait.

But he didn't know what car they were in, nor what airport entrance they were going to use, and that made the Russians' job much harder. The place was a labyrinth; they'd already passed a gate marked "VIP," so it was clear they were being directed away from any obvious entrance that Balakin's people might be watching.

Without warning, a white van sped out of a side street and fell in behind them, following so closely that the bright white light of the headlights flooded the Porsche with a cold glow.

Emma hit the accelerator and the Porsche jumped forward. But the van sped up, too, its engine grinding from the effort.

Orlov grabbed the handle above the passenger door and gripped it tight.

"Is it them?" he asked, his voice rising. "Did he find us?"

"I don't know." Emma's voice was tight. The headlights were blinding, and she squinted into the mirror, trying to make out the features of the van's driver, but it was impossible. She could see nothing but a shadow.

When she looked straight ahead again, golden dots hovered in her vision and she blinked them away with effort.

"I don't know who it is, but I don't like how they drive," she said.

An airport entrance loomed to their right, and Emma saw the number six mounted at the top of it.

Three gates to go. They were so close.

"Can you lose him?" Orlov asked.

Emma looked around the low-roofed warehouses doubtfully.

"Maybe."

She sped up again until she was going double the speed limit on the narrow street. At the next intersection, she spun the wheel, turning so hard the tires screeched.

The van followed with effort, taking the turn so fast it started to tilt onto two wheels.

Left, right, right again . . . Emma drove blind, completely uncertain of the route she should take or whether she'd find herself at a dead end.

Finally, they found themselves alone on a dark street lined with parked cars. It must have been an employee parking area. Emma slammed the Porsche into reverse and backed into a parking space between two work trucks and cut the engine.

The sports car went dark.

A second later the van tore around the corner and sped by them. As it passed, Emma saw that it was a older model van, the registration plate too smeared with mud to read. The front seats held two men—one, dark-haired and slight, the other bulkier. But that was all she could see before the van turned the corner and disappeared.

Neither was Fridman or Balakin, of that she was certain.

As soon as the van was out of sight, she started the Porsche's engine and floored it. They tore out of the parking space and back on to the narrow road.

Every muscle in her body felt strained and tight with the urgency to get out of here, to get back to Britain. She didn't know who those men were, but she was certain that Balakin was hunting her now, as well as Orlov.

Left, left, right . . . she retraced their steps, her mind utterly focused on remembering every landmark, every corner, until they were back on the airport perimeter road. Now, though, they were speeding around the airport, past the signs for gates seven and eight, tires squealing on every bend. The Porsche liked the speed, it clung to the road on the bends, until at last gate number nine appeared, and Emma pulled in front of it.

The second the car stopped, two armed guards melted out from the shadows, shouting commands in Italian.

Emma lowered the window, cut the engine, and raised both hands off the wheel. When Orlov, huddled in the passenger seat, didn't move, she turned to him and barked, "Show your hands!"

Slowly, his arms rose.

The soldiers looked young; the one on Emma's side still had peach fuzz on his cheeks, and his large eyes watched her with suspicion as she spoke clearly and slowly.

"My name is Anna Case. You should be expecting me."

She saw the recognition in the young soldier's face.

Lowering their guns, the two soldiers conferred, the second soldier checking something on his phone against the license plate of the car.

"Anna Case?" As the young soldier spoke, his gaze moved from her face to the silvery silk dress with its smear of blood, the high-heeled shoes on the backseat, to Orlov, who sat frozen with terror in the passenger seat, his hands still in the air.

"Yes," Emma said. "We are expected."

Instead of opening the gate, though, the soldier held up his phone and took a picture of them. Emma flinched, but as she watched, he typed something—presumably sending the photo through to someone else. Someone with more authority.

"Wait here," the young man said.

The two soldiers stepped back, huddling over their phones and talking quietly.

"What the hell are they doing?" Nick whispered.

"Being careful." Emma kept her eyes on the soldiers, her nerves on edge.

Ripley had done all he could, but the Italian government would be fully within its rights to arrest them both and take them in for questioning. Her very presence here was an international incident waiting to happen.

Suddenly, both men straightened and put their phones away. The older one walked to a small metal box and pushed a button.

With a rattle of metal that seemed deafening in the quiet, gate nine began to slide open.

The younger soldier approached Emma. "Can you step out of the car, please?"

She opened the door without hesitation, but Orlov panicked.

"Where are you going?" He moved to open his door but the other soldier stopped him, closing his door firmly.

"Please stay in the car, sir," he said in perfect English. "She's perfectly safe."

"I want to know where you're taking her," Orlov protested, his voice rising.

Barefoot, Emma followed the young soldier a few feet from the car, where he stopped and turned to face her.

The breeze cut through the flimsy material of her dress, but she hardly noticed.

"Don't go inside the airport, we're not certain its secure." The soldier spoke quietly and fluently. "We're searching it now but we haven't had time to complete our work. There are no passengers, but the staff have not all been cleared."

"Understood," she said.

"Your plane is there." He pointed to where the white jet Orlov had rented stood waiting, its long pale wings juxtaposed sharply against the night sky. "It's been searched thoroughly by our team. The pilot's already on board—your people have checked his background and found no issues. You are fueled and cleared for immediate takeoff. Leave the car with me. We'll take care of it."

He was no ordinary soldier, Emma realized as she listened to his calm commands, he was military intelligence all the way.

For a split second, she saw her younger self in those cool, confident brown eyes. So smart and certain. Did she still have that assurance? Or had the last year hacked away at it? She didn't like that she didn't know the answer to that.

But all she said was "There's a handgun between the front seat and the central console. I took it off a Russian operative earlier tonight."

If this surprised him, he didn't show it.

"We'll take care of it," he said.

"Thank you for everything," she said. "I hope we can return the favor some time."

His expression didn't waver. "I hope you don't have to."

Emma hurried back to the car, the long skirt swaying around her, her feet increasingly numb on the rough concrete. As she approached, the other soldier said something to Orlov and stepped back.

Still clearly angry, Nick threw the door open and jumped out.

Emma reached into the backseat to retrieve the loathed silver heels. The tracker they carried was expensive, and neither Martha nor Zach would appreciate her abandoning them in Rome simply because she hated them.

"What's happening?" Nick demanded. "Are we being arrested?"

"No, we're leaving." Emma stood straight, the shoes dangling from her fingertips as she pointed across the tarmac. "That's our plane. Let's go home."

26

Minutes later, they were in the warmth and light of the Dassault Falcon. This time there was no flight attendant to bring them champagne. In fact, the only other person on board was the pilot.

Any resentment he might have felt about being dragged out of bed must have faded when he'd spoken to the Italian soldiers, and his air of urgency and tension was clear. The second she and Nick reached the top of the steps, the pilot pushed a button and the stairs folded in. The doors closed and locked.

Emma saw his sharp eyes take in her torn bloodied dress, and Orlov's exhausted expression. Most pilots, she reminded herself, started out in the Royal Air Force. He must have been one of them, because he didn't ask any questions.

"We've been cleared to take off quickly," he told them, quietly. "Belt yourselves in. I'll get you home."

As soon as he'd disappeared into the cockpit, Orlov collapsed into one of the beige leather armchairs and sank into himself, silent and morose.

Cold and exhausted, Emma would have loved to do the same thing, but her work wasn't finished yet.

While the pilot finished his final check, she searched the cupboards at the back until she located a blanket and a refrigerator holding bottles of water. She handed one bottle to Orlov, who accepted it grudgingly.

Emma took the chair next to him and broke open the other bottle. She drank most of it in one go. The second she sat down her muscles began to ache, and she could feel the bruises forming from her fight with Fridman. Until now, she hadn't allowed herself to notice them. Wincing, she clipped her seatbelt in place and covered herself in the blanket. As the adrenaline that had kept her going receded from her bloodstream, she began to shiver.

The Falcon began to taxi down the runway. Emma could feel the power of the engines through her feet, it seemed to her they could probably lift a plane three times the size of this one.

Nick still hadn't spoken, and she leaned toward him and said, "Are you OK?"

He swung around slowly to face her, a look of absolute despair on his face. "I think Vladimir Balakin could find us anywhere. Even here. I'll never be safe."

The plane began to gain speed. Emma noticed his fingers digging into the leather arms of his seat.

She was distantly conscious of the fact that she should be terrified too. After all, Balakin was a resourceful man. If he wanted to shoot down this jet, he could find a way. But somehow, she trusted that young soldier. She would never put anyone on a plane that had a chance of crashing back down again, and she didn't think he would either.

Still, as the Falcon's wheels left the ground, she closed her eyes for just a moment, feeling the emptiness of the air. Then she opened them again to watch as Rome, eternal, beautiful, and dangerous, receded into the distance, until it was nothing more than a glimmer of light.

Only when they reached cruising altitude, did she turn back to Orlov. His face was paper white and his eyes were squeezed shut. He looked like he might be sick.

Emma unbuckled her seatbelt and went to the back again, where she retrieved a bottle of Lagavulin whisky she'd spotted earlier and two glasses.

When she'd sat back down, she put the two glasses on the small table between them and filled them, pleased that her hand was completely steady. Wordlessly, she pushed one across to him, then she picked up the other and took a long drink.

She didn't much like whisky that smelled like it had been rescued from a burning house, but she did like the way the warmth of the alcohol seeped into her veins and chased out the chill that seemed to have settled there.

Nick didn't touch his glass, and sat watching her balefully.

Emma gestured at the untouched glass of whisky. "You'd feel better if you had a sip of that."

"I'll drink when I want to," he growled.

She waited, watching him patiently, until at last he picked up the glass and took a reluctant swallow.

Almost immediately color began to return to his face. In moments, he'd downed the rest of the whisky.

Emma refilled the glass with more of the whisky and said, "Nick, we would like to make a deal with you."

He regarded her warily. "What sort of deal?"

"You tell us exactly what Russia is planning to do at the G7," Emma said. "And we will protect you from Vladimir Balakin."

She saw the information hit—the convulsive tightening of his fingers around the glass, the dilation of the pupils. But Orlov recovered quickly. "How will you protect me? I was in Rome for one night and they found me. If they want to kill me, they'll kill me. They've probably already killed my son."

It was time for Emma to set all her cards on the table.

"We have people in place to protect your family in Russia," she said. "If you help us, we'll do our best to get them to safety."

Orlov's head snapped up. "What are you saying? You can do this, *inside* Russia?"

Emma nodded.

For this to work, Andrew Field at MI6 would have to agree to help, but he wouldn't refuse. Not if they prevented an attack in Scotland. For that, he'd pay any price.

"But you have to tell us everything. We need to know precisely what Balakin is planning," Emma said. "We know you're working with him."

"It wasn't my idea." He met her gaze directly. "I have been very careful to have no connections to the Russian government. I know how they work. I have had nothing to do with them my entire life."

"So how did you get tangled up in this?" Emma asked.

"Leonid Fridman came to my office four months ago." Nick rubbed his red-rimmed eyes. "God, I wish I'd never let him in that building. But he said he owned an oil support company in Russia that wanted to move to Britain and work with North Seven. They had a new system for cleaning oil and it sounded interesting, so I said yes." He let out a breath. "Of course it was a lie. Once he was in, he showed me pictures of my son at school, at his friend's house, going to a party . . . He said he was watched all the time, and that I would never see him again if I didn't help him with something the Russian government was planning."

He leaned toward her, his dark eyes pleading. "I was trapped. Peter's birth was not planned, but I love him as if it were. Please understand—he's just a *child*."

His voice trembled on the last word, and Emma could see the helplessness in his face.

"Why didn't you call someone?" Emma said. "Ask for help?"

"Who would I call?" He made an impatient gesture. "What's your number at MI6? How do you report something like this? I was on my own."

"So you decided to go along with Russia's plans," Emma began, but he cut her off, his voice sharpening.

"I didn't *decide* anything. I was forced to go along, and I went along. They said all they wanted was to use my house. They said nobody would notice because I'm not a spy." He made an impatient gesture. "I don't remember it all, but they said all they wanted was to meet at my house to plan."

"To plan what, exactly?" Emma held his gaze.

Orlov glanced over his shoulder, but the pilot was locked in the cockpit. They were completely alone.

The plane's engine faded into the background.

"An assassination." Nick's voice was flat.

Emma's stomach lurched.

"Who?" she demanded. "The US president?"

Orlov shook his head slowly. "Too difficult. Balakin thought there was no way."

"Then *who*?"

A fine line of tension as tight and palpable as piano wire seemed strung between them. Nick's hand tightened around the glass with such force she thought it might break.

"The prime minister," he said, hoarsely. "And anyone else they could get after him." He lifted his head to meet her eyes. "They want a bloodbath."

Emma sank back in her seat. She longed to get up and walk away from this conversation, but there was nowhere to go.

She unbuckled her seatbelt and threw the blanket onto an empty chair. Picking up her water bottle, she took a sip before trying to speak again. But her voice remained steady.

"Why do they want a bloodbath? What is their goal?"

He held out his hands. "Punishment. Britain supported Ukraine and other Russian enemies. They want revenge. To humiliate Britain, that is the only goal."

Emma heard her mother's voice in her head: *Russia never forgives or forgets.*

"I need to know how it's going to work," she said. "And exactly who's going to do it."

Orlov reached for the whisky bottle. "I don't know everything," he warned, as the amber liquid sloshed into his glass. "Only what they let me hear. But I'll tell you what I can." He glanced at her. "You'll keep me safe? Because I didn't want any part of this, and I still don't."

Emma thought of Michael Primalov, struggling to make a new life for himself miles from everyone he knew.

But all she said was "We'll keep you safe. It's a promise."

It was nearly four in the morning in the UK when they landed in Edinburgh. During the flight, Emma had switched from whisky to coffee, and she felt hyperalert, as if she might never sleep.

When the stairs were lowered, she descended first, the silver shoes back on her feet one last time. The icy North Sea breeze caught her dress and sent it billowing around her as she walked to where Adam stood waiting, his face as tired as her own, next to a black Volvo SUV.

His dark eyes took in the smear of blood across her torso and the purple bruise blooming above her left eye.

"Good trip?" he asked quietly, glancing past her at Orlov, who was fumbling his way down the steps.

Emma gestured at her dress. "Well, this is Leonid Fridman's blood so it wasn't a complete waste of time." Glancing back to make sure Orlov couldn't hear, she said quietly, "He's cooperating. We need to get him to the office."

Adam nodded and opened the back door. "This way, Mr. Orlov."

Nick Orlov gave him a look of pure distrust. "Who the hell are you?"

"I'm your guardian angel," Adam told him. "Welcome home."

SUNDAY

13 October

SPECIAL TO THE PRIME MINISTER
EYES ONLY
SECURITY LEVEL: TOP SECRET
RISK LEVEL: HIGH

Private communication

*From: Hayley Mir, Operations Director,
Secret Service*

We've had a late request for a meeting with Italian leaders regarding an incident last night involving a British security officer who was attacked in Rome along with a Russian-British dual national. The incident relates to the G7, and the threats the event has received. The officer involved is with the Agency, and was undercover investigating those threats. The dual national is currently in our custody in Edinburgh.

This situation is developing at this time. The threat is still live. We are working with C and Andrew Field from MI6 and with Charles Ripley at the Agency to neutralize this situa-

tion. We have put your flight to Scotland on hold until Monday at 08:00 while our work continues. We'll meet with you shortly to fully brief you on the situation.

Your security has been enhanced during this time, and all law enforcement at Number 10 have been informed. You will receive further updates throughout the day.

27

On the drive back into the city, Emma, sitting in the front passenger seat, suddenly remembered that Mackenzie had called earlier that night.

Sitting in the passenger seat, with Adam behind the wheel and Orlov silent in the backseat, she held her phone to her ear and checked the message.

"Hey, I'm sorry to call so late. I've been looking into the name Blake and there's something I didn't tell you earlier. Remember the case I told you about when we first met? The girl murdered in the park? The suspect in that—who I still believe was the killer—was named Finlay Blake. I didn't mention it because I thought it was bound to be a coincidence but now I'm not so sure. Blake's a real thug—I think he's killed people in the past, but we've never been able to pin it on him. He's smart and he's violent. He's got his fingers in every bad pie you can think of. I've been pulling in some favors, asking a few of my old contacts in his world and . . . I don't know, Emma, he could be the one Orlov was talking about on the phone. Call me when you get this."

Emma hung up the phone and looked back at Orlov, who was staring morosely out the window at the dark, quiet streets blurring by.

"Nick," she said, and his head jerked up. "Who's Blake?"

"What?" He looked at her with confusion. They were both exhausted now, but she needed him to focus.

"You mentioned someone named Blake yesterday," she said, carefully omitting who he'd been speaking to at the time. "You said you wouldn't meet him. Who is he?"

"I don't . . ." Orlov rubbed his fingers against his eyes. "Did I tell you that? I don't remember . . . He's someone Balakin wanted me to meet. He said he was a local fixer. But I never met him. I refused."

"What's his first name?" Emma asked.

Orlov shrugged. "I don't know. I don't think anyone ever said."

When they reached the office building, Emma limped behind Orlov and Adam into the elevator. By now, Orlov was too tired to ask questions, but when he stepped out into the long, unfinished office, he gave the exposed wires and cinderblock walls a look of disbelief.

Ripley and Zach were standing at the long table. Martha, who'd been sleeping with her head on her desk, jumped up.

"Mr. Orlov." Ripley walked over with his hand outstretched. It might as well have been ten in the morning—his jacket was on, his shirt clean and crisp. Emma could see the shadows under his eyes but Orlov would never know that they weren't ordinarily there. "Thank you for coming. Could you take a seat over here?"

Glancing up, Emma saw that the wall screens had been turned off, and for the first time in days there were no pictures of the stone manor house on the walls.

Martha ran across the room to her. "Christ, look at you," she said, taking in the damaged dress, Emma's hair falling out of the carefully placed clips, the bruises on her face.

Emma handed her the fake diamond earrings. "Somehow, I didn't lose them."

"I don't care about the earrings, you idiot," Martha said, gently. "You must be freezing. Let's get you some warm clothes."

In much the same way Emma had forced whisky on Orlov on the plane, now Martha placed a steaming cup of sweet tea in her hands and made her drink it while she dug out jeans and a warm sweater from her racks of clothes, along with a pair of sturdy boots.

Emma kept an eye on Nick as she cleaned up. Ripley, Adam, and Zach had settled him into a chair and were plying him with tea and biscuits. Once, Nick looked up and caught Emma's eye and gave her a baffled look that made her smile.

A few minutes later, changed and warm, she joined the others around the table. It was still dark outside and the row of bare windows reflected their images back at them. Quickly and concisely, she told the others what Nick Orlov had told her during the long hours on the plane.

"The plan is targeted assassination of the prime minister, and anyone else they can hit, Monday afternoon, Carlowrie Castle," she said.

Adam gave a low whistle but Ripley showed no emotion.

"Weapons?" Ripley's voice was short.

"Guns," Emma said.

"How many shooters?" He was taking notes.

Emma glanced at Orlov, who shook his head.

"Unknown," Emma said. "Mr. Orlov refused to be involved, so we only know what he heard during the meetings in his house."

Without another word, Ripley picked up his phone and dialed a number. After a long moment, someone answered.

"Hayley, I'm very sorry for phoning you so early, but you said to call you when we knew the details. We've got them." He walked away from the table, talking quietly.

Emma guessed it must be Hayley Mir, the sharp-eyed woman from MI5 who'd been at the meeting in the secure room back in London when all of this began.

Ripley was on the phone for less than a minute, and when he returned, Adam asked Orlov, "Could you tell us more about the weapons?"

"Balakin brought them into the country himself, in diplomatic bags," Orlov said. "He said they had been seized by Russian soldiers fighting in Ukraine. He thought it would shame Britain if their prime minister was killed with a Ukrainian gun."

Adam and Emma exchanged a look.

"Where did he store the guns?" Emma asked. "At your house?"

"No. Balakin brought them to my house on the first day, and Fridman loaded them into my Land Rover and took them away." He met her eyes. "I wish I knew more. But I was trying very hard not to be part of this."

"We understand," she said.

He nodded, his lips tight, and for the first time since she'd met him, his eyes grew bright with unshed tears.

"I love this country. I would *never* hurt it." He turned to Ripley and Adam, his hands clenched. "This country took me in and accepted me. You have to see, I was attacked. My life and my family were attacked."

It was Ripley who responded. "I think anyone would have struggled to stand up to Vladimir Balakin the way you have. You refused to do what he wanted even when you knew he might kill you or your son. You are saving lives by talking to us." He angled forward, holding Orlov's gaze. "I've spoken to our people in Russia. Your son is on his way out of Russia, along with his mother. We've arranged accommodation in Poland. I'll let you know as soon as they've arrived safely."

At that, Orlov crumpled. Burying his head in his hands, he wept, his shoulders heaving with great, painful sobs.

"Thank you," he whispered, through his tears. "Thank you. Thank you."

Outside the office windows, the sky had begun to warm from black to pale gray. A new day was beginning.

Leaving Orlov at the table, Ripley motioned for Emma and Adam to join him in the small storage room adjoining the office.

"I think he's done for now." Ripley raked his fingers across the top of his head. "I need to talk to Andrew and make sure Leonid Fridman and Vladimir Balakin are blocked from entry into the UK. They will be expecting this, however, so I don't think they'll even try to get back in. That can't be their plan."

"Yes, that's the problem, isn't it?" Adam's sturdy intelligent face grew intense. "We know what they intend to do, but not when they're going to do it. They must have known there was a possibility they'd be shut out of the UK once we were on to them. So, what's their plan B?"

They all fell silent. Through the walls, Emma could hear the traffic beginning to rumble on the streets below as the city woke up.

"Nick Orlov may know know more than he thinks he does," Ripley said. "That's my hope, but he's too worn out to give us more right now. We'll let him rest and then question him again this afternoon."

"Mackenzie's looking into this Blake person," Emma said.

Ripley frowned. "Remind me who Blake is."

"The name came up from the listening devices in Orlov's office, so I asked him about it, and he says a guy named Blake was a local fixer for Balakin," Emma explained. "But Nick's never met him and doesn't know his first name."

Adam glanced at his boss. "Sounds like a long shot."

"Yes, but worth a bit of time." Ripley turned back to Emma. "Work with Mackenzie on that. Find out who he is." He paused. "Oh, one more thing. There's been a request for a meeting about what happened in Rome. Our Italian friends want some clarification about your presence in their nation."

Emma's stomach flipped. "How bad is it?"

Ripley made a weary gesture. "If we prevent this attack, they'll give us a medal. London's now working with us. Hayley Mir from MI5 is on her way to Scotland, Andrew is as well, and they're both bringing staff to back us up. There are six Russian nationals of interest in Scotland, and we're looking for links to Balakin now.

We're going to use this office as Gold Command headquarters, so things are about to get very busy."

"Six?" Emma was stunned. "Can they be investigated in time?"

"They have to be," Ripley said. "That's what the teams coming up today will be doing. It's going to be a large operation, moving very fast."

"Does no one think . . ." Adam paused, and Ripley gave him a puzzled look. "Does no one think we should cancel the G7? Balakin's plan is pretty far along. I know he and Fridman are both out, but the guns are already in the country. Isn't this still too risky?"

"The prime minister has been fully briefed and he's decided to go forward. He has all the facts, and he's trusting us to keep the meeting safe. So, here's what's going to happen." Ripley pointed to Adam. "You're going to get Orlov to the safe house. Afterward, come back here—I want you working with MI6 on this." He turned to Emma. "I want you to sleep for at least three hours before you get back to work." Seeing her rebellious expression, he held up his hand. "I don't care if you do it in a hotel or on the floor right here but you have to sleep or I'm sending you back to London, do you understand?"

Emma nodded meekly. There was no point in arguing. But she was daunted by the task ahead of them. The G7 started in one day.

.   .   .

When they left the storage room, Nick Orlov was no longer at the long table. Instead, he was standing at a window looking down at the street.

While Adam and Ripley moved off talking quietly, Emma walked over to Orlov.

"Hey," she said, touching his arm. "Are you OK?"

When he turned to look at her, his eyes were raw and red, but he smiled. "They're getting my son out. I'm really free of Balakin. Of course I'm OK. I will tell your people everything I know. If I can help you stop this attack, I will."

There was a passion in his voice that hadn't been there before, and Emma believed him completely. The cage Vladimir Balakin had put him in had been unlocked when his son was saved.

It made such sense to her that he'd not sought help—he hadn't known who to turn to, and he was being watched. Too much had been at risk for him. But he clearly despised Balakin, and that would make him a useful source for the Agency. Ripley would extract everything Orlov knew about the Russian spymaster, and that information would be hugely valuable.

She leaned back, pressing her shoulders against the window's cold glass. All night long she'd been thinking about this moment, and now she had her chance to set something right.

"Look," she said, hesitantly, "I owe you an apology. I'm sorry I lied to you. I hope you understand—it was the only way to be sure I was getting the truth."

His eyes held hers, and she could feel him looking for any deception. But for once, she really meant what she'd said. She was sorry. Nick Orlov was a good person, caught up in something he couldn't control.

"It's not easy, what you do," he said. "And I understand why you lied." He paused, his warm brown eyes searching her face. "But I did like Anna Case. And I'm sorry she's not real."

Emma thought of that kiss, and the way her body had responded.

"Yeah," she said, with a wry smile. "I'm kind of sorry, too."

He tilted his head. "So it's Emma, right? Maybe we could meet when this is all over?"

Before Emma could reply, Adam called over. "We're ready for you, Mr. Orlov. I'm going to take you to get some rest."

Nick looked at Emma.

"Go on," she said, ignoring that last question. "Adam will take care of you."

With some reluctance, Orlov turned and walked over to where Adam was waiting.

"Call me Nick," he said. "All my guardian angels do."

When they'd gone, and the room grew quiet, Emma gave in to Ripley's demands that she should rest. In fact, she slept soundly, stretched out on a pile of coats in Martha's corner of the office until she was woken by the vibration of her telephone.

Mackenzie's name was on the screen, and Emma answered without lifting her head from the rolled up jacket she was using as a pillow. "Hi, Kate."

"Are you back?" Mackenzie asked.

"I am." Emma sat up stiffly, and reached for a bottle of water.

"How'd it go?" Mackenzie asked.

"Orlov's cooperating with us, and we know what they're planning," Emma said, taking a sip.

When she didn't volunteer more, Mackenzie prodded her. "Which is . . . ?"

"I'll tell you when I see you." Emma set down the bottle and stretched gingerly, testing the stiffness of her muscles. "What's up? Any more news on this Blake person?"

"Nothing at all," Mackenzie said. "But that's what's weird. I've been asking around. Nobody's seen Finlay Blake in days. He's simply disappeared."

28

Half an hour later, Emma met Mackenzie at a pub called the Bull and Lamb, in one of Edinburgh's rougher quarters. It was noon, and the pub had only a few customers.

Emma still wore the sweater and boots Martha had found for her, and she'd topped those with a worn leather jacket that fit in well here.

Mackenzie's faded jeans also attracted no attention.

They ordered fish and chips from a surly bartender, and took a table with a good view of the room.

When they were seated, Mackenzie studied the purpling bruise on Emma's temple.

"You look like shit," was her assessment. "Did Orlov do that to you?"

"It was Leonid Fridman." Emma touched the bruise lightly. "But in this case, trust me, you really should see the other guy."

Mackenzie grinned. "I believe you."

As Emma filled her in on the basics of what they'd learned from Orlov, though, they both quickly grew serious.

"What you're saying is, we know what they want to do, but not who will pull the trigger or when they might do it?" Mackenzie asked.

"Exactly. That's why we're interested in Blake. All Orlov knows is that he's a local working with Balakin. He got the impression he was being paid to help. A kind of hired muscle, I guess."

"That sounds like Finlay Blake." Mackenzie lowered her voice, although no one was near enough to overhear. "This is one of his hangouts. I think the bartender works with him. Blake makes most of his money dealing meth and cocaine. I spoke with a few contacts I really trust—nobody's seen him in days. One of my guys says he's got nothing to sell because Blake hasn't turned up with his usual deliveries. I must have spoken to half the criminals in Edinburgh, and the consensus is no one has a clue where to find Finlay Blake."

She fell silent as the bartender, his arms rippling with muscles and tattoos that covered every inch of exposed skin, approached with two large plates of food. The chips piled in golden heaps around the fish.

Suddenly realizing she was starving, Emma popped one into her mouth and devoured it, relishing the salty heat.

"God, this is delicious," she said, surprised.

"Yeah, the food's quality here," Mackenzie agreed. "Criminals don't have time for bad grub."

For a while they ate in silence until suddenly Mackenzie spoke again, her voice low but passionate.

"The thing about Blake is he has no soul. There's just something missing inside him; he was wired wrong. There are people like that, you know. I've seen it more than once—a man who can't tell right from wrong, or worse, someone who can see the difference but doesn't give a shit—that's Finlay Blake. He doesn't care about anything except himself." She paused. "I tell you one thing though: he wouldn't do this for anything but very serious money. He's already doing pretty well dealing and stealing."

"The Russians are not short of cash," Emma said.

"How much would they pay for something like this, do you think?" Mackenzie reached for her water.

"I think they'd have offered him a million pounds," Emma said.

Mackenzie, who had just taken a sip, choked. "A *million?*" she sputtered. When she'd recovered, she said, "Blake would sell his soul for a million pounds. He'd sell his country for much less."

"Why would he do it at all, though?" Emma mused. "There are huge risks. He would get life in prison."

"He should have got life for killing Skye Johnson in the park that night." There was bitterness in Mackenzie's voice. "He could have got life three times at least if we'd had the evidence we needed to bring him down. But we didn't. We failed, and I think that made him feel impervious. He thinks he's smarter than us, and he's not wrong." She pushed her plate away. "Christ, I hate that murderous bastard."

"So, you genuinely think he might be our guy," Emma pressed.

Mackenzie made a back-and-forth gesture with one hand. "I mean, yes and no. All I know for certain is he's a criminal for hire, who will do anything for that kind of money. And he's gone underground."

It wasn't, Emma thought, even nearly enough to go on.

"Wait." Mackenzie's attention fixed on something across the room. "Those two guys who just walked in. One of them is a mate of Blake's." She gestured at the bar where two men in jeans and T-shirts stood talking, heads tilted together.

As the women watched, one of them waved the bartender over and asked him a question. They spoke for a second, their faces suddenly dark and secretive.

"Give me a second." Taking her empty water glass, Mackenzie got up and strolled nonchalantly to the bar, and waited as if planning to order. Deep in conversation, the three men didn't notice her at first, even though she stood within reach.

Emma watched from beneath her lashes, careful not to look obvious.

When the bartender finally spotted her, he said something quickly to the men before walking over to her.

"What do you need?" His voice was brusque.

Mackenzie held out the glass and said something Emma couldn't hear. The bartender took the glass, filled it, and pushed it back toward her, but his body language made it clear he wanted her to go away.

Mackenzie walked back, a look of frustration on her face.

"I could swear they're talking about Blake, but I didn't hear enough," she said quietly as she sat down again. "They're very careful."

"We need something concrete." Emma paused to think, and then said, "Do you know where Blake lives?"

Mackenzie nodded. "I can take you there. Why?"

"I want to search the place," Emma said.

Mackenzie's eyebrows rose. "Do you have a warrant?"

"Warrants are for cops. We take a different approach." Emma wiped her hands on her napkin and picked up her car keys. "I just need to make a stop at the office on the way."

They drove back into the city center through the labyrinth of security road closures. Emma had rarely seen more police on the streets—tactical vans were parked in rows of fifteen—but the streets were quieter than they would be on a weekday, and it didn't take them long to reach the office building.

By now, it was one o'clock, and they arrived to find the long, unheated office bustling, with not just the Agency staff but also intelligence and security staff from MI6, MI5, and Special Branch. Zach was in the middle of the throng, typing a thousand miles an hour, along with several other tech experts who must have come in that morning from London.

Mackenzie and Emma walked straight past them to Martha's racks of supplies. Emma dug through a box she kept in the corner and found a set of lockpicks, which she slid into her pocket.

Taking out a slim, black-handled knife, she slid it into her left boot.

Mackenzie's brow knit as she watched her. "Expecting trouble?"

"Always." Emma glanced to where Ripley stood talking with a tall woman with short-cropped dark hair and tawny skin. Their conversation was intense—he didn't seem to have noticed her walk in with Mackenzie. Emma recognized her as Hayley Mir. "Wait here. I'll be right back."

Mackenzie stayed by the racks of clothes as Emma walked over to the crowd gathered around the table, and slipped through them, pulling a laptop closer and opening MI5's browser. She typed in the name "Finlay Blake" and read the information in his file. It took only minutes to read all it contained—a short summary of his prison sentences. All had been brief stints, one each for car theft, assault causing grievous bodily harm, and burglary.

She caught Ripley's attention, and waited until he strode over to meet her.

"What's happening?" he asked, his eyes flitting from her to Mackenzie, waiting across the room.

"Finlay Blake has gone missing, and Kate really thinks he might be our guy," Emma explained. "We're going to search his house."

"Have you got anything at all that makes you think she might be right? Or are you fishing?" Ripley asked. He sounded tense and distracted.

"I'm not certain," Emma said, slowly. "There's nothing in his records that makes me like him for this. But Kate knows him better than I do, and she's confident. I trust her judgment."

He didn't immediately reply. Again she got the sense that something was wrong.

Emma frowned. "What is it? What happened?"

He answered slowly, choosing his words. "I've just been speaking to Hayley Mir. They've traced the press leak of information about the case. It came from the police."

Emma didn't hide her disbelief. "The *Scottish* police?"

He nodded.

"But the only Scottish police officers who really know about the investigation are Graham Brodie and . . ." Emma's heart contracted, and she drew a breath. "Ripley, you're not saying you think it's Kate?"

"I'm not saying anything," he said, "except the leak came from the police."

Emma glanced back to where Mackenzie stood waiting, her phone in her hand.

"I trust her," she said, but her chest felt hollow. Hadn't she learned in the last year never to trust anyone? After all, if MI6 officers could be traitors, couldn't Kate Mackenzie be a liar?

Of course she could.

"I don't think she'd do that," she said. But her voice was flat.

"You're probably right," Ripley said. "Just be careful how much you tell her."

They both knew it was too late for that. If Mackenzie was the person leaking, then she could tell the papers about the assassination plot, about Orlov, about this office.

It would be devastating.

"Where are you going now?" Ripley asked.

"To search Finlay Blake's flat, see if we can find evidence linking him to Balakin."

"Do you need backup?"

Emma considered this offer. Backup was a luxury they hadn't had in days. "I don't think so," she said. "If he's not there, we'll be fine. If he is there and we show up looking like a gang, we'll get nowhere."

Ripley nodded. "Message me all the addresses Mackenzie has for Blake, and I'll get Zach to check CCTV, see what he can find.

Oh, and one more thing. Wait here." He walked over to the table and took something from his briefcase. When he returned, he held out a card. "Keep this with you."

Emma took it and turned it over. It was jet black and bore only the words "His Majesty's Security Service," the official government crest with a unicorn and lion, and a phone number. "There are a lot of us out there right now stepping on each other's toes. I don't want any accidents."

"Copy that." Emma slid the card into the pocket of her jeans.

"Ripley." A man in his twenties wearing a suit with no tie, his hair neatly cut, interrupted them. "Can I borrow you for a moment?"

He had the polished look and plummy accent of MI6, Emma thought. Fast track, most likely.

"Stay in touch," Ripley told her as he walked away. "And keep your wits about you."

Emma squared her shoulders and turned to walk over to where Mackenzie stood waiting, expressionless as a statue, but observant, as all detectives must be.

"Right. Let's go get our man," Emma said.

29

Finlay Blake lived in a surprisingly pleasant neighborhood east of central Edinburgh, in a modern apartment building where the walls and balconies were so clean and white they might have been picked up in Scandinavia and dropped by accident in Scotland.

The front door had a buzzer entry system and a very good lock. Emma and Mackenzie lingered out front, pretending to wait for a friend until someone walked out, leaving the door swinging slowly shut behind them. Emma grabbed it before it could close, and she and Mackenzie slipped inside.

"His flat's on the second floor," Mackenzie said, heading for the stairs.

Emma followed. All the way here her mind had been working, looking for any clues she might have missed that told her Mackenzie wasn't trustworthy, seeking any sign that she was capable of betrayal. But she could find nothing. Mackenzie was clearly bitter about how she'd been treated by the police, but even if she wanted revenge for that, she'd take that revenge on the police force, not on Emma or the Agency. She seemed to know plenty of things the police had done wrong, or mistakes that had been made, but there was no indication she'd released those to the media. So why would she leak about the most important operation she'd ever been part of? One that could save lives?

It wasn't logical.

But then she hadn't seen Jon Frazer's betrayal when he was working right beside her. Or when he was in her bed.

For the first time in her life, Emma didn't trust her own judgment.

She must have been silent for too long, because Mackenzie gave her a curious look as she stopped in a wide, clean corridor on the second floor.

"Everything OK?" she asked.

Emma met her gaze. Mackenzie's vivid blue eyes were clear and puzzled, but unwavering.

"Everything's good." Emma pulled the lockpicks out of her pocket. "Which one?" She gestured at the row of identical doors.

"Number twenty-two," Mackenzie pointed.

Stepping to the door, Emma tapped lightly with her knuckles. No answer.

They'd passed one man in the stairwell, but the corridor was empty and hushed. Emma could hear nothing from inside the flat—no radio or television, no shuffle of footsteps.

"Keep an eye," she told Mackenzie, and dropped to one knee.

The door had a single lock, standard issue, mass-produced. Probably installed by the company that constructed the building, which looked to be no more than ten years old.

It was foolish, Emma thought, for criminals to have bad locks. But they often did.

She inserted the first pick, a slim, long hook. Taking a deep breath, she emptied her mind of betrayal and loss, murder and guns. She could feel her heartbeat slow, sense the cool air entering her lungs, and the warm air leaving.

Some people meditate to deal with stress. Emma picked locks.

She slid in the second pick and found the tumbler inside. They both heard the click when the lock gave.

"Come *on*," Mackenzie whispered, admiration in her voice.

As she stood up, Emma turned the handle and the door swung open.

"Finn?" Mackenzie called, pushing the door open cautiously. "Are you home?"

But Emma knew he wasn't. The apartment had that cold, airless feel places take on when nobody has been there in a while.

The living room was neat and furnished in a masculine style — black leather sofas grouped around a vast television, four straight-back black chairs at a table. The kitchen was so spotless it looked unused. There was nothing on the counter except a pod coffee-maker.

"Neat as a pin," Mackenzie observed, as she began opening drawers and cupboards, revealing a small supply of cups and glasses.

"I'll take the living room," Emma said. But there was little to search in the sparse space. She pulled up cushions and peered under the sofas, before heading to the bedroom.

This too was almost obsessively orderly. There was nothing of interest here. The closet held only a few items, all of them in dry cleaner bags.

The smell of cleaning chemicals made Emma's nose itch as she lifted out a plaid shirt and held it up. It would fit a broadly built man.

A shoulder bag tucked into the corner proved to be empty.

She turned her attention to a small desk in the corner. There was space for a laptop on top, although it appeared Blake had taken that with him.

Like the closet, the drawers were virtually empty — a couple of pens, paper clips, a rubberband.

Emma sat down in the chair and looked around the desk, which held nothing except a pencil and a notepad.

The place bore all the hallmarks of a carefully planned escape. No pictures, no identification — nothing that connected it with Finlay Blake. It could have belonged to anyone.

"What do you think?" Mackenzie walked into the room, and looked around. "Anything here?"

"Nothing. Wherever he's gone, I don't think he's planning on coming back." Emma gestured at the half-empty closet. "He took most of his clothes."

Mackenzie's brow furrowed. "Where's he going, then?"

"With a million pounds?" Emma shrugged. "Barbados? Mexico? Somewhere he thinks we won't look."

"Damn." Mackenzie sat on the edge of the neatly made bed. "We can't catch a break."

Emma searched her face and saw nothing there but worry and concern. She took this case personally. It couldn't be acting—she didn't see any of that in Mackenzie.

And if she wasn't acting, then she wasn't the person leaking.

"You need to know something," Emma said. "Someone inside the police is leaking to the press. Only two people have firsthand access to our work—Graham Brodie . . . and you."

A series of microexpressions swept across Mackenzie's face— confusion, wariness, and then a cold fury.

"You think it's me." Her voice was flat.

"If I thought it was you, I wouldn't be telling you any of this." Emma held her gaze steadily. "I want to know what you think is going on. Because someone is leaking top secret information, and there's going to be an investigation."

"Well, it's not me." Mackenzie's tone was clipped. "This might surprise you but I don't have journalists' phone numbers in my phone." Reaching into her pocket she yanked out the device, unlocked it with a touch of her fingertips, and held it out. "Take it. See for yourself. Look through my texts. Have it all. There's nothing in there I'm ashamed of."

"I believe you." Emma didn't reach for the phone. "But they'll say you used a burner, or you used a messaging app. Or you met the reporter in person."

Mackenzie's shoulders sagged just a little as the full weight of what they were talking about hit her. It was as if she'd been physically struck.

"So what I need," Emma continued, "is to know who did this. If it wasn't you, who was it?"

"Graham Brodie, of course," Mackenzie's tone was infinitely weary. "The answer is right in front of you. This is classic Graham Brodie."

Emma remembered the sharply dressed, amiable man on that first day in Edinburgh. "Graham is the best cop I know," Ripley had said. He'd told her later he'd worked with Brodie on something ten years ago when Brodie was a detective and a Russian national had been murdered.

Now Brodie was deputy chief of police in Scotland.

"But why would he take that risk?" Emma asked.

Mackenzie let out a long breath. "Graham Brodie has what you might call political ambitions. Everyone knows he's planning to run for office when he leaves the police force, and he's been buddying up to the press for the last three years, feeding them information that makes him look good, and someone else look bad. This will be a triple win—it will make the government in Westminster look bad, and everyone around here will love that, and it will make him look great, while he throws me and my boss under a bus." Her voice was bitter.

Emma fell silent. If Mackenzie was right—and Emma believed her—then she needed to talk to Ripley. But now was hardly the time.

"Leave it with me," she said. "I'm going to deal with it."

Clearly this didn't help, because Mackenzie gave her a look of absolute skepticism. Emma held up her hand. "I get it. But I trusted you with information I wasn't meant to tell you. Now I need you to trust that I will fight your corner . . ."

Her voice trailed off as she looked down at the notebook she'd forgotten she was holding. It had been on the desk when she sat down. It had branding from what looked like a local company—

J&B Construction, and in the light streaming through the window, she could see the faint imprint of handwriting.

"Hang on," she said.

She'd seen a blank sheet of paper in one of the drawers, and now she took it out, and placed it over the top of the notepad and used the blunt tip of the pencil lying nearby to shade in the page.

"What is it, a note?" Mackenzie stood and leaned over her shoulder as the carbon covered the paper, and gradually words began to appear in careless, hurried writing.

"Tommy 8 pm."

Emma held up the page so they could both see it clearly.

"Any idea who Tommy might be?"

·   ·   ·

Mackenzie directed her out of the pleasant streets to Edinburgh's western fringes, down where the air smelled of brine and a constant cold breeze blew in off the Firth of Forth.

By unspoken agreement they were letting go of the leak issue and focusing on the case. It was a relief to both of them.

As they drove, Mackenzie explained. "Back when I was working in homicide, I investigated Finn Blake. He trusts two people in the world—Tommy Wilson and Craig Stewart. He grew up with them. He knows their families. They're more like brothers than friends. Craig is inside now, doing eight years for armed robbery. But Tommy's out." She paused. "It's funny, I'm forty-two years old, and in a way, I watched them all grow up. I think Tommy was only a wee lad—maybe fifteen years old—when he was first arrested. I was a patrol officer back then and I helped bring him in. It was thrilling." She gave a dark smile. "But he's been arrested many times since then. The excitement wanes."

Emma said, "You said there's something missing in Blake. Are they the same?"

Mackenzie considered the question seriously. "No, I wouldn't say that. I find it hard to imagine Tommy murdering anyone.

Maybe that's why he idolizes Finn. Tommy's a small-time criminal, a born follower. Finn is ruthless, a leader. Even though Tommy must know he's done truly awful things, his moral scale is not particularly reliable and he can find reasons to justify it—the police are unfair, life's stacked against them both, they deserve more . . ." She ticked them off on her fingers. "But he's not like Finn." Her tone was definitive. "Finn's in a category of his own."

They stopped in front of a simple row house on a quiet street, where worn blue paint flaked away from the windows, and the front garden was overgrown with weeds that brushed against Emma's ankles as they walked to the front door.

While Mackenzie knocked, Emma hung back, keeping an eye on the neighboring properties. But everything looked peaceful.

It was one of those streets where working people lived; a bit rough around the edges, but with a neighborly feel. The house next door had a number sign shaped like a duck in a bonnet. One across the street had a handmade mailbox, carved from wood. Some of the houses had neat front gardens with colorful flowerbeds. But not Tommy Wilson's house.

When the door opened, a small, thin woman in a faded T-shirt and jeans looked at them with suspicion.

"Wha' dae you want?" she demanded.

"Shar Wilson," Mackenzie smiled, her accent suddenly thickening. "Do you remember me? I'm Kate Mackenzie. We met a few years back after the bother up the road there when old Steven was shot. Do you ken?"

"Yeah, I ken." Shar fixed her with a steady untrustful look. "Who's dead now?"

"Ach, nobody, and there it is. I just need to have a word. Can I come in?" Mackenzie's tone was easy but her hand pressed against the door hard, catching Shar off guard and sending it flying open.

The entrance corridor was crowded with coats hanging from hooks and stacks of plastic boxes filled with things Emma couldn't quite make out, leaving the dark hallway claustrophobically narrow. At the end of it, half hidden by an open door, a short, stocky man stood watching.

"Ah, Tommy." Mackenzie beamed at him. "Just the man. Do you have five minutes for a chat?"

By the time she'd finished the sentence, she was already inside. Emma, right on her heels, had to admire her technique. With no warrant, Mackenzie had no right to come in uninvited but she'd somehow rendered an invitation unnecessary.

"I'm a little busy right now, Mack," Tommy objected, in defiance of his appearance. In a T-shirt and cotton shorts, his fair hair standing on end, it appeared he'd been asleep until the knock came to the door.

"This won't take long. I apologize for disturbing your day." Mackenzie turned to his wife. "Shar, a cup of tea would be lovely, if you don't mind. We won't be a minute with your Tommy."

The thin woman hovered for a moment as if some part of her mind was aware she was under no obligation to make tea for anyone but then the power of suggestion won out and she turned into the tiny kitchen, muttering unhappily to herself.

"Now, Tommy, shall we go in here?" Mackenzie maneuvered him into a crowded living room. Emma followed but remained in the doorway, keeping an eye on Shar at the same time.

"Now, do you ken where your mate Finn Blake's got to?" Mackenzie was asking pleasantly. "He didn't show up for work on Friday, and they're worried about him."

Tommy gave a small, nervous laugh. "Oh, is that all it is? Finnie's gone missing again, has he? No, I don't know where he's got to this time."

"Oh, really? That's a shame." Mackenzie kept her tone easy. "Only when was the last time you saw him, if you don't mind?"

"Who me?" Tommy looked surprised, as if it had never occurred to him that he might be asked this question. "I don't know. I haven't seen him in days."

"Days, is it?" Mackenzie asked, sympathetically.

"Oh, aye." He scratched his cheek, fingernails rasping against unshaven whiskers. "Last Wednesday, I think. I saw him down the pub. Yes, that's the last time."

"Now, that's strange, Tommy." Mackenzie gave him a direct look. "Because I heard you met Finn Blake last night at eight o'clock."

It was a gamble—they had no idea what day that note had been written.

But Tommy blanched and took a stumbling step back from her. "No, that wasn't me. It must have been some other short bastard. I was home last night."

"Come now, Tommy." An edge had entered Mackenzie's voice. "I think you ken exactly where Finn is right now."

"You leave him alone, Kate Mackenzie." Shar shoved Emma aside and stormed into the tiny living room, clutching two cups of tea, which she slammed down on to the small table with such force, the hot liquid sloshed into a puddle. "If he says he didn't see Finn, he didn't see him."

But Mackenzie kept her focus on Tommy, who was watching her anxiously. The heating wasn't on and the crowded flat was cold, but even from where she stood, Emma could see the nervous sweat beading his hairline.

"Tommy, we've got ourselves a problem," Mackenzie said. "It looks like Finn might have committed a terrible crime. If you get yourself caught up in that, I can guarantee you we'll get you. And this time you won't get a year or two inside and out for good behavior by Christmas. This sort of crime we take very seriously. That's why my friend Emma is here today." Tommy's neck swivelled as he turned to look at Emma, standing silently in the doorway. "She's with MI5, Tommy. And the spies don't mess around. You'll be looking at twenty-five years." She glanced at Shar. "Twenty-five years in prison, and you don't get benefits while you're doing time. You might lose this place. The council doesn't look kindly on this sort of crime. You'll find no sympathy in their offices."

Shar, who had opened her mouth to argue, shut it again. There was a pause, while she and her husband looked at each other in a kind of silent debate. Shar's brow creased, but Tommy shook his head with slow worry, like a dog trying to shake off a bee.

But Mackenzie had got through to Shar. She grabbed his arm.

"Tell her, Tommy. Tell her what you know." Turning to Mackenzie, she said fiercely, "It's all Finn's doing. He's the one who dragged Tommy into this. I told him to have nothing to do with it." She angled her body to include Emma in the discussion. "Finn gets everyone all confused. But Tommy never did much of anything. He just drove some things for him. That's all."

Mackenzie gave Emma a significant look, and Emma's heart quickened. She bit back all the questions she wanted to ask. Shar and Tommy knew Mackenzie, in some way they trusted her. She had to leave her to handle this.

"Now, Tommy," Mackenzie focused on the small man, who seemed to be wilting in the face of three angry women. "Those things you drove for Finn. Did they happen to be guns?"

30

With his wife urging him on, Tommy told them everything.

Finn Blake had called him four days ago and asked for his help. "He needed to move something. He said it was a big job. Didn't tell me what it was, but he said it was important and that's all I needed to know," he said, puffing his chest. "Finn's my pal and I'll do anything for him, and he'd do anything for me."

Shar shoved his elbow. "Tell him how much he's paying."

Tommy looked at Mackenzie without shame. "He's paying me twenty K. I got five grand up front."

He sounded amazed and delighted at his good fortune.

"So he asked you to help him hide some guns." Mackenzie's tone made this sound perfectly reasonable, as if anyone would have done the same thing.

Emma watched her with disguised admiration. In just a few minutes, she'd gone from locked out of this house to sipping tea on the sofa with Tommy and Shar, both of whom now seemed desperate to tell her everything.

The police used different techniques to intelligence—blunter and with less finesse—but when it worked it was glorious to see.

"Yeah, he said he thought you lot were watching him and

could I just put 'em in a safe place until he needed 'em," Tommy explained.

"Did he tell you what he needed the guns for?" Mackenzie asked.

Tommy shook his head. "Didn't 'ave to. He's a mate."

Shar intervened eagerly. "All Tommy did was take them where Finn told him, and left them there."

Mackenzie pulled out a notepad and pen and held them out to Tommy. "I'm going to need that address."

"I don't need to write it down," he said. "I can tell you. It's at J&B's yard. The little one in town."

Emma saw a flicker of recognition in Mackenzie's face.

"Is that the one over by Clarence's Pub?" Mackenzie asked.

Tommy nodded enthusiastically. "That's it. He said no one goes in there much these days, and they'd be fine, long as they . . ."

His voice trailed off and he looked suddenly secretive. Shar frowned at him, and he wouldn't meet her eyes.

"Long as someone used them soon?" Mackenzie suggested. "Is that what he said, Tommy?"

That was enough. Emma caught Mackenzie's eye and made a questioning gesture. Mackenzie spoke quickly. "J&B is a big local construction company. They have two yards—one outside town, and a small one off Milton Street, down by the train line. They don't use the small one for much—it's just storage."

Suddenly Emma remembered the heading on the notepad she'd found in Blake's flat. The one where he'd written the note about Tommy. It had said J&B at the top.

Emma picked up her phone and dialed, walking to the door.

Behind her she heard Mackenzie ask Tommy, "Where in the yard did you put the guns?"

"In one of them little sheds, at the back."

An unfamiliar female voice answered Emma's call. "Operations."

As she stood in the cold, claustrophobic corridor, Emma heard Mackenzie say, "How many guns were there exactly, Tommy?"

"This is Makepeace 1075," Emma spoke quietly into the phone. "I may know the location of the guns."

As she explained the place Tommy had described, behind her she heard Tommy say "Five. I unloaded the bags myself. There were five guns in long waterproof bags. I unzipped one of the bags to look inside, it was a beautiful weapon—an M24 sniper rifle, American made."

"Tommy was in the army," Shar told Mackenzie. "For a while."

Emma said into the phone, "There should be five weapons in that shed. Count them. If any are missing, let me know. And be careful—Blake could be with them."

"Understood." The woman's voice was clipped and rushed.

The line went dead.

Emma returned to the doorway of the small living room where Shar still clutched her husband's arm, her face pinched with worry.

"Where did Blake say he got the guns?" Mackenzie was asking, her tone patient and unhurried.

"Someone give 'im," Tommy said, vaguely. "Friends of his."

He glanced at Emma, but Mackenzie, motioned for his attention. "Keep your focus on me, Tommy. Tell me what Finn was going to do with the guns?"

The small man shifted slightly. His gaze, suddenly crafty, shifted from Shar to Emma.

"Finn didn't tell me. He said he'd call if he needed me." He paused. "He never called."

"And you're sure you don't know where he is? Tommy? Shar?" Mackenzie's voice was gentle, cajoling. "It's very important that you tell me the truth."

"Like Tommy told you, Finn said he couldn't say," Shar said. "He told us the cops would come and it was best if we didn't know."

Mackenzie glanced at Emma, who nodded, and she stood up.

"Well, I appreciate your candor, Tommy, you've been very

helpful," Mackenzie said. "Now, I'm going to need you to do it all again down at the station . . ."

Both Tommy and Shar erupted.

"He told you all he knows," Shar began, furiously.

"I did what you asked . . ." Tommy complained.

"We only need to make sure we've got all the details right," Mackenzie explained calmly. "It's just a formality but you know how we are with our paperwork. If it isn't written down in triplicate it never happened. Just do me a favor and sit tight until we can get an officer out here to pick you up, there's a good lad."

"It'll be my people coming to talk to you," Emma interjected, smoothly. If Mackenzie's boss was leaking to the press, they couldn't hand Tommy Wilson over to him or they'd be reading about it in tomorrow's papers. "They'll just need a few more details. It shouldn't take too much time."

She and Mackenzie hurried down the crowded hallway and out the front door. Emma dialed as she walked. As they reached the pavement, she said into the phone, "This is Makepeace 1075. I need Special Branch at 374 Sycamore Street to collect two witnesses who are known associates of Finn Blake. Names Tommy and Shar Wilson. Please note witnesses are cooperating. This collection is for written statements and further investigation."

She had to fight to keep her exhilaration out of her voice. They had almost everything they needed now. All that was left was collecting the guns and finding Finlay Blake.

She could hear the woman at the other end typing notes, sending the assignment to the right team.

"Is Ripley there?" Emma asked.

"He's leading the unit at the construction yard," the woman said.

"If he calls in, tell him I'll meet him there."

She unlocked the car and turned to Mackenzie. "They're on their way to get the guns. Let's go."

They jumped in and Emma pulled out into the street, tires

squealing. Her pulse was racing. They had them. They had them all.

As Mackenzie guided her back to the center and then down a steep hill, Emma found herself smiling.

"That interrogation was picture perfect," she told Mackenzie, as she navigated the narrow street. "A masterclass."

"Stop. You're making me blush." Mackenzie's tone was dry, but she looked pleased. "Anyway, Tommy Wilson's a fool, so it wasn't as hard as it might have been. Blake only keeps him close because he's loyal. Turn left here."

"Nonsense, you played him like a fiddle." Emma slowed to take the sharp turn onto a narrow street that wound along the old train line.

The construction yard was tucked between the railway and a steep hill. It was, as Mackenzie had said, small. Mostly it held storage sheds, and pallets stacked with lumber.

"Blake really could be hiding out here," Mackenzie said as they pulled in. "It wouldn't be a bad spot."

Emma could see the gates had been forced open, and a chain cut. Four cars were parked haphazardly, and people in dark jackets were searching the site.

Emma spotted Adam's wiry hair and muscular form as soon as they left the car, and she and Mackenzie ran over to join him.

"We found the guns," he said, as they walked up. "Right where you said they'd be." He pointed at a wooden shed in one corner of the small lot where the largest group of agents were clustered, looking inside.

Something in his voice made Emma's throat constrict.

"How many?" she asked.

He paused, and she knew the answer before he spoke. "Four."

"Damn." Emma said it softly, the breath knocked out of her. "He got one out."

"Any sign of Blake?" Mackenzie asked.

"Negative." Adam wiped his forehead with the back of his

hand. "This is a full manhunt now. We're going to need your help. We've put a trace on Blake's phone, but if he's smart he'll have junked it. We're in the process of freezing his bank accounts but it takes time and that's one thing we haven't got." He paused. "I'm Adam by the way. I don't think we were ever introduced."

"Mackenzie." She shook his hand awkwardly.

"Emma." Ripley strode up to join them, his black coat swirling around his long form like a cloak. "Great work. And to you, as well." He directed the latter to Mackenzie, who flushed slightly at this praise. "We are one step closer to Finlay Blake. Now we have a single gun and a single man to find and we are so *close*."

Excitement had brought hectic spots of color high on his cheeks, and his narrow grey eyes were blazing.

"We're heading back to the office to get everyone working on this," Ripley continued. "Zach is tracing Blake's last known movements on CCTV, although there are far fewer cameras here than London. But we should get enough to put a picture together."

He considered Mackenzie for a long moment. Emma knew he was thinking about the leak and how much to trust her, but then he said, "Mackenzie, can you take Emma to Blake's hangouts, and do a physical search?"

Mackenzie fairly snapped to attention. "Yes, sir."

Emma watched him with interest. Would he do this if he believed Mackenzie was the person leaking? Had he begun to doubt Graham Brodie? But there was no time to ask.

"Excellent. Adam, let's go." Ripley glanced at Emma. "Stop by the office before you go out, you'll need a proper weapon for this. Blake's too dangerous for us to take chances."

He motioned impatiently at them and barked, "Everyone get moving. We have a killer to catch."

MONDAY

14 October

Private communication

From: Hayley Mir, Operations Director, Secret Service

Sir, our investigators continue to search for suspected Russian agent Finlay Allen Blake. All his known locations have been searched and are being watched. He was last seen 9 October, when he and an associate moved five long guns believed to have been brought into the country by Vladimir Balakin in his diplomatic bags, and then transported by Russian operative Leonid Fridman, until they were given to Finlay Blake. Blake hid the guns at one location in central Edinburgh. It is our understanding (via GCHQ Listeners) that he'd been asked to divide the guns and hide them at five locations, so at least one would survive even if others were found, but that he failed to do so.

As you know, Russia strongly denies any involvement in this operation. Balakin is now in Moscow. Leonid Fridman is being treated in hospital in Belarus after an altercation with a female British intelligence officer.

The risk to the G7 remains high. Security has been reinforced around the full perimeter of Carlowrie Castle. Flights from Edinburgh Airport will be redirected during the G7 away from the castle, and the airspace above it will be closed. All off-site gatherings and meetings have been canceled until Blake is captured. Due to the heightened security situation, we've requested and received an agreement from Scottish authorities to close all roads completely when you and the other leaders are transported from the airport to the castle. Our confidence is high that Blake is in hiding in the Edinburgh area and will be captured.

With security so critical, the continuing leaks from the police remain a threat. I have personally spoken to the head of Police Scotland, who assures me a full internal investigation is underway. I've received transcripts of an interview with Graham Brodie, who denies any knowledge of the leaks. He states strongly the leaks must be coming from a detective working with our teams in Edinburgh, Katherine Mackenzie.

You should know that Brodie is scheduled for early retirement in May, and his own political ambitions cannot be ignored in this. Damaging the party in power in Westminster could be beneficial to Brodie's future plans.

The article below, published at midnight last night, is the result of the most recent leak. Charles Ripley, from the Agency, says this could not have been leaked by Kate Mackenzie, who was with his team all of yesterday.

THE SCOTSMAN
Page One

14 OCTOBER

GOVERNMENT REFUSED TO CANCEL G7 DESPITE DANGERS

BY ALEX LOUIS

As the leaders of the free world arrive in Edinburgh today for the Group of Seven annual meeting, the government in Westminster is refusing to take actions to keep them safe.

Sources inside the operation to secure the gathering tell *The Scotsman* a plot to attack and possibly kill one or more of the participants has been identified, and the attacker remains at large, despite a massive security operation that has sprawled across the city.

The unidentified attacker is believed to be known to police, but after one of the biggest searches in recent history over the weekend, his whereabouts are unknown.

Police and security vehicles were spotted on Sunday at a J&B Construction yard near the rail line, and I am reliably informed that officers located a cache of weapons believed intended for use by the missing attacker.

Despite these dangers, the government insisted in a statement late Sunday night that "The G7 meeting will go forward as intended. The meeting locations are secure, and we have absolute confidence in our security services to keep all participants safe."

The Scottish First Minister declined to comment for this article, but it is our understanding that both the Scottish government and the police are deeply concerned about security plans, should the G7 go forward in the face of these threats.

Many will be questioning the government's judgment on this.

31

Emma woke up to find herself lying on a cement floor in a dark, windowless room. Her muscles ached, and for one frozen moment she thought she'd been kidnapped. Then someone stirred next to her, and she remembered where she was.

She and Mackenzie had searched for Finlay Blake until three in the morning, by which point they'd both been exhausted. Emma had tried to send Mackenzie home, but she'd refused. By then, a storage room on the fourth floor had been converted into a makeshift dormitory, with sleeping bags borrowed from an army base nearby. The bags kept them warm, but did nothing to soften the hard floor.

The clock on her phone told her it was just before seven o'clock. She could hear other people breathing and rustling as they shifted in their sleep, and faint voices from the office on the other side of the door.

Slowly, she sat up and unzipped the bag, trying not to wake the others but, seconds later, the person next to her did the same. Emma could just make out Mackenzie's rumpled hair in the shadows as they both got stiffly to their feet and folded their sleeping bags.

They picked their way over the sleeping bodies and slipped out. After the darkness, it was like walking into a wall of light.

"Jesus," Emma muttered, raising an arm to shield her eyes as they ducked into the toilets to splash water on their faces at a long row of sinks and clean their teeth using small tubes of toothpaste and disposable bamboo toothbrushes that had appeared during the night.

As they stood at the mirrors, Mackenzie sniffed the fabric of her top suspiciously. "I really need to change clothes soon," she announced, as they headed back into the main room.

But as they stepped into the crowded room, they were instantly reminded that it didn't matter how they looked or how stale their clothes were.

Over the last twenty-four hours, the unfinished office had been converted into a full Gold Command—the wall screens had been expanded to cover one entire wall. The long table had been joined by five more long tables. Chairs had been acquired somewhere by somebody and scattered around the room.

Martha's disguises were no longer needed, and she'd packed up during the night and returned to London on an early plane, freeing the space in that corner for use by Special Branch, who were coordinating with MI5 on the airport motorcades.

At the same time, MI6 was busy checking the people brought in by each country for intelligence operatives who might use the situation to gain an advantage. All seven countries were allies, of course, but no one could really be trusted. MI5 and Special Branch were protecting Carlowrie Castle, where the meetings would take place.

In the midst of all of this, the Agency was tasked with finding Finlay Blake.

Ripley, who seemed never to rest, was sitting with Zach near the windows. The screens on the wall in front of them showed CCTV of Blake's apartment building, his mother's house in Glasgow, which was also being watched by police, Carlowrie Castle, and the storage yard where they'd found the guns.

Emma and Mackenzie grabbed coffee and protein bars from a

table that had been turned into a makeshift kitchen and walked over to join them.

"Good, you're awake," Ripley said, as they sat down.

"Any progress?" Emma asked.

"Two reported sightings early this morning," Ripley said. "Both probably wishful thinking, but Adam and the others are out investigating."

Police had put out a "man wanted" report overnight, releasing Finlay Blake's image and name to the press, but saying only that he was wanted in connection with "police enquiries."

It was a gamble. By downplaying why he was wanted, his picture would get less attention, but putting it out at all risked an overload of false reports that could bury the police for days. This way they hoped to raise awareness without being overwhelmed.

"Should we go help them?" Emma asked, eagerly.

"No, those are under control but more are coming in all the time." Ripley rubbed a tired hand along his unshaven jaw and turned to the younger man across the table. "Zach? Anything?"

"Coming in now." Zach glanced up at Emma. His brown curls were in absolute chaos this morning, but he alone did not look particularly tired. "We've had a few that are blatantly bogus and I've junked those already. This one is more interesting." He scribbled something on a sheet of paper and handed it across to her. "It's a café. The owner says a man who looked like Blake came in just after he opened today. It could be nothing, but the guy sounded positive, according to the dispatcher who took the call. Said he knows Blake, and this was definitely him."

Mackenzie looked over Emma's shoulder at the address. "That's on the west side," she said. "He could be crashing with one of his contacts over there, someone I don't know."

"Let's go." Picking up her cardboard cup of coffee, Emma grabbed her coat off the rack where she'd left it the night before and pulled on the boots that rested underneath it. She felt her coat pockets for the small knife, and slipped it into its place inside the sturdy boot.

While Mackenzie crouched to put on her shoes, Ripley motioned Emma over. She followed her boss to a low metal safe in a corner. As she watched, he pressed his thumb against a reader and the door swung open to reveal a neat row of gleaming silver and black handguns.

"There's been another leak," he told her quietly. He lifted one from the shelf and checked the chamber with a swift movement of his wrist. "Did Mackenzie spend any time alone yesterday evening?"

Emma shook her head. "I was with her constantly."

"That's what I thought." Ripley retrieved a bullet clip from a cardboard box and snapped it into place.

"I don't think it's her," Emma told him. "I really don't."

He flipped the loaded gun over in his hand and held it to her, the barrel pointed down.

"Nor do I," he said, simply.

Emma took the pistol, checking the safety while Ripley pulled a shoulder holster from the lower shelf.

"It's Graham, isn't it?" she said.

He sighed. "It's a damn shame. He's a good cop. MI5 has requested his removal from the operation, but Graham insists it's Mackenzie leaking, which makes it complicated."

Emma shrugged off her leather jacket and strapped the holster over the sweater she'd now been wearing for two straight days. When she put the coat back on, the gun was invisible, but it felt bulky and obvious under her arm.

"I'll handle Graham." Ripley's eyes met hers. "Be careful out there."

"Always."

She kept her tone emotionless, but just having the gun made her heart rate quicken. She was a former soldier—guns didn't intimidate her. But it was extremely rare for weapons to be issued like this in Britain, and the fact that they were being issued now was simply a reminder of how very dangerous this operation had become.

Everything felt more intense now. The prime minister was scheduled to fly at eight o'clock that morning. The US president would follow at nine. And then the French and Canadian leaders were to arrive at the same time after that, then the Italian leader. And so on. Each flight arrival required a secure motorcade to Carlowrie Castle. It wasn't far at all—the castle was on the same side of Edinburgh as the airport, but that didn't matter. A lot could happen in five minutes. A lot could happen in five *seconds*.

Emma and Mackenzie walked out into unexpected sunshine. In fact, the day was everything the Scottish Tourism Board could have wanted—bright, crisp, and cool—a perfect October morning. The sun had an amber edge to it, as if it were struggling to shine with winter tugging on its sleeve, but for now the light held on, nearly the same color as the turning leaves in the trees.

As Emma and Mackenzie climbed into the BMW and headed out, they saw a pack of press gathering on a corner, cameras bristling. Uniformed police patrolled the pavements in groups of two and three, and a helicopter hovered low above the ancient stone buildings.

Since the decision had been made to keep the G7 meetings all at the castle just outside of town, there was less need to close streets in the city center, and traffic was actually better than it had been for the last few days. The night before, Emma had been issued a sticker for the car—a simple unobtrusive design, a black crown on a white background, but it made the car instantly recognizable as official to any roadblock or security patrol. It would help, as Mackenzie put it, if the shit hit the fan.

"Left at the corner," Mackenzie said, and yawned. She still clutched her cup of coffee. "It's not going to be him," she told Emma. "We're not that lucky."

"But if it *was* him, then that means he's on the opposite side of town from the castle," Emma reasoned, "and he has to get through intense security to get over to the G7 site. That gives us a chance to track him."

It took them under fifteen minutes to reach Terry's Café, a modest-looking joint on a busy street, where workday shops and pubs sat shoulder to shoulder. Emma parked in the red zone out front and they jumped out and ran inside.

Every seat in the café was taken, and the air smelled tantalizingly of sizzling bacon and very good coffee.

An amiable looking fifty-something man with dark hair and skin, wearing a blue T-shirt that said "Terry's" beneath a white apron, stood at the stove.

From the counter, Mackenzie flashed her badge. "We're looking for Terry Smith."

"That's me." He wiped his hands on a towel and stepped out from behind the counter. "I've been waiting for you."

Mackenzie said, "I understand you think Finlay Blake came in here this morning?"

"I don't *think* it. I know it." He had a south London accent. "Blake comes in here all the time when he's working this side of town." He gave them a look. "You know what he does, right?"

"He's a drug dealer, among other things," Mackenzie said, shortly. "We're aware."

"Then why don't you get him off the bloody streets?" The man's voice rose slightly. "He's a menace."

"That is exactly what we're trying to do," Emma interjected. "Please tell us what you saw today."

"I'll do better than tell you. I'll show you." Smith motioned for them to follow and led the way behind the counter into a tiny, very crowded office, where stacks of paper and fluorescent sticky notes threatened to subsume anyone who dared enter.

"Bloody taxes," he muttered, gesturing at the piles. "Got to do 'em every quarter like a curse." He turned the monitor of an aging computer to face them. "I got robbed last year, so I got CCTV. Cost a mint and took me months to figure it out, but now I'm a bleeding expert. This was recorded this morning."

He pressed a button and an image of the café appeared, clear and bright. "This was just after I opened at six today. Watch the door." Smith pointed at the screen.

On the monitor, the door swung open and a stocky man walked in. He had a distinctive rolling gait, his steps lighter than his sturdy build might have indicated. Blake had brown hair worn parted on the side. This man's head was shaved, but when he looked in the direction of the camera, the round face was clearly that of Finlay Blake: the same narrow eyes, and, looking closely, Emma saw the small tattoo of a cross on the right side of his neck that she remembered noticing when she'd looked at his MI5 files.

Emma's breath caught. Mackenzie looked at her. "That's him."

On screen Terry Smith hesitated but then stepped forward to serve him. At that hour they were alone in the café, and the rows of tables were clean and empty. The two men spoke briefly and then Smith turned to the stove.

"Blake's nervous," Mackenzie said softly, pointing at the screen. "Look."

As he waited for his food, Finlay Blake fidgeted, alternately looking over his shoulder at the door, and staring at his phone. When Smith handed his food to him in a Styrofoam box, Blake paid with cash and left immediately.

"He got a bacon and egg sandwich to go, and cup of milky coffee," Smith said. "Scared the hell out of me. I'd seen the news before I opened up and I knew you was lookin' for him. And there he stood, bold as brass, asking me for food."

"Did he tell you anything at all about where he was staying or what he was doing?" Emma asked.

Smith met her eyes directly. "No, and I didn't ask. I figure if you're looking for him enough to put his face on my television it's bad." He turned to Mackenzie, somehow instinctively seeing her as the real cop. "What'd he do anyway?"

"We can't say," Mackenzie told him. "But you were right to be worried."

"I knew it." Smith looked both gratified and nervous.

"Did you see where he went when he left?" Emma asked.

"He walked out the front door, turned right, and disappeared." He glanced at her. "I turned around and called you. By the time I hung up, he was long gone."

Emma pulled out her phone and walked away. Behind her she heard Mackenzie say, "You did the right thing, Terry. Can I get a copy of that film emailed to me?"

Emma didn't call the main number this time, she called Ripley, who answered on the first ring.

"It's him," Emma said. "He was in this café at six A.M. He's on foot, and he's shaved his head. We're sending the footage to you now."

"Good." There was relief in Ripley's voice. "I'm sending local police to canvas the area. Stay there, work with them."

"Copy that." Emma looked up and down the busy street, excitement kindling inside her. "He was *right here*, Ripley. One hour ago. We're getting close. We're going to get him."

32

Ten minutes after Emma made that phone call, a police transport van pulled up in front of Terry's Café and eight uniformed officers spilled out.

Their sergeant was a tall, gregarious man with auburn hair. Emma walked over to introduce herself, but before she could speak, he looked past her shoulder and said, "Hey, Mack. What are you doing here? Slumming?"

"I'm just doing my part to catch the bad guys as usual," Mackenzie said. "This is Emma Makepeace from MI6 . . . sort of. Emma, this is Sergeant Dowell."

"MI6 sort of?" Dowell laughed. "That sounds sinister." Glancing at Emma he said, "I hope you haven't been listening to anything Mack says about me. She's jealous, you see. I'm the best they have. I'll find your guy for you."

"That's what we're hoping," Emma said. "He was here a little over an hour ago. He's shaved his head, so we've got new pictures for you. Can I send it to your phone?"

Using the CCTV footage from the café, Zach had captured a still image of Blake and cleaned it up until they had a clear shot. It was surprising how ordinary he looked, how normal, with his round face and dark eyes, his scalp still pale from being recently exposed to light. He could have been anyone you passed on the street. Just a normal bloke.

Killers never look like killers, that was the problem.

"Ah, he's shaved his head and thinks it's a cloak of invisibility," said Dowell, amused. "Probably thinks he can change his DNA by drinking bleach as well. Come on, lads." The last sentence was directed at the officers who clustered around him. "You'll all get this picture on your phones: I'm sending it to the group now. We'll be working with these two ladies; one of them's from MI6, sort of." He shot Emma a cheeky wink. "Go door to door, show everyone the picture." He glanced at Emma. "What are we looking for if he's left the area?"

"How's he traveling—did anyone see him get in a bus or was he in a car? Is he alone or is someone helping him?" Emma raised her voice so they could all hear. "Anything that could help us locate him. This man is very dangerous. He may be armed. Be careful."

Dowell turned back to his team. "You heard her. Now split up. You lot do the south side of the street; the rest take the north." He divided them into groups. "Stay in contact with me. If you see him, *do not engage*. Call me and request backup. Understood?"

The officers dispersed on the street, moving quickly. Emma and Mackenzie worked with them, stopping people on the street, showing the picture of Blake over and over again.

"Have you seen this man? You, sir? Have you seen this man?" And on and on.

But Blake, it seemed, was a ghost. No one had seen him walk out of Terry's Café. No one knew where he'd gone.

After two hours, they were flagging.

Emma hid her disappointment. They'd missed him by minutes. And now it was as if he'd never been here at all.

"What do you think?" Mackenzie asked. "Should we try somewhere else?"

As she spoke, her phone rang. She looked at the screen, and then stepped back to take the call.

"Kate Mackenzie." She paused. "Yeah, Kayla, what've you got?"

There was a long silence.

When Emma glanced over, Mackenzie's forehead was creased with thought. "And you really think it's similar? Any ID on the guy? No?" She glanced at Emma. "Let me see what I can do."

Ending the call, she stepped closer to Emma. "That was my old partner from homicide. There's been a murder this morning, not very far from here. The victim is a man in his late thirties, they're still IDing him. He was killed on the street, his throat slashed. But here's the thing, you remember the girl in the park?"

Emma nodded.

"This killer has the same MO—the same style." Mackenzie sounded puzzled. "It's unusual, you see—hands tied, throat slit, body left face down."

"But you thought Blake did the murder in the park." Emma looked at her. "Are you saying you think he killed this guy too? Or were you wrong back then?"

Mackenzie held out both hands. "I don't know. I'm sure that was Blake's kill in the park. So . . . I think I need to go see this crime scene. But I haven't got my car—"

"I'll take you," Emma cut her off before she could finish the sentence. "Let's go."

Mackenzie directed her off the main street and down a winding tangle of small side streets that led down a steep hill until they reached a patrol car, its lights flashing, blocking the road.

It had taken them less than five minutes to get here from Terry's Café. Walking, it would have been fifteen.

Emma and Mackenzie exchanged a glance.

"It's close," Mackenzie said.

Emma pulled over, and they both jumped out. As she walked, Emma could feel the weight of the Glock 7 against her left arm.

When they reached the long strip of blue-and-white crime tape that stretched across the narrow street, Mackenzie flashed her badge and said, "We're expected."

"They're over there." The young female officer let them through and pointed toward a group of people standing at the edge of a small lawn.

The body was in a driveway, surrounded by a cluster of police and forensics experts.

"Mackenzie!" A small woman in a blue wool coat, her wavy auburn hair pulled back tightly, called them over.

As they neared her, her freckled face broadened into a wide smile.

"It's good to see you, Mack." Her lilting Edinburgh accent marked her as a born-and-bred local.

"Thanks for calling me, Kayla." Mackenzie gestured at Emma. "This is Emma Makepeace, from . . ."

"I'm with Intelligence," Emma interjected, firmly. "Can you tell us what happened here?"

Kayla Edwards had the experience of a longtime cop, and her face betrayed no emotion as she absorbed this, but her quick eyes studied Emma with interest as she explained the situation.

"Our victim was knifed—throat slit. Man in his fifties. He lived on this street. Just there." Kayla pointed to a modest terraced house a few doors down. "We got ID from a neighbor. His name's Dennis Marrs. Apparently he's a landscaper. No prior convictions. Clean record. Neighbors loved him—said he was divorced, minded his business, kept a beautiful lawn."

Turning to Mackenzie, she continued, "I thought of you straightaway. It looks like your perp. It's a different kind of victim—he's never killed a man before as far as we know—but this has his hallmarks. The same serrated knife, the same cable ties used to bind the body, the blow to the head with a hammer to knock him out at the start."

They walked over to the crowd, Kayla pushing through with firm politeness, until they could all see the crime scene.

The body had been rolled onto his side, and Emma and Mackenzie crouched down to see more clearly. Dennis Marrs wore faded jeans and an old gray jacket that had bunched around his waist when his hands had been forcefully pulled back and bound.

There was a dark pool of blood beneath him and his shirt was so soaked, its original color could not be identified. Emma could smell its metallic tang in the air as she studied his face, the eyes staring past her at nothing.

"You're right," Mackenzie told Kayla as they straightened again and stepped away to let the others do their work. "That's got to be the same kind of knife."

"Did he have any connections to Finlay Blake?" Emma asked. "Did he get mixed up in drugs at all?"

"Not if the neighbors are telling the truth," Kayla said. "We're searching his house now, but so far we've turned up no drug paraphernalia and no evidence of criminality. We'll keep looking, but my experience tells me there's nothing there." She glanced at Mackenzie. "That's the weird thing with this one; he has cash in his pocket and his phone. If it was Blake who killed him, he took nothing as far as we can tell."

Emma looked at the body, the legs sprawled, the hands purple where they'd been bound too tightly.

"Nothing taken," she murmured. "Then why kill him?"

Something tugged at the back of her brain, a slight warning that made her stomach tighten even before she'd had time to think it through.

This man could hardly have been a threat to Blake. If he wasn't a threat, then the only reason to kill him was if somehow Blake would benefit. If somehow killing Dennis Marrs would help Blake.

"Where was he going?" she asked.

The two detectives regarded her blankly.

"When he was killed," Emma said. "Where was Marrs going?"

It was Kayla who answered. "We think he was headed to work. His neighbors said he always left the house before seven."

"But today is Sunday. Where does he work?" Emma's voice was curt.

"He's a landscaper—"

"I know," Emma interrupted. "But where specifically was he working?"

"We're trying to find that out," Kayla said. "His neighbors said he had a new job that required weekend work. But he had no work identification on him when we found him."

Again Emma felt that sharp clear sensation that this was important. Dennis Marrs mattered to this case, somehow. Blake had cared about him enough to kill him on the first day of the G7.

Stepping back, she lifted the phone and called Ripley.

"What have you got?" His voice was taut and expectant, as if somehow he'd known she'd call.

"I need you to check our list—does a man named Dennis Marrs work at Carlowrie Castle?" Emma kept her voice measured but excitement thrummed in her veins, and she waited impatiently as he relayed the question to Zach. There was a pause and then . . .

"Yes, there's a Dennis Marrs on the list," Ripley said quickly. "He's one of the groundkeepers. Why?"

"Dennis Marrs is dead," Emma said. "I think someone stole his work identification." She paused. "Ripley, it's got to be Blake. This is how he's getting in."

33

The drive across Edinburgh to Carlowrie Castle seemed to take forever. Every bus, every taxi, every red light got in their way.

"Come on, come *on*," Emma muttered, as a delivery truck lumbered ahead of her, as if time were of no matter in its day.

It was nearly ten o'clock. All the leaders had arrived at the castle now except the prime minister of Japan, whose plane was landing at this very moment. They had to get to the castle before his motorcade left the airport or they risked being stuck in traffic until it had passed, and that could cost them half an hour, maybe more. They didn't have that kind of time.

Mackenzie had already guided her through every shortcut she knew, but it was Monday morning and the roads were very busy.

The records at the castle showed that Dennis Marrs had shown up for work about an hour after his death, scanning his government-issued pass at the gate. The guard who let him in had never seen him before, and had no idea that it wasn't actually Marrs holding the pass. He'd glanced at the picture and, deciding Blake looked enough like the image, let him pass.

Marrs had been carrying nothing in his hands—no long bag. If so, the guards would have searched it. But they all knew that didn't matter. The castle grounds sprawled for acres. Blake only needed to find a quiet stretch, and throw the bag over the fence. Then he could go collect it once he was inside. That had to be his plan.

"I knew it," Mackenzie kept saying softly to herself, punching her fist against her denim-clad knee as the BMW weaved through traffic. "I knew it was Blake. I could feel it."

"I could, too," Emma said. "But he's smart to do it this way. Getting that ID was very clever."

"But the cold calculation of it. He ate his bacon and egg sarnie, drank his coffee, and then murdered Dennis Marrs." There was disgust in Mackenzie's voice, and Emma couldn't blame her.

"He's a born assassin," Emma agreed.

She followed signs for the airport and then turned off the roundabout toward the castle, driving so fast Mackenzie grabbed the door handle.

The grounds of Carlowrie Castle almost bumped up against the periphery of Edinburgh Airport—that was one reason it had been chosen for the G7 in the first place, and she was grateful for that decision now.

When they reached the gate, two security officers headed straight for them. Emma tapped the crown sticker on the windshield.

"I'm Emma Makepeace," she said. "I'm expected."

Mackenzie pulled out her badge and showed it to him.

The guard studied the list in his hands, and examined both their faces, before opening the gate.

It's far too late for that, Emma thought as she gunned the engine. *You already let him inside.*

She followed the long smooth drive through a sprawling parkland of velvety green lawns and huge oaks with leaves just beginning to tinge with amber. Seen from a distance, the castle seemed to float above the grounds, like something from a fairy tale, its pale, vine-covered towers and turrets ageless and fanciful.

It was an odd place for a castle, Emma thought, but then it had never been a fortress. The castle was a Victorian creation, built by a nineteenth century businessman, who hadn't lived to see its completion.

"Have they swept the inside of the castle?" Mackenzie asked, as they pulled into the car park with a squeal of breaks.

"They have," Emma said. "And the leaders are all being kept indoors. But, there are windows everywhere. He just needs one clean shot." She slammed the handbrake on and reached for the door handle.

They left the car at a sprint, running to where a group of men and women in the plain dark suits of intelligence officers stood conferring. Even from a distance, Emma could hear the buzz and hum of two-way radios. Hayley Mir from MI5 and Andrew Field from MI6 were both in the group, and Ripley was at the center, his phone in one hand and a sheet of paper in the other. His long, craggy face had that bright intensity it took on when an operation was running full bore, and everything was at stake.

"Where do you need us?" Emma asked as she neared the group.

"We're searching the grounds in quadrants. Adam and Patrick are taking this section." The paper in Ripley's hand turned out to be a simple tourists' map of the grounds, across which several lines had been drawn in blue ink, and he pointed at an area directly in front of the house. "Special Branch are here." He indicated a section of greenhouses and garages near the rear of the house. "I want you and Mackenzie to take this section here." He tapped a stretch of green at the far edge of the castle grounds. "Pay special attention to the storage buildings, and there's a hilly area that might provide cover for him, so be careful there." He looked up at her. "We've got people watching every inch of the fence line, so he's on the grounds somewhere. Let's bring him in."

Emma and Mackenzie needed no more information; they headed off side by side, running down low stone steps, and then onto a gravel pathway bounded on both sides by lush hydrangeas covered in fat, pink blossoms.

Mackenzie lagged slightly behind, and Emma could hear her breathing was already labored.

"This way," Emma called, pointing to a well-tended walk on their left.

"Do you want to split up to cover more ground?" Mackenzie replied, her voice shaking with each thump of her boots. "Christ, I'm out of shape."

"No." Emma's reply was immediate. "We stick together."

She was intensely conscious of the holster strapped to her shoulder, and the heavy gun it held there. Mackenzie, she knew, had no weapons at all. She'd been trained to de-escalate and calm dangerous situations, but Finlay Blake would not de-escalate. He was cornered and ruthless, he was going to fight to the death.

The gravel path was not straight as it had appeared on the map, but curved across the beautifully maintained grounds, under the shade of a row of birch trees and then into a section that had been left more wild.

Emma slowed her steps and Mackenzie slowed too. Her face was red with exertion and she was clutching her side, her breath coming in wheezy gasps.

When Emma gave her a questioning look, though, Mackenzie shook her head.

"I'm fine," she gasped.

Taking her at her word, Emma turned to study the area around them. She could see now that the search wasn't going to be easy. The castle grounds covered more than thirty acres. The area closest to the house was a manicured picture of perfection, but out here the property was much more rugged. A forested area stretched ahead, as far, she suspected, as the edge of the property. And she thought she could see the tops of the outbuildings Ripley had mentioned through the trees in the other direction.

So many places to hide.

There'd been no time to do this right, she realized. She didn't have any comms to connect her to the other search groups. They were moving to quickly to organize it, or Ripley had been too busy to think of it.

She just had her phone, and when she held that up, her signal was very weak — just one bar. And, after a second, even that disappeared.

"Phone signal's weak," she told Mackenzie quietly. "Stay close to me. All eyes."

Mackenzie nodded.

Emma stretched out her arms, motioning for distance as the path ended and they headed into the forest. Mackenzie moved to the right until there was four feet between them as they walked through the trees, their footsteps silent on the soft, loamy soil.

Emma reached under her jacket to unsnap the strap holding the gun. She could feel the hard hilt of the knife press against her ankle with every step.

It was curiously quiet here, given that there was a motorway close by, and the airport just beyond that. The sounds of the outside world seemed far away, replaced by the rustle of branches in the breeze, and the soft songs of the birds. It felt so isolated, it was hard to believe that right now at least a dozen people were searching the grounds around them. They might have been completely alone.

Craning her neck, she looked up at the tree branches above her head, seeing fragments of that brilliant October blue between the dark green of the leaves and pine needles.

I would climb a tree if I were him, she thought, and motioned for Mackenzie's attention, pointing up and around, making sure she also thought to look overhead.

Mackenzie nodded silently. Her color had returned to normal and she was moving carefully.

A sudden rustle in the bracken made them both stop, mid-step.

Mackenzie gave her a questioning look, and Emma pointed to the left, to where shrubs covered the forest floor. They stepped slowly closer. Emma reached under her jacket, her hand hovering near the Glock.

The rustle came again and her breath caught. Then a squirrel shot out of the shrub and flew with incredible speed up the trunk of a pine tree, where it stopped to look down at them accusingly.

Mackenzie exhaled and shook her head, smiling.

"Bloody squirrels," she whispered.

They resumed their search, moving back and forth through the woods until they felt certain Blake wasn't there.

By then, they'd reached the fence—a surprisingly ordinary wire barrier, with a strip of barbed wire at the top. On the other side, they could see more forest, stretching into the distance.

They turned right, following the fence for ten minutes until the ground became more uneven, and a low hill appeared ahead.

Emma motioned Mackenzie closer and whispered. "Let's head that way. We need to check the outbuildings."

Mackenzie nodded, and they began climbing up. There was no path here, and the ground was soft from the recent rains, but the incline was gentle. After about ten minutes they reached the highest point, where a bench had been placed for the more adventurous wanderers who made it this far to take in the views.

Emma stood on top of it and scanned the grounds. The castle turrets, one topped by a jaunty banner, looked small in the distance. She could see the dark shapes of people moving around the grounds in groups of two, and that was comforting in a way. They weren't really alone, but there was no sign of anyone in their quadrant. This area, so far from the house, felt deserted.

"There," Emma said quietly, pointing to a low roof at the foot of the hill to their left. "We need to search those buildings next."

Going down the hill was faster than going up it, and they spread out leaving space in between them as they made their way down the gentle green slope. Emma was getting thirsty, and she knew

Mackenzie must be, too, although she never once complained. They'd been walking for nearly an hour now.

They'd complete a full search of their section, then go get some water and regroup, Emma decided. It might be more effective for all the searchers to form a single line across the grounds, sticking together. She'd discuss it with Ripley.

It took only a few minutes to reach the buildings she'd spotted from above. They proved to be old, disused storage, perhaps from when the grounds had been used more for farming or hunting. Now, they were rotting, the weatherworn doors hanging half open. One roof had already collapsed.

They approached the first building with caution. The door gaped, and Emma moved it gingerly with her elbow, wincing as the rusted hinges squeaked until it opened wide enough to see inside. Through the light of the open door and broken window at the other end, they could see that the old shed was empty. The dirt floor bare—nothing to hide behind.

"Clear," Emma whispered to Mackenzie, who nodded agreement.

The next building was smaller, but its door was closed.

They walked toward it, cautiously.

Mackenzie turned to her and whispered, "Do you want me to check the back?"

The words were barely out of her mouth when the deafening *crack* of a gunshot split the pristine silence, echoing across the castle grounds.

Crack . . . crack . . . crack . . .

Mackenzie stood stock-still, one hand outstretched.

"Kate . . ." Emma said. The Scottish detective pulled her jacket back and looked down to where a bloom of dark blood had appeared on her shoulder and begun to spread.

She looked at Emma in wordless shock, and then her knees gave, and she *folded*—there was no other word for it—to the ground.

34

A high hum of fear filled Emma's head, a noise like the sound of electricity coursing down a wire. She barely felt herself moving toward Mackenzie, crouching beside her, barely knew she was reaching inside her jacket, her fingers finding the Glock pistol just as another gunshot *cracked*, shattering the peaceful landscape.

Emma heard the bullet slam into the wall behind her, sending fragments of wood flying through the air.

He was on the hill. He must have followed them from the woods, watching as they climbed, lying low as they searched for him, and then taking the high ground, so he could pick them off.

She'd been so stupid. Why hadn't she realized they should have stayed on the hill? That view of everything was his now. He could pick off the searchers one by one.

She had to warn Ripley.

"Mackenzie!" Emma said, urgently. "Can you hear me?"

There was no answer. All the color had drained from Mackenzie's skin, and through her layers of clothing Emma couldn't even see if she was breathing.

She couldn't help. Emma was going to have to do this alone.

Jumping to her feet, she grabbed Mackenzie's jacket, and

pulled with all her strength, dragging her toward the abandoned building.

It never ceased to amaze her how heavy a human body was. Even a small one weighed a hundred pounds, and Mackenzie wasn't small. It took everything Emma had to move her, but she was not going to leave her alone and exposed.

Sweating from the effort, she used her own weight as a tool to drag the unconscious woman toward safety. She was almost there when the gunshot came again.

Emma threw herself on top of Mackenzie, shielding her with her own body. But the shot flew high over them.

It seemed to Emma that Finlay Blake wasn't comfortable with the gun. The shot that hit Kate must have been beginner's luck, because the rest of his shots went far wide, and there were long gaps when he didn't fire.

That gave her a chance.

As soon as the echo from the shot faded, Emma jumped up and pulled the door open, and with a cry of effort dragged Mackenzie into the shelter of the ancient shed and slammed the door shut. She knew they weren't safe here—the walls were too thin to offer protection—but at least Blake couldn't see them anymore.

Panting, she took Mackenzie's wrist in her hand. Her skin felt cool and dry, but Emma detected the faint flicker of a pulse. Her own heart was racing, and it could have been her own blood she could feel coursing through her veins, but she prayed it wasn't.

Pushing the fabric of Mackenzie's jacket aside, she found the bleeding wound and pushed her hands against it. The blood was warm, soaking Mackenzie's sweater.

Warm blood is hope, Emma reminded herself. Warm blood is life.

"Hold on, Mackenzie," she said. "Just hold on. I'm here."

She tore off her jacket and the shoulder holster, throwing both on the ground before pulling her sweater over her head. She pressed the soft garment against the wound.

Still applying pressure with one hand, she pulled out her phone with the other and dialed.

She didn't wait for Ripley to speak. "Finlay Blake is on the hill at the back of the property. He's got a view of everything and a sniper rifle. He can see you, Ripley. He can see everyone. I need backup and I need an ambulance. Mackenzie is down. Repeat: Mackenzie is *down*."

Her voice broke on the last word.

As if from a hundred miles away, she heard Ripley try to calm her, and then the sound of him giving orders, calling Adam and the others. His steady, urgent voice was like a blanket thrown across her shoulders as she pressed the sweater firmly against the bullet wound.

"You're OK, Kate," she whispered to the unconscious figure beside her. "I'm here. I've got you."

As she spoke, Blake's long gun cracked again outside. Emma dropped the phone and threw herself down, draping her arms protectively across Mackenzie. The shot blasted through a high part of the shed wall, sending fragments of wood and dust flying, and letting in a perfect "O" of light.

Her chest felt tight with fury. He was still firing. He was going to shoot and shoot until he killed them all. That was his plan now that he'd been prevented from hitting the target he wanted.

Looking down, Emma saw the Glock in its holster lying on the dirty floor next to her. She watched her hand reach out and pick it up. And in that instant she knew what she was going to do.

"Stay here, Kate," she told Mackenzie. "Don't give up."

Reaching out with one hand, she pushed the rickety wooden door open, and angled her body so she could see out.

"Finlay Blake!" She raised her voice, shouting at the long curve of the green hill. "Stop this now. It's over."

Her own words floated on the breeze, seemingly to nothing and no one.

Behind her, Mackenzie stirred and moaned, and Emma's heart jumped. She was alive. But for how long?

She tried again.

"Give yourself up, Finn. It's over."

This time, she was rewarded with mocking laughter.

"Who do you think you are?" a voice asked. "This isn't your business. You should have stayed home."

Emma stiffened. The voice was close. Blake had come down the hill.

"This is the end," Emma said, simply. "We know the plan and we know who's behind it. We found the guns. Balakin and Fridman are gone. They left you all alone to take the heat, Finn. And we're going to get you. There are people coming for you from everywhere. If you give up now, you'll get credit for that when it all goes to trial. Take this chance I'm offering you, Blake. It's the only one you've got."

This time there was a pause before he responded.

"I don't believe you. You'll never let me walk away from this."

"Of course you can walk away," Emma forced her voice to stay steady. "I personally guarantee if you put that gun down, no one will hurt you."

He didn't reply.

Emma tried a new tack. "My friend is wounded, Finn. We need to get her out of here. I'm sure you didn't mean to hurt her, but I need to get her to a hospital."

In the distance, Emma heard voices and, in the distance, the steady thump of helicopter rudders, and her heart quickened.

"Listen, Finn, they're coming. It's over. Put down your gun. Everything's going to be OK. I promise."

"Everything will be OK," his voice repeated, much closer now, and Emma saw him step out from behind a tree and stride toward her, a rifle pressed to his shoulder, pointing at her. ". . . if I make it OK."

Emma's breathing stopped. Time stood still. She couldn't feel the breeze through the door against her skin or hear the birds in the trees. It was just her and a gun.

In that uncanny silence, she saw her left hand rise to steady the Glock 17 she held in her right. She saw Blake at the end of the barrel swinging his own gun to her face, and she heard a gun fire.

For one split second she didn't know if it was her gun or his.

Then she felt the kick of the revolver, and she knew.

As Finn Blake flew backward, the rifle tumbling from his hands, Emma drew a shuddering breath that didn't seem to reach her lungs.

She didn't wait to see him hit the ground; she knew the shot had been true. Instead, she dropped the gun and turned back to Mackenzie, whose eyes did not open as Emma pressed both hands against her left shoulder. Her blood felt colder now.

"I'm sorry," Emma whispered. Tears filled her eyes. "I'm so sorry. I'm sorry. I'm sorry . . ."

35

For Emma, the next twenty-four hours were a blur.

It turned out she'd never hung up when she called in the attack, and the shooting was followed aurally by everyone in the operations room. Ripley told her later he'd thought she'd been hit until he heard her talking to Mackenzie.

"I've rarely been more worried for you," was how he put it, when she finally saw him again.

Four Special Branch officers had arrived seconds after the shooting, having, as one of them informed her later, "run like the wind to get to you."

In the confusion, they'd approached her—the only person conscious—with guns drawn, shouting for her to get down, but Emma refused to lift her hands from Mackenzie's wound. She kept repeating, "I need an ambulance!" until, at last, an officer moved her aside and took over first aid.

"The ambulance is coming, lass," he'd said, gently. "Let me help her."

"She's a police officer," Emma told him, brokenly. "She's one of us."

It wasn't necessary; he'd been telling the truth. Within minutes, a helicopter ambulance had thudded across the sky, landing a short distance away, and soon paramedics were swarming across the scene.

Finn Blake was pronounced dead at the scene, but Mackenzie was lifted onto a stretcher and carried with extreme care into the chopper.

The same officer who'd treated Mackenzie walked over to Emma as the ambulance took off. Emma barely glanced at him as wind from the rotors whipped her hair into her eyes.

"You did good," he said. "They'll take care of her now."

He was over fifty, with graying hair and knowing eyes. She had no idea who he was with—MI5, MI6, or Special Branch—but he'd stayed with Mackenzie, and she was grateful for that. But she couldn't find the words to thank him as she watched the helicopter take away the only partner she'd ever had.

At that moment, Charles Ripley strode out of the tree line, his face white and tense, his black coat swirling around him.

"Emma." He walked straight to her. She saw him take in the blood that covered her hands to the elbow and soaked the T-shirt she'd worn under the sweater.

"Is any of that hers?" he asked the man next to her.

The man shook his head.

"She lost so much blood," Emma told Ripley, her voice cracking.

"They can give her more." It was all he said before pulling her into a hug. As she buried her face in his coat, it struck Emma that in all the time she'd known him, Ripley had never hugged her before. She breathed in his scent of Dunhill cigarettes and clean fresh air, and she refused to cry. Not now.

Finally, he released her and she stood up straight.

"Blake is dead?" Again, the question was directed at the officer next to her.

"Oh, very," the man replied. "She took care of that." He smiled at Emma. "We haven't been introduced, by the way."

Ripley turned to Emma. "This is Tom Stone, from Special Branch. Tom, this is Emma Makepeace. She works with me."

"A pleasure to meet you, Emma," Stone said. "Your reputation precedes you, and even that doesn't do you justice."

Emma couldn't think of anything to say. This conversation seemed to be happening to someone else. As if he knew this, Stone shifted his focus to Ripley.

"We'll have to go by the books on this. We'll need to take her in so the Scottish authorities can oversee the investigation. Someone from my office will keep an eye on her."

"She can't be identified." Ripley's voice was firm.

"We'll make sure nobody identifies her," Stone agreed.

"There's a leak inside the police," Ripley said, and the man nodded.

"Oh yes, I'm well aware," said Stone. "It's my understanding that the Scottish First Secretary has had a word with the Chief Constable this morning, and that the situation is now in hand." He turned back to Emma. "Is that your gun?" He pointed at the Glock lying in the dirt next to the dark stain of Mackenzie's blood.

Emma looked down at it. "Yes."

"When we run it through" — he began, but Ripley finished the sentence for him.

"—The system will ask you to contact MI5 for information about this weapon. Yes."

"Fine then," Stone said, reasonably. "I just like to know what I'm dealing with."

Turning to Emma, he said, "We're going to need to bag your hands now and take you in for questioning. Do you have any other weapons?"

"There's a blade in my right boot," Emma told him. "I need to know how Mackenzie's doing."

"We'll let you know as soon as we have an update," he said. "Can I please have that knife now?"

Reaching down, Emma pulled the knife from her boot, flipped it over, and held it out handle first.

He took it. "Now, I need your phone."

Ripley objected, but Stone raised a hand to stop him. "I'll make sure its kept safe and the contents protected. That's what I'm here for, Charles. Really, after all these years you should trust me."

Holding her phone, Emma glanced at Ripley, who gave a reluctant nod. She handed it to Stone, who turned to a younger man who stood nearby with a small case open beside him.

"Bag these," Stone said. "And then do her hands."

The younger man placed each item in a plastic bag before putting them in the case. When he'd finished, he approached Emma, who held out her hands. He slid a plastic bag over each hand, and fixed it carefully at the elbow. This would protect the blood and gunshot residue for testing later.

After that, there'd been a long walk across the grounds, Emma at the center of a phalanx of security officers, and then she'd been in the backseat of Stone's car and they'd driven back into the city.

It turned out the police headquarters weren't far from the office building she'd gone to every day that week, and that was comforting in a way.

Stone had been true to his word, and he'd stayed with her as polite Scottish officers ran tests on her hands for gunpowder residue, before leaving her in an interview room alone while Stone went off to talk to someone about her case.

There, in a scratched mirror on the wall, she'd seen the truth of how she looked. Blood was smeared on her face and in her hair, her hands and clothes were soaked in it. As she stared at herself, the door opened and someone handed her a blue track suit and asked her to change out of her clothes and place them in a plastic bag.

Finally, then, she was taken to a shower room and allowed to wash the blood off, and Emma stayed in there a very long time, sobbing quietly as the warm water washed the evidence away.

All that day, Emma did everything she was asked. They brought her food she couldn't eat, although she managed a cup of tea. Whenever anyone came to the door, she asked the same question: "Can someone please tell me if Kate Mackenzie is alive?"

After several hours the interview room door opened again, and Stone returned. This time, with him was Kayla Edwards, the small, auburn-haired detective Emma had met that morning at the murder scene. When she recognized Emma, her eyes widened but she recovered quickly.

"Emma . . . Makepeace, is it? I just need to ask you a few questions." Her eyes searched Emma's face. "It shouldn't take too long. Mr. Stone here has filled me in on the basic facts."

"That's fine," Emma said. "Please, can you tell me—is Mackenzie . . . ?"

She didn't finish the sentence. She'd asked so many times.

"She's alive." Kayla's voice was steady. "But barely. She's been in surgery for hours."

Stone sat with them as Kayla walked Emma through everything that had happened. She was patient and compassionate, and Emma liked her instantly. She described the search of the grounds with as much detail as she could recall, and Kayla took copious notes, asking only occasional questions. When she had everything she needed, she stood up and held out her hand to shake Emma's.

"They're going to want to keep you overnight and interview you in the morning. I'll speak to the officers in charge and see if I can get you out of here as soon as that process is over. But we've got one dead man and an injured officer, so you can imagine this is going to take a little time."

She left, promising to check on Mackenzie and let Emma know how she was.

There's no place in a police station to sleep except a cell, so that was where Emma spent the night: on a hard cement bench.

But the officers were kind, and brought her chocolate bars and steaming cups of tea, and to her surprise, Emma slept dreamlessly.

The next day, Emma was taken from her cell in the morning for more questioning. In many ways, it was a repeat of her conversation with Kayla the day before. Again, Stone was at her side as they asked the same questions, just more frequently, repeating the same points over and over. By then, her head had begun to thud.

Kayla interrupted after about an hour to give her an update on Mackenzie.

"She's still alive, but the doctors say the next twenty-four hours are critical. She's lost a huge amount of blood."

Emma was allowed to rest after that, as much as she could in the tiny, windowless room, with its hard bench. As she sat staring at the wall, she kept replaying the moment of Mackenzie's shooting over and over in her mind.

She'd lost track of time by then, with no outside light, and no clocks. Still, she sensed it was late when the door to her cell again opened with a creak of metal against metal.

"Right, then," a cheerful female officer said. "You're free to go. You'll be called back to give evidence as the case progresses but we have no more questions at this time."

They kept Emma's clothes as evidence, so she walked out of the building in the blue track suit. When she'd collected an envelope containing her few remaining things, including her phone, she stepped out to find Ripley waiting for her outside in the cool evening air, a Dunhill blue smoldering in his hand.

"They kept you long enough," he said, and a smile creased his tired face. "But you're free at last."

Emma looked up at the stars with surprise. She hadn't realized it was so late.

She waited until they were in the car to ask the question.

"How's Mackenzie?"

"She's alive," he said. "I think she's going to make it."

Emma sagged back against the smooth seat and closed her eyes as he started the car and pulled out into the quiet street.

She was going to make it.

THURSDAY
17 October

THE SCOTSMAN
Page One

THE G7 FINISHES ON A HIGH

BY ALEX LOUIS

After two days of meetings at Carlowrie Castle in Edinburgh, a royal visit with His Majesty the King at Holyrood Palace, and even a wee dram of whisky in a local pub, the leaders of the world's most powerful nations left Edinburgh, saying the annual gathering of the Group of Seven had been a stellar success.

Agreement was reached on critical issues including immigration, as well as oil and gas production. On the last day of the gathering, the group agreed to further sanctions against Russia for its continued war against Ukraine and other malicious meddling in elections, which the group condemned in the strongest terms. The sanctions are intended to cripple the Russian economy over the long winter.

The threats of violence did come to pass when a lone armed man attempted to disrupt the gathering at Carlowrie Castle, but security forces shot and killed him at the scene.

One police officer was injured in the incident, and is recovering in hospital. Police are not at this time identifying the attacker or the injured officer.

36

The Royal Infirmary of Edinburgh was at the edge of town, a huge, white building bounded by city on one side and fields on the other.

It was late morning when Emma walked in from the cold. The weather had been wildly unpredictable for the last few days, bringing torrential rain one minute, bright sun the next. At the moment, it was the latter, and the blue Scottish sky was almost painful to look at.

The astringent scent of disinfectants that was a hallmark of every hospital reminded her that it had been just over a year since she'd spent several days in a London hospital after a Russian bullet passed through her shoulder.

It still ached in the cold, but otherwise, it had healed completely, and if it weren't for the scar above her clavicle, she might have forgotten it ever happened.

The thought cheered her as she stopped at the front desk to check in and ask directions, before making her way through the confusing tangle of hospital corridors. Mackenzie would probably be the same, she told herself. She'd heal.

She found the room after what felt like endless walking, and tapped lightly on the door before pushing it open.

Mackenzie lay in a narrow bed, a pale blanket pulled up over her hospital gown. She looked smaller somehow, as if the injury had diminished her. Her dark hair was wild against the pillow, and her skin was the color of the sheets she lay on. She seemed to be connected to a hundred machines by wires and tubes.

The sight made Emma's breath catch in her throat.

Without a word, she pulled a chair closer and sat next to the bed, setting down the bag she'd carried, and taking Mackenzie's hand. Her fingers were cool and dry, but she was alive. Completely and utterly alive.

Emma's touch seemed to rouse her, and Mackenzie murmured in her sleep, before opening her unusual blue eyes.

"There you are," Emma said, gently.

It took a moment or two for Mackenzie to fully wake, her fingers tightening around Emma's as she realized who she was.

"I am . . ." she said haltingly, ". . . so glad . . . to see you. I've been . . . worried."

"*You've* been worried about me?" Emma laughed. "You're the one in the hospital bed."

Letting go of Emma's hand, Mackenzie reached for the controls that tilted the bed up, raising it until she was sitting straighter.

"Could I have some water, please?" Emma picked up the plastic tumbler on the table at her elbow and passed it to her. Mackenzie sipped carefully through a straw before speaking again.

"They shoved a tube down my throat during surgery," she explained, sounding much more like herself as she set the tumbler down. "And I swear to god that did more damage than the actual bullet. I can barely speak." She cast a glance out the window to her right, at the bright morning. "How many days have I been here? Do you know?"

"Four," Emma said, without hesitation. "You were in intensive care for two, and then yesterday you started to get your shit together."

Mackenzie gave a short laugh, holding up a hand, tubes dangling like confetti. "Don't make me laugh. It moves things around that shouldn't move."

"I'd ask how you're feeling, but I think I know," Emma said. "Did anyone tell you what happened?"

Mackenzie nodded. "I had detectives in here twice asking questions and giving me their opinions." She smiled. "It's ironic. The department ignored me for two years because I did something they didn't like, and now they can't get enough of me."

Her tone was less bitter than amused, and Emma thought she understood. There's something about being shot that makes you suddenly incredibly pragmatic. It's hard to get stressed about work with a bullet lodged in your shoulder.

"What do the doctors tell you?" Emma asked. "How long do you have to stay here?"

"A few weeks. I'll be here, and then I've got to go to rehab, and learn how to take care of myself. They seem to think getting shot makes you forget how to take a shower. Maybe they're right. I've never been shot before."

"I have," Emma said. "I never forgot how to wash my hair, but it did take about four weeks before I could raise my arms high enough to do it."

"That is not what I wanted to hear." Mackenzie gave her a slight smile. "Who shot you?"

"I never got his name," Emma said. "Some Russian."

"Some Russian," Mackenzie reported with a snort of laughter. "You spies have the oddest lives."

"I can't argue with that." They exchanged a smile. "Oh, by the way, I brought you some things." Emma lifted the bag onto the edge of the bed, careful not to jostle her, and dug through it pulling items out. "A hair brush, some toothpaste, slippers, incredibly comfortable yoga trousers, and a couple of jumpers. If you're anything like me, as soon as they let you out of the clown suit, you'll want real clothes."

Mackenzie's eyes filled with emotion, but all she said was "Thank you."

There was a pause as Emma searched for the words she wanted to say. Mackenzie beat her to it.

"They told me you saved my life," she said. "You kept pressing against the wound, trying to stop the bleeding. They said I would be dead without you. Thank you."

Emma suddenly didn't trust her voice enough to reply.

"He was on the hill, wasn't he?" Mackenzie continued. "I've been thinking about it, and I think he followed us out of the forest."

"I think the same," Emma said. "I think if we'd stayed on top of that hill, he'd never have shot you. But we went down and suddenly we were sitting ducks."

"But we had to check those buildings, because that's where I would have hidden if it were me," Mackenzie said.

"I know." Emma sighed. "By the way, Tommy Wilson is going to take part in the official inquiry into Finlay Blake. His wife has turned into an absolute martyr for the cause of justice, and she seems determined to badger him right into the witness stand."

"God bless Shar Wilson." A fond look spread across Mackenzie's face. "She should have married a better man but she loves her Tommy, so she's spent her adult life trying to convince him to just get a job and stop stealing. Someday she might succeed."

"Someday," Emma agreed.

"And Nick Orlov? What happens to him now?" Mackenzie asked.

"Nick's already back home," Emma said. "They kept in hiding precisely until the end of the G7, and then he said he'd had enough. He's hired a private security firm we recommended, and he's got a personal bodyguard, but I can't see that lasting." She smiled ruefully. "That man loves freedom and Scotland just about equally. I think he should run for office. He'd get my vote."

"He'd get more than your vote, I reckon." Mackenzie tapped her hand. "You fancy him."

"I don't," Emma said, but she laughed. "Well, I do, but I wouldn't trust him around other women so it would probably be a bad idea."

"So what happens next for you?" Mackenzie asked. "Back to London and vodka martinis, shaken not stirred, or whatever it is you do down there?"

"I'm flying back this afternoon," Emma said. "The rest of G7 went off without a hitch. If the Scottish police don't throw me in prison for shooting Finn Blake, they might give me a promotion."

"Lucky you." Mackenzie sighed. "I guess I'm back to the drug wars, if I ever get out of here."

"Actually, that's one reason I wanted to talk to you." Emma hesitated, moving the bag back on to the floor, arranging it carefully in place before looking up again.

Mackenzie observed this with puzzlement. "What's going on? Are you asking me out on a date?"

"Not exactly." Emma paused. "I just wondered if you'd ever thought about coming to work with us. I think you're good, and I think you have a lot to offer. We're always looking for smart people like you."

Kate Mackenzie gave her a look of frank astonishment. "You're offering me a job?"

"I guess so."

"Is this a reward for nearly dying?" Mackenzie asked.

"It's a reward for being a bloody good partner," Emma said. "I'm not sure it's an actual reward, though. You'd have to try out the job first and see if it was reward or punishment."

Before Mackenzie could respond to that, a nurse bustled in. "Oh good, you've got a visitor," she enthused, before setting about a lengthy series of tasks, unplugging one cable and plugging in another, removing something from a canula in Mackenzie's arm, and then attaching something else after a great deal of fussing about with saline and anti-bacterial wipes that left their clean, as-tringent scent lingering in the air.

When she finally left, reminding Mackenzie that lunch would be served in an hour, the room felt oddly quiet. Emma could hear machines beeping down the hall, and the sound of voices and the soft shushing of rubber-soled shoes moving swiftly across lino-leum. It was a comforting kind of noise, she thought. A things-are-under-control cacophony.

Mackenzie lay still, her fingers worrying the edge of the cream-colored blanket, and Emma wondered if she'd forgotten what they'd been talking about before the nurse interrupted them. But then Mackenzie cleared her throat.

"I'm honored," she said. "But I don't think I'd be any good at it."

Emma tilted her head. "Why do you say that?"

"First of all I don't know what it is you do. I can't think that all of this," she waved one hand at the room around them, "is your normal job." She continued quickly before Emma could tell her that it more or less was quite normal. "And second, I think I'm a good cop, and I enjoy being a cop. I like talking to people. I like listening to them. I don't know if I'm ready to leave that behind."

"You're a great cop," Emma told her. "Watching you work has been fascinating. You draw people to you and convince them to tell you the truth. I've watched you do it and I still don't under-stand how you do it. But the simple truth is, that would also make you an excellent spy. It would just be different people, different cities. Bigger stakes."

Mackenzie didn't reply right away. She looked past Emma, her brow furrowed, as if she were envisioning this alternative future.

"I don't know." Her fingers plucked at the white cotton blanket covering her. "I can't imagine leaving here and starting over. This is home. I've been to London once in my life, and I don't know much about Russia. How would it work?"

"We would train you," Emma said. "And you would fly through the training."

Mackenzie's eyes searched hers, and then she shook her head. "I can't imagine it. I don't think I could do it."

Emma reached out and touched her arm. "Don't worry. I understand. It was just a thought. You see, I've never had a partner before, and working with you . . . well. It changed things for me." She paused. "Just, do me a favor, and don't write it off. Think about it, while you're getting better. Who knows? You might change your mind."

Before Mackenzie could reply, Emma's phone rang. With an apologetic gesture, she answered it.

"Makepeace."

It was Ripley. "Emma, we've got a bit of a situation. Leonid Fridman is flying to Paris. We've spoken to our friends in France, and they are very open to us having a conversation with him about his activities. They'd like us to send a team, and I want you to be on it. How soon can you get to the airport?"

Emma's heart jumped. She turned to Mackenzie.

"How far is the airport from here?"

"Thirty minutes, if you're lucky."

Emma spoke into the phone. "Thirty minutes, Ripley. I'm on my way."

She stood up and slid the phone into her pocket. "I've got to go."

Mackenzie watched her with amusement. "Another big case?"

"Something like that." Emma pulled out the keys to the BMW. When she reached the door, she paused and looked back. "I understand everything you've said, but as far as I'm concerned, the job offer still stands. If you ever need me, just call. My number's in that bag."

She turned toward the door, but Mackenzie's voice stopped her.

"Hey, Makepeace, you know what? I'm glad I met you."

Emma turned back and smiled. "Call me Alex. That's what my family calls me."

ACKNOWLEDGMENTS

I'm so grateful to my wonderful editors Selina Walker and Anne Speyer, who offer wisdom and guidance at every step of this journey. I couldn't do this without them. Many people contributed to this book, and I owe them all a debt, especially Charlotte Osment, Meredith Benson, Joanna Taylor, Emma Thomasch, Sarah Breivogel, and Allison Schuster, but I know there were many more people behind the scenes who worked hard to make this series a success.

As always, huge thanks to Madeleine Milburn, Hannah Ladds, Liv Maidment, and everyone at the Madeleine Milburn Literary Agency who keep everything running smoothly and make it possible for me to keep writing.

I owe a huge debt to my amazing PR, Tory Lyne-Pirkis, who makes sure everyone finds out about Emma Makepeace, and who puts my books into more hands than I can count. Also, she literally walks me to interviews in Shoreditch because I cannot find anything there on my own.

I'm so lucky to work with Emma Waring, who brings joy to my working days, and makes sure I show up for interviews and meetings at the right time and in the correct location.

Finally to Jack, my husband and best friend in the world, you make everything better. This one is for you. Always and forever.

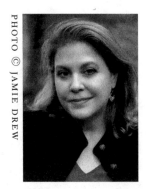

AVA GLASS is a pseudonym for a former crime reporter and civil servant. She is the author of *Alias Emma* and *The Traitor*. Her time working for the government introduced her to the world of spies, and she's been fascinated by them ever since. She lives and writes in the south of England.

avaglass.uk
X: @AvaGlassBooks

ABOUT THE TYPE

This book was set in Electra, a typeface designed for Linotype by W. A. Dwiggins, the renowned type designer (1880–1956). Electra is a fluid typeface, avoiding the contrasts of thick and thin strokes that are prevalent in most modern typefaces.